Traitor in the White House

MI Agent Skip Daggard is NSA's topgun-now he's
running for his life through the tunnels of Washington,
D.C.

By

T.S. Pessini

ISBN: 1-4140-1894-0 (e-book)
ISBN: 1-4140-1893-2 (Paperback)
ISBN: 1-4140-1892-4 (Dust Jacket)

This book is printed on acid free paper.

1stBooks - rev. 08/30/06

ACKNOWLEDGE

A writer can sit at his or her writing place and create, during long, lonely hours at the keyboard when most people are still sleeping warm and snug in their beds, yet it takes many people to get a book into the hands of readers. I would like to thank Mary Ann Chapman, a teacher of English at Frostburg State University, Frostburg, Maryland, who volunteered to edit my manuscript. Mary Ann is not only my editor, but my mentor, teacher, counselor, and dear friend. Richard Rank, who chided me for four years, "Is that novel finished yet?" Brad Barkley, a Barnes & Noble award winning author and a teacher of "Creative Writing" at Frostburg State University, Frostburg, Maryland, who challenged me to write this novel. Lisa Hall at VITALink who helped me design my cover, and John Richards, US Army Retired, who provided technical information. Fred Powell owner of Main Street Books, Twila Fike who owns Twila's Restaurant, and Vern and Freda Sines who own and operate S&S Market, Walter Augustine, and Patty Wells all of whom have supported me in my endeavors. And my wife, Erroll Jean who watched me struggle, lending her encouragement for me to "drive on" and proofreading. But most important, to my daughter, Tammy who spent many hours proofreading and printing.

T.S. Pessini

DEDICATED

To the military and civilian men and women of NSA, Military Intelligence, CIA, FBI, BATF, and to all those who serve in the Intelligence Community around the world.

Chapter One
The Interception

White House Communications Center
White House, Washington, D.C.
Saturday—0030 hours

The code lock clicked, and the single steel door swung open. Sergeant First Class Anderson spun around pointing her US Army issue Colt .45 at the figure in the doorway. "You startled me, Skip!"

"I can see that; ever vigilant huh?"

MI Chief Warrant Officer Skip Daggard closed the heavy door behind him. "Sorry, honey," Skip said to his operations sergeant as he entered the White House Communications Center.

"You should be home sleeping, darling, especially if you plan to leave for New Jersey at 0600," SFC Anderson said placing the weapon back into her shoulder holster.

"Yeah, I know, but there's a hellacious thunderstorm topside. Since I couldn't go back to sleep, after pulling myself out from under our bed, I thought I'd spend some time with you."

Chief Daggard hung up his army issue black overcoat on the coat rack. He placed his black umbrella in one of the appropriate holes at the base of the coat rack. Then he stepped over to SFC Anderson planting a juicy kiss on her lightly coated red lips. Daggard slipped off his denim sports jacket, and hung it over the back of a standard military issue chair, then plopped down onto the gray cushioned seat. Skip leaned back in his chair clasping his hands together resting them against the back of his head.

Chief Daggard glanced at the dedicated communications circuits for Camp David. The green systems function LED lights were glowing indicating all systems normal and active but the circuits were devoid of traffic at this time. "All quiet on the mountain?"

SFC Kristine Anderson looked up from several messages she was cataloging, "Yes, Skip everything is quiet. Sergeant Mott and I changed the KW 100 sandwiches at 2300. He is on duty until 0700 when Staff Sergeant Hoboken and his day staff come on line.

"By the way, sweetheart, I have been meaning to ask you something…"

Daggard glanced at Kristine, "Yeah! What?"

"When are you going to take *me* home to meet your mother? After all, we have been engaged for sixteen months now."

Skip glared at Kristine through blank blue eyes as he shifted in his chair lowering his hands to armrests-his knuckles turning white. He loved her Germanic facial features, her fleshy one hundred and twenty pounds and her slender long legs, yet, once again questions. Why, Skip wondered, was she always probing? 'I want to meet your mother. I want to meet your family.' Hell! His family believed he was dead except his mother. She knew the truth.

What should he tell his lovely? This twenty-seven year-old pretty? After two years with Kristine, he has yet to share his secrets. Should he start now? Hell no!

"You may never get to meet my mother, Kristine. She isn't doing well…cancer. Monday was the first time I had spoken to her in thirty-four years. Now that my career is coming to an end, my mother isn't in danger any more.

"Besides, this may be the last time *I* get to see her."

Kristine gulped down the last mouthful of her coffee. She dropped her left arm banging her Mickey Mouse coffee cup against the console table edge.

Skip and Kristine stared at each other across the six feet of aisle space between the two communications consoles.

It was moments like this, which Kristine feared the most because Skip's eyes seemed to penetrate her sanctuary; invade her inner self. And it was *this* self she kept private and secret. She had to for her self-preservation.

Skip broke the trance. "Since you're in a *lovable* mood, I think I'll scan the phone lines before I head back to our apartment."

He swiveled his chair to the left placing a headset over his thinning reddish gray hair, and plugged the jack into the port labeled White House.

"OK," Kristine mumbled turning back to her task both mad and frightened for provoking him.

Skip Daggard fitted the small sponge type earpieces into his ears. Instantly, he became lost in the world of eavesdropping where nothing else existed: The world he had come to love and hate.

Military Intelligence Chief Warrant Officer Skip Daggard thought about his life. He had lived, killed, and loved across the US and the world for thirty-seven years while engaged in the protection of the American people, the cause of freedom, and the doctrine, which is dearer to the American way of life than life itself. Now his career was winding down. The White House Commo Chiefs' position was his last stop. From here, there would be retirement, marriage, and the mountains of West Virginia. But if that damn Ash Blonde doesn't stop agitating the water there isn't going to be a wedding.

Soon the closed confinement of buildings without exterior windows and rooms like this one with their deck gray painted walls and floors and security doors and windows will be behind him. No more hidden basements. No more secret out-of-the-way field stations or disguised microwave satellite dishes and no more killing.

Right now, however, Skip felt content because he had finally fallen in love, an emotion he had lost in Vietnam. Retirement was fast approaching, and at last he could go home.

The next few moments were going to change all of that!

While scanning channels, Skip thought about the day he had informed his mom that he had been inducted into the intelligence field. His induction came with his new assignment out of Nam to Colorado Springs at NORAD. Although his mission as a communications technician was real, his covert mission was to learn NORAD's protective and subversive missions in the overall scheme of the Military Intelligence Community because some of his future assignment successes would depend on that knowledge. He had been assigned to an army MI unit, which was responsible for trafficking and repairing communications equipment at Ent Airforce Base, Colorado Springs, Colorado.

Ent was an overflow link, or relay station, from Cheyenne Mountain to all Middle American US Air Force Bases in NORAD to include Andrews Air Force Base in Maryland and NSA at Fort Meade, Maryland. Daggard's official duties would require his presence at the Cheyenne Mountain Facility once a month.

On the days Skip was scheduled to work at the mountain facility, he always tried some ploy not to go; every time those humongous steel doors shut, he felt trapped.

But actually his career as an operative had begun when he had been assigned to STRATCOM and the 1st Signal Brigade in Vietnam. This was his first assignment after graduating AIT at Fort Gordon, Georgia in the spring of 1968.

He had been attached from the 1st Signal Brigade to the 29th Signal Group, Bang Pla meaning land of many fish, Thailand. STRATCOM was so covert that none of the four hundred and fifty enlisted men knew the complete mission of the communications site. However, Skip befriended two American civilian operatives who shared some secret knowledge with him.

Skip's fact-finding information came to him piecemeal as well. One afternoon while on duty the maintenance chief, SFC Haig took Skip into the major's office. "I have a special assignment for you, Daggard," Haig said, "we have a satellite site sixty miles north of here. We provide tech support. They're having equipment problems so I'm sending you and Sergeant Richardson, our crypto tech."

"Why me?"

"Because it's your turn," said the sergeant.

Skip shook his head and looked over at Kristine's rigid back. He began turning the channel dial switching channels on the White House switchboard panel while thinking about his mom. After thirty-four years, he could still see her standing in the doorway. He had knocked on the eighteenth century hard wooden door.

The Revolutionary Historic Mills House was situated at the corner of Early and Mill Street directly across from Alexander Hamilton Elementary School in historic Morristown, New Jersey.

His mother opened the door, but before she could scream out her delight, he had grabbed her placing his right hand over her mouth. "*Who's home?*" he had whispered in her ear.

"Your sister, Mary," She whispered back. Always trust mom to go with the flow.

After a short hug, Skip had pleaded with his mom, "Pretend I got zapped in Nam, mom; that I never made it home."

Then he told her who he worked for, and that his code name "Snoopy" had buried Skip Daggard. He watched her tears cascade out of her eyes, but saw, too, her recognition—she understood.

It was better for him to hurt her now, than have her taken and tortured, and used against him later.

Skip knew the subversive world and all of its cruelties. Of government plots and truths better left unsaid. Who would believe him anyhow? Government sanctioned eavesdropping on friend, foe, and the American people all under the guise of security and the best interest of the US Government and American public.

Covert operations in which even partners didn't know who was doing what, nor did half the Intelligence Community. The CIA kept things to themselves as did NSA and MI. And the president was kept in the dark all the time simply because he was classified as "a four year player," which meant he was fed information on a need-to know-basis.

Skip leaned back in his chair thinking about all the time lost without his family. He bent forward gently caressing the imaginary face of his mother on the blue field of the frequency modulation screen. "I'm sorry, Mom," he said as tears welled up at the corners of his eyes, "it has been a long time, but I'm coming home today."

Skip automatically stopped on the channel with voices. He glanced to his left and saw the Secretary of State's green LED light aglow as well as the amber LED light indicating the Russian Embassy in Washington, D.C. He eavesdropped on the conversation for ten seconds. 'Da, Da, Da.' was all he could differentiate.

Chief Daggard jumped back from his communications console sending his chair careening across the floor. SFC Anderson jumped from the sudden activity rotating in her chair to look at Skip. His slight tan complexion had turned sunburn red, and his icy blue eyes were narrowed to horizontal slits.

"What's the matter, Skip?" It was his instantaneous rage she had come to fear.

"Is the recorder on? Switch to line four. Mark the tape and record the tape counter numbers and time."

The urgency in his voice frightened her as much as the hideous expression on his face. Kristine switched the dial on the recorder, marked the tape's edge with a dot from a black magic marker, and wrote down the counter numbers and time on a single sheet of paper.

"What's going on, honey?"

"Either the Secretary of State or someone else is in his office upstairs is code-talking to someone in the Russian Embassy."

"What caused you to jump and scare the crap out of me?"

"Listen."

They listened, but the conversation was encrypted. A language coding system Skip pretended to be unfamiliar with. The conversation lasted five minutes at which time Kristine marked the tape with a dot and recorded the end of conversation counter numbers and time over the start figures.

Skip looked at her and spoke out in a sarcastic tone, "You're supposed to be a linguistics expert; the perfect little analyst! What kind of language is *that*?"

She shrugged-lying.

Skip looked at her suspiciously. "Run the tape back to the beginning mark and we'll listen again.

"Can you identify anything?"

Should she tell him? Did she dare? And then what? How will he react?

Kristine feathered her hair using her fingers of both hands, "I think," she began, "the prominent language sounds like Prussian. It is an extinct Balto-Slavic tongue that has been displaced by German. There seems to be Old English mixed with Latin and Greek Mythology terminology's, but the numbers…"

"Replace certain vowels," Skip said.

Kristine stared at him.

"Old Prussian, huh? One of the Slavic Languages-like Russian?"

Skip stood over Kristine as he queried her. He leaned down towards her so that their noses almost touched.

Kristine turned away gathering messages together so Skip couldn't see the sweat seeping from her pores and beading together on her forehead. "Perhaps the late sixteenth or early seventeenth century," Kristine said looking at papers in her trembling hands.

She knew she had said too much. "Yes, like…like Russian," she answered turning around to face him, throwing the papers on the counter top. Kristine gulped down her fears as she studied his facial expression-blank.

She looked into his eyes. Skip's rage had subsided, but his pupils remained dilated. Kristine shivered because she saw her reflection in the blue of his eyes. She rose from her chair. "But why would these speakers be conversing in encryption?" She used this tactic to get Skip focused on this development and not on her responses.

"Why indeed," Skip said, "this is code specific, Kristine. For instance, I heard both speakers respond and answer with three "da's" at the beginning of the conversation. We didn't get that on tape.

"So, let's analyze the "da's," Skip said as he sat down at Kristine's console pointing for her to take her seat.

"Da is Russian for yes. The speaker in the Russian Embassy picked up the receiver and said, 'Da, da, da.' The caller said the same thing, 'Da, da, da.'

"Both speakers say yes three times, which means that they are identifying themselves."

"*Really?*"

Skip began to work through the code out loud, "Yes, yes, yes. Yes it is I. Or, yes, yes, yes, SOS using the distress signal, which could mean…"

Skip leaned forward and wrote SOS on the left side of a sheet of paper, and SOS on the right side. He closed his eyes trying to remember who spoke first.

"It was the receiver who spoke first, then the caller," Skip said, "and the one who made the call is upstairs in the secretary's office."

Skip leaned back in his chair nibbling on the tips of his fingers of his left hand. "*Schmirnoff!*"

"*What?*"

"The receiver emphasized the first and third "da" and the caller emphasized all three da's."

Skip leaned forward again. He picked up his pencil and lined through the "O" on the left side of the paper. "When I take out the "O" it leaves "SS."

There was a long pause before Skip blurted out, "Secretary Schmirnoff," then wrote it down.

Kristine stared at the name Skip had written on the paper. Then she watched as Skip wrote Secretary of State under the SOS on the right side of the paper.

Skip sighed heavily for a few seconds pondering his accusations. He rubbed his chin with his left hand massaging his skin with his thumb and forefinger.

"Ok," Skip said as he sat upright, "now let's test my theory."

Chief Daggard went into his office. A few minutes later he emerged with a laptop computer. He connected the laptop to the recording device using a five-prong audio cable and rewound the tape. "This is a VMRAS, honey, which is an acronym for "voice modulation recognition system. First I will eliminate the Russian Ambassador by comparing his voice with that of the receiver's."

Skip began the tape after he had programmed the laptop to modulate the ambassador's voice. As he and Kristine watched the spikes and valleys appear on the computer screen it was apparent the voices did not match.

Next, Skip programmed the computer to play Secretary Schmirnoff's voice, and he reran the tape. No question about the comparison of the modulation spikes; it was a perfect match. Then Skip programmed the Secretary of State's voice recognition analysis program in and checked it against the caller from the White House. The modulation spikes revealed a perfect match.

Skip sat rigid with his hands clasped on the console's table edge and stared at the computer screen while the tape continued to play.

"Skip, time has elapsed."

"Don't worry! I know how to adjust the counter and time on the recorder so no one can tell there had been any elapsed frames."

Daggard rose slowly placing the palms of his hands on the table on either side of the computer.

Kristine watched in feared awe of Daggard's transformation as he hissed out his words, "Why is the secretary having an encrypted conversation at 0045 hours with Secretary Schmirnoff?"

"I don't know, but your cloak and dagger life has made you too paranoid and suspicious of everything. I suppose you're even suspicious of me," she declared.

Kristine rose from her chair to swing a right round-house at him when she saw the truth in his eyes, "You bastard!"

Her hand never reached his face. Skip caught her wrist in his left hand and gently drew her into his arms. "It's my life, Kristine. Being suspicious is how I've stayed alive," and he kissed her, "besides, you're someone to be suspicious of, after all, why would a beautiful, fairly decent figured, twenty-seven year-old, slightly imperfect Venus be interested in a fifty-six year old washout?"

Kristine hugged him placing her cheek against his and whispered, "Because you are the best there is, but sometimes you frighten the hell out of me, sweetheart."

The clicking of the receiver brought them back to the situation. Skip reached over and pushed the stop button on the recorder. He disconnected the audio cable from both the recorder and his computer, then uploaded an encryption-decoding program.

While the program was uploading, Skip went back to his office at the back corner of the comcenter. He retrieved a splicing device from his safe and returned to the work area.

"Here," Skip said, "use my handy-dandy hand-held two-in-one homemade device. I want you to place the device on the counter, slide the tape along the silver base-plate, and push down on the top of the splicer handle. This will allow you to cut the section of tape from the reel."

Kristine measured the length of magnetic tape from mark to mark using the tape counter numbers she had written down as her guide.

Skip returned from his office again with a top secret Key Code Guide. "Okay, honey," Skip said as he watched her work, "how's it coming?"

"It looks like a huge stapler, Skip. I cut the left end."

"Now turn the splicer around and cut the other end," he said as he began thumbing through the Code Guide.

"The cutting edge cuts the tape giving the tape a smooth edge, which makes splicing tapes back together a perfect job.

"It will take an expert to determine if and where a splice occurred."

Chief Daggard looked up the page he needed according to the calendar Julian date and Zulu time, which is five or six hours ahead of standard time depending on the season. He placed the guide face down as SFC Anderson handed him the ribbon of tape.

Skip attached a special electronic tape reader to his computer in the keyboard port, and placed the tape on the glass window, similar to those on register machines that read the bar codes on products, and closed the tape lid. Then he connected a small speaker at the speaker port. Daggard said, "Now let's see and hear what these two had to say."

Skip typed in a code and hit the start key. The computer fed the tape through the reader, which took forty-five seconds. What came out was scrambled-garbled, but some Russian letters were identifiable like the inverted "R" and the upside down "V": 1's and 0's were laced throughout the printout on the screen.

These binary codes are now called computer language; however, in many electronic communications devices the numbers in combinations of seven represent the start/stop codes, but in this case the 1's and 0's represented certain vowels.

"Remember I said the binary code is replacing certain vowels? I can identify the Beowulf language-Old English, but those other words..."

"Those other words and phrases are Prussian," Kristine said.

Skip looked at her for a few seconds then said, "Yeah! And this shit is all garbage, and I can't decipher it using this cryptic Key Code Guide, and my program can't decode it, and..."

Sergeant Anderson looked over at Chief Daggard. His face was aflame and his eyes had narrowed to slits again. He was rising in a quick, smooth motion drawing his weapon.

"*Skip!*"

"I'm going up to see the secretary."

"*No you're not*! You just sit back down and put that thing away."

"That son of a bitch needs killing!"

"Based on *what*?"

Daggard glared at her through the pencil lines of his eyelids. Amber flames permeated from his eye sockets. Kristine knew this rage. She knew she had to get him under control before Skip stormed upstairs and shot the secretary.

She felt like she was dealing with the notorious Doctor Jekyll and Mr. Hyde. Kristine sucked in her breath and shouted, "Skip! Skip!" She moved in and wrapped her arms tight around him. "Skip!" She felt his body tense then begin to tremble. In a few seconds he answered her. "What?"

Skip always feared this time. When he was out of control. Those blackouts when he was in posttraumatic stress disorder. He was a raging animal in this condition—a viscous killer out for blood. PTSD was his mental memento from Vietnam.

Kristine still held onto him as she said, "Skip, turn it over to the Secret Service. Let them handle it."

"Turn *what* over? I don't have any concrete evidence of anything," Skip said as he holstered his weapon.

"Exactly! That's what I was trying to tell you. What can you do?"

Chief Daggard placed his hands on SFC Anderson's shoulders and moved her to arms' length from him. "You're right, Kristine. What proof do I have that the secretary is up to no good? But I have a friend who can help me."

"Where?"

"Oh damn," she thought as he turned on her.

"Right now *you* don't have a need to know," he hissed at her.

Skip went to Kristine and hugged her when he saw the hurt in her eyes. "Okay, honey! I'm sorry for that remark."

Skip leaned into her and whispered in her ear, "I have an analyst friend at NSA. Shhh!"

Kristine whispered back in his ear, "Always so secretive! Do you think the comcenter is bugged?"

Skip shrugged his shoulders, "No! I removed seven of the little tattletales three years ago. After a week of playing games, the Secret Service stopped posting their devices. But you know me!"

"I'm beginning too," Kristine said, "but even if we are together for another thirty years, I have a feeling I will never truly know you."

Skip ignored Kristine's comment as he packed up his equipment except the slicing device. "I'm going to put the decoding devices away. Then I'll put the tape back together and fix the figures."

When Skip returned to Kristine's workstation, he was carrying three twelve inch reels of magnetic tape. He placed each reel next to the one on the recorder before Skip found a match of color, density, and width. "Figures," he said, "that it would be the third reel that matches."

"Be more optimistic, honey; at least you have a match."

Skip unraveled a length of tape along the counter. "Place the ribbon you had cut from the recorder, Kristine and lay it on top of the tape I just unreeled.

"Make sure the ends align perfectly," he said holding the reel steady, "now use the splicer to cut a matched edge."

Once she had made the splice, Skip lay the reel down. He picked up the splicing device and the blank length of tape Kristine had just cut, and aligned the left ends of the tapes on the base of the device.

Daggard hesitated about twenty seconds, then he told Kristine to complete the splicing. He talked her through the process. "Make sure the ends overlap a sixteenth of an inch. Once you are satisfied, gently squeeze the handle and base and hold them together for thirty quick counts, then release your grip. Do the same with the right ends."

When Kristine was finished, Skip inspected her work. "Good job, honey!"

He looked at the clock. "Thirty minutes have elapsed," he said taking two small reels from a bag.

Skip attached the left reel to the take-up reel on the recorder and stretched the encrypted section of the tape lengthwise. "Ok, Kristine select the dubbing and rewind buttons simultaneously, then drag the right reel on the recorder with your hand."

As the reels turned, Skip placed his index finger of his right hand on the record button. When the tapes were equal, he pushed the button. The recorder was now on the proper counter numbers and tape length.

Next, Skip took up the section of tape Kristine had cut from the recorder and threaded it into the spindle of a tiny spool. He unraveled a paper clip and poked the straight clip through a hole in the spindle turning the reel until the tape was wrapped around the spool. Skip took a small elastic band and secured the tape in place. Then he placed the reel into a metal container the size of a snuff can.

Chief Daggard dropped the canister into the left inside pocket of his denim sports jacket. "All right, honey," Skip said, "I am going to put the splicing device away then head to NSA."

Skip slipped into his sports jacket, then went to the coat rack and donned his raincoat. He stood at the steel door with his hand on the doorknob staring at the floor.

"What's wrong, Skip?"

Daggard had his back to the room and Kristine. When Skip spoke, he spoke to the floor, "Have you ever had a sense of foreboding? I don't want to open this door. I have a premonition that when I do our world is going to change. My sixth sense is warning me, 'Skip, stay here. Let the world go to crap.' Yet, I know I have to go, Kristine."

Skip tucked his umbrella under his left arm and pushed the white button on the silver plate mounted on the wall between the steel door and the steel barred window. The lock clicked and he pulled on the doorknob.

Kristine came to his left side. Skip turned his head—they kissed. "I'll call you," he said and stepped out into the luminous corridor in the basement of the White House and closed the steel door behind him.

"See you later, Sam," Skip called out to the FP guard as he passed through the East Gate of the White House going to his vehicle parked at the dead end.

Skip inhaled deeply the aromatic fragrance of Cherry Blossoms as he unlocked his car door. He stood by the opened door enjoying the sweet smell thinking about the secretary. "I should go back and kill him," Skip whispered to the warm early morning air."

Chief Daggard drove out of D.C. using the Greenbelt Route 495 to Route 295 north. Just before he entered the beltway, he stopped at a phone booth and made a call. Skip was reluctant to use his cell phone in case someone was eavesdropping.

Chapter Two
The Verification

White Marsh, Maryland
Saturday—0110 hours

"Did you see how bright the moon was tonight?"

"It wasn't very bright!"

"Because of walls."

"Walls!"

Charles Demois was replacing the receiver in its cradle when his wife, Claudette muttered, "What time is it? Who was that, Charles?"

"I have to go in, honey. Seems there's some kind of glitch in a system. It's ten after one. Go back to sleep!"

Charles stared at Claudette while he slipped on a pair of black jeans. He smiled because she had her face hidden under a facial pack.

"What's so funny?"

"How am I going to find your lips under all of that gunk?"

"It's not that difficult," Claudette said pulling him down for a kiss.

Charles looked at himself in the full-length mirror attached to their bedroom door. He liked what he saw. He stood five feet and eight inches. His black, short-cropped hair was free of gray, and his ebony shin was smooth. Laugh wrinkles had formed at the corners of his brown eyes, and dimples creased both sides of his full lips.

Charles Demois was impressed with his image. He would turn sixty in October, and retire from the agency on January 1, 2005.

Charles had spent twenty years in the US Air Force as a cryptologist in Military Intelligence.

His index finger traced the four-inch scar along the right side of his face. The scar was almost invisible now a memento of his teenage years in Baltimore as a gangbanger.

Chuck, Charles' nickname, pulled on a black turtleneck sweater. He couldn't rationalize his choice of dark clothes, except for the fact that "when Skip Daggard calls in the middle of the night," Chuck recalled, "stealth is required."

After tying the laces on his black sneakers and rising from their bed, Chuck looked over at Claudette who was resting her head on her right elbow watching him. "Going incognito?"

"Ha, ha, ha," Charles chuckled," "I want to be comfortable because I don't know how long this will take."

Chuck drove away from his classic brick four square style home in White Marsh. He entered Route 695 from Route 1, then paid a toll and began driving over the Francis Scott Key Bridge.

Demois could barely make out Camp Carroll to the left of the bridge. Camp Carroll was a hexagon shaped battlement constructed under the supervision of Colonel Robert E. Lee of the United States Army in 1855. The small fortress was the first strategic defense position enemy ships would encounter trying to enter the Baltimore Inner Harbor. Charles glanced to his right and saw lights illuminating Fort McHenry, the second fortress of defense for Baltimore. He could barely see the floodlights lighting up the American flag on Federal Hill, which was the third and final defensive earthwork of Baltimore by sea invaders. During the War of 1812 Fortress McHenry was the primary defense engaging the British war ships while the small battery detachment on Federal Hill played a minor role in the fray. However, the Redcoats were able to dispatch longboats to Eastpoint landing a fairly good sized force of infantry because the eastern shore of the harbor had no defensive positions; therefore, Camp Carroll was built thirty-nine years after the conflict. On the dawn of September 14, 1814, Francis Scott Key a lawyer and US negotiator wrote the poem "Defense of Fort M'Henry," from the *flag of truce ship* when the American flag was still visible over the fort after a twenty-four hours bombardment by the British fleet.

The poem was set to music to the melody of "Anacreon of Heaven," but published in Baltimore in November 1814 under the title "The Star-Spangled Banner." The United States Army first sang the song in 1895 during the raising and lowering of the American Flag. In 1931 Congress passed a resolution making "The Star-Spangled Banner" the U.S. national anthem.

As Charles rode over the bridge, he tried working out scenarios for reasons why Skip wanted to meet him at NSA, which represented the "walls" part of their conversation. But why meet at this ungodly hour? Demois gave up trying to second-guess Skip as he turned off the beltway ramp onto the Baltimore/Washington Parkway, Route 295 heading south towards Fort Meade and NSA.

South Maryland, Route 295
Saturday—0115 hours

As Skip Daggard drove along the Greenbelt, Route 495 towards Route 295, Skip pondered over a question: Why was the loop around the Washington corridor dubbed the Greenbelt? Perhaps when the route was named, the beltway was rich with flowers, trees, and green grass. But due to all of the construction in the past twenty years the only highway still in trees and grass in some sections was Route 295. However, even that had changed since Skip had come to Fort Meade in 1982. Now Route 97, a four-lane highway ran from Route 1 all the way to Cranesville, which eliminated Doresy Road, an old two-lane highway.

New developments dotted the landscape from Baltimore eighty miles out to Frederick, Maryland. Where farmers raised crops a few years ago, single family and townhouses grew. The entire Baltimore/Washington corridor is in growth upheaval to include Route 270 from Frederick to Washington.

Driving, for Skip, was a spark for thinking and he thought now. What was the secretary doing conversing in code with Schmirnoff? How did Kristine know all the mixtures of the dialogue, especially the obsolete Prussian words? Yeah, she's a linguist, Skip answered himself, but he was compiling pieces and constructing a puzzle of Kristine and Skip Daggard didn't like the picture he was creating. "If she's Russian I'll have no option but to kill her," Skip said out loud.

As Skip Drove north on Route 295, he let his mind wander. Frames of his life flashed into his consciousness. His mind began selecting certain frames—holding them longer for Skip's scrutiny. There they were scenes that passed in slow motion resurrecting the causes of Skip's induction into Military Intelligence. His mom crying and pleading with him when Skip had informed her of his decision to enter the army in the military police. Because of her begging, Ship elected communications. He would become a technician so his mother wouldn't have to worry about Skip being on the front lines. Unknown to Skip and his mother, he would be placed in more danger.

Next came the big surprise! Mr. Bolk, the History Chair and Mr. Bent, the high school principal, approached Skip one April day just before graduation. "We have a proposition for you Skip," Mr. Bolk had said.

"Yes," Mr. Bent had added, "we want to send you to college with all expenses paid: tuition, books, dorm, and meals."

He couldn't believe it, especially from Mr. Bent. During Skip's sophomore year, Mr. Bent tried to expel him permanently. Now he wanted to send Skip off to college. "I ain't goin' to college; I'm going to war! Besides, what would I have to do for this free package?"

"All you have to do," Mr. Bolk said, "is teach here for six years once you graduate."

"Teach *here*, at Morristown High? You're crazy! Any way, I'm joining the army in August."

Christ, Skip thought, was that *really* thirty-seven years ago? Skip Daggard also entertained the idea that if he had taken that scholarship how different his life would be. Those two decisions: Dropping the MP's as his mother had pleaded; and turning down college became the most crucial decisions, which resulted in his life as a "spook."

NSA
Fort Meade, Maryland
Saturday—0210 hours

Chief Daggard came off of Route 295 at the Ft. Meade exit close to NSA. He turned right onto Route 32, Annapolis Junction heading east. Skip turned left at the first traffic light onto Canine Road and proceeded around NSA's main building to the external parking lot near the barracks of the United States Air Force Military Intelligence Squadron.

Agent Daggard drove his dark blue GMC two-door Yukon Sport Utility Vehicle into the north parking lot then selected a parking space so he faced the Air Force building, Skip could see NSA in his rear view mirror. His position provided him with a 360-degree view.

While waiting for Charles, Agent Daggard scanned his old haunt. The cement barricades of the eighties were gone—replaced by a twelve-foot high chain-linked fence topped with three strands of barbed wire encircling the entire complex. Yet the cement barricades had not disappeared; they were simply placed inside and along the fence perimeter.

The 29th MI Group, his old unit, had been reorganized into the 704th Military Intelligence Brigade, to which he was now assigned, but attached to the White House Communications Center.

Skip felt naked-exposed because his was the only vehicle in the parking lot. He slid down in his seat so only his head was visible. Skip surveyed the area by moving his head in slow sporadic movements. As Daggard continued his surveillance, he came to realize what had been driven home years ago was absolute—the only constant in life is change.

In Nam, he had been assigned to the 1st Signal Brigade, attached to the 29th Signal Group, which became the 325th Signal Battalion, all because of change and restructuring. From there, he was secretly attached to DIA via ASA, which no longer existed. And that's when he, Specialist Fourth Class Skip Daggard disappeared and became a covert operative for Military Intelligence and the Intelligence Community. His name was buried; replaced with a Code Name: "Snoopy." During nineteen-ninety, Daggard's Code Name was deleted, and he became himself once again, that is, in his name only. The internal Skip Daggard would never be the same.

During the beginning of his intelligence career, Skip had adopted a policy that he maintained throughout his service: I see nothing, I hear nothing, and I know nothing—tunnel vision. Ironically, Hogan's Heroes, one of his favorite TV shows depicted Schultz, a German guard at a prisoner of war camp, who embraced the same philosophy.

Change is inevitable and is usually brought on by need or necessity. It was both need and necessity that was instrumental in creating what is now configured as the "Intelligence Community."

In 1942, William J. Donovan, who had commanded the fighting 69th during World War One, advised President Franklin D. Roosevelt of the need for a special organization to conduct intelligence activities. President Roosevelt gave his blessing, and the Office of Strategic Services (OSS) was created headed by Donovan.

When the war ended, the three branches of OSS were incorporated into a new federal intelligence structure. The Research and Analysis Branch was assigned to the State Department. The Counterintelligence and Secret Intelligence Branches were assigned to the War Department, then reassigned to the Central Intelligence Group (CIG) when the CIG was formed in 1946. Eighteen months later, the CIG was restructured and became the Central Intelligence Agency (CIA), responsible for counterintelligence operations.

These changes were created during World War II because there was a problem with sharing information between the two military branches, the army and navy. This created a paradox, and General MacArthur and his G-2 (Security Group) complained. These complaints resulted in an investigation in 1944 by Colonel Henry Clausen.

Colonel Clausen stated his findings to a Joint Congressional Committee in 1945. "Information," Clausen said, "should not be monopolized by one service or the other, but have it distributed by one agency on and overall basis."

To insure a cohabitation of shared information and to achieve the benefits of a centralized structure, the Defense Department established the Armed Forces Security Agency (A.F.S.A.) in 1949. The function of the A.F.S.A. were strategic communications intelligence.

This unified cryptology approach exploded into massive operations, which resulted in the abolishment of the A.F.S.A. on November 4, 1952, and the National Security Agency (NSA) was created and housed at Fort Meade, Maryland. Today, it is one of the most powerful entities of the Intelligence Community.

NSA North Parking Lot
Fort Meade, Maryland
Saturday—0230 hours

Skip watched the white van approach. The van stopped three parking slots away from him and to his right.

"I hope this is worth my time," Chuck said as he slipped from his white Ford custom van.

"Have I ever bothered you when it wasn't worth your time, partner?" Skip said getting out of his SUV.

"I suppose not," Chuck said, "but the last time you used our code I ended up firing more bullets in that fifteen minute fray than I did during my two tours in Nam."

"Ah, the dull life of an analyst. I provide you with exuberant excitement and you throw a shit fit."

"That's what you call *excitement?* Being shot at? Your kind of excitement I can do without, especially since I am eight months shy of retirement."

Both men laughed as they approached the fence gate and FP guard facility. They showed their badges. The metal gate opened, sliding on its track. Skip and Chuck crossed the compound to the front or north entrance where they signed in at the front desk with the Desk FP officer on duty in the main lobby. They rode an elevator to the basement in silence.

Chuck was familiar with Skip's MO so he didn't bother asking any questions. Besides, how could Skip be involved in anything? The powers that be tucked him nice and neat away in a basement corner in the White House. Yet Chuck knew something was amiss because Skip didn't use their code except in severe emergencies. Maybe Skip found his duties at the White House comcenter boring, and decided to play a prank on old Chuck.

Actually, MI agents perceived the White House Communications Chiefs' position to be a prestigious assignment, but Skip took his assignment from NSA to the White House as being put out to pasture.

Charley-Echo Group NSA
Fort Meade, Maryland
Saturday—0245 hours

When Skip and Chuck entered the comcenter in Charley-Echo Group, Chuck took Skip directly to his office. "All right partner, what's up?"

"I've intercepted an encrypted message between the Secretary of State Kelly and Secretary Schmirnoff in the Russian Embassy. I need you to decipher it for me."

Chuck stared at his friend for five seconds, then filled his coffeepot at the sink next to his desk. Chuck shook his head, "You do realize that you are a problem child! That's one reason you got stuck with the White House. Only you, Skip-only you can be placed out of circulation and still manage to come up with a boner."

Skip sat rigid glaring at Chuck. "Pretty damn cranky before you have your cuppa joe aren't you?" Skip said as Chuck was measuring coffee grounds.

No one spoke until the coffee had stopped brewing. The two men sat at Chuck's desk sipping at the strong steaming beverage. "If you're going to drink coffee, Skip drink coffee. Why do you put all of that foreign matter into it?" Chuck said as he watched his friend add sugar and evaporated milk.

"You never experienced army 'joe' have you? Of course not, living in luxury as a "Zoomy." One time in Nam I went for a cuppa java. I had to look around to make sure I was in the mess hall and not the motor pool as the goo oozed out of the spout. I ate my dredge with a spoon."

Chuck sipped his coffee watching his friend's facial distortions as Skip explained army coffee.

"Then there was another time when I used a spoon to stir what looked like machine oil and smelled like turpentine. The mess sergeant was trying to pass it off as coffee. When I withdrew the spoon all that was left was the stem. Besides, I like my coffee with pet milk and sugar."

Skip and Chuck laughed heartily at Skip's description of army coffee in Vietnam. Both men then sat relaxed, sipping their coffee in silence, enjoying the moment. Skip studied their surroundings realizing how much he missed NSA. But he would never disclose that to anyone.

Chuck's office was an enclosed ten-foot wide by ten-foot long square room at the south end of the comcenter. The solid sections of the walls were four feet high. The remaining eight feet sections were made of glass panels. Venetian blinds were drawn up allowing for viewing both from anyone inside the office and the personnel working the comcenter floor. Chuck's desk was metal, and situated five feet from the right wall, which was solid.

Daggard disrupted their universe. "My Aunt Mary is responsible for turning me on to drinking my coffee this way.

"When I was eight, I started spending a few weeks during my summer vacations at the Violet farm in Florhem Park where my Uncle Clarence worked as caretaker. While my Aunt Mary was preparing breakfast she'd say, 'Skippy, go out and fetch some eggs for breakfast.' I'd come back from the hen house with four chicken eggs for her and Uncle Clarence to share and one duck egg for me.

"Aunt Mary had my coffee ready with cream and sugar—man was it good! I'd eat that huge duck egg, bacon, sausage, and toast and savor four cups of her sweet coffee. I've been hooked on a quarter ounce of evaporated milk and two heaping spoons of sugar ever since. Now it's two cups of coffee a day with one sugar each, but I still allow myself one shot of evaporated milk in each cup.

"Why are you dressed in black, Charles? Are you trying to disguise yourself?"

"Shut up! Look at you; don't you ever change?"

"Nah, I have more jeans and cowboy boots in my closet than most stores have for sale."

Skip and Charles laughed as they picked up their second cups of coffee from the coffee bar in Charles' office. They left the office through the center doorway and stepped over to DAESY.

As Charles powered her up by pushing the main system power button, Daggard studied the system intently for a few minutes before he spoke. "Compact isn't she, Charles? I remember when we needed floor space of forty feet by twenty feet to house a system like this."

"Impressive, huh? That's modern technology for you, Skip. As you can see, DAESY is composed of one PC sized computer with a backup system. They are connected to a duel multiplex configuration capable of duplex operations; they can send and receive simultaneously. She has three information storage units: one for storing outgoing messages, one for saving incoming messages, and one for messages created for in-house purposes..."

Skip interrupted Charles, "Yeah, Charles modern technology. Hell, Charles when I went to Teletype School in '67' they were still teaching tube theory. We were using World War II Klineschmit equipment right through 1982. And look, we still have thirty-five thousand tape decks in use because the military spent Boo-Ku bucks on these magnetic tape readers."

"Yeah, I know, Skip. In some respects we are far advanced in certain fields, but we haven't made many improvements in other areas. But if you don't mind can I finish bragging about this baby!"

Skip Daggard shook his head.

"DAESY has a one hundred gig replaceable hard drive, a printer, scanner, and a magnetic tape storage unit. The whole system uses no more than a rectangle of floor space of four feet by six feet."

Skip stepped back shaking his head as he handed Charles the small silver canister. Charles removed the lid. "What's this?"

"The tape I need decoded."

Charles took the tiny spindle from its housing and removed the rubber band. Then he unwound the tape. Next, Charles placed the leader of the tape on the glass plate of the special tape reader attached to PC1, the main operating system, flipped a switch which removed DAESY from the on-line circuit to her off-line system. This prevented any distant ends DAESY may be connected to from receiving the information that's on the tape.

The magnetic tape was fed through the tape reader within a nano second. That's faster than a person can snap his or her fingers. Lights began flashing as DAESY came to analytic life. Within thirty seconds the printer created a hard copy of DAESY's response.

"Damn, Charles I hope the enemy doesn't know about this *baby*!"

"Awesome, huh?"

Skip nodded his head.

Charles looked at Skip and smiled. "It's a good thing we don't have flies in here, Skip because you would have swallowed them. Reach down and pick your chin up off the floor; you're drooling."

Both men stepped over to the printer on the right side of the system, and read the decoded type. "You have to notify the Secret Service immediately, Skip."

"No! You know me better than that. Right now I don't know who can be trusted or who's involved. The Secretary may not be acting alone."

Skip stood in front of the printer with his eyes closed. "I mean analyze the situation, Charles. Kelly and Schmirnoff can't be the only two involved; there must be others. I mean…"

A soft humming coming from DAESY interrupted Skip's conversation. He looked at the computer system and saw a flashing red "SEND" light. Skip jumped. "*What* the hell is going on Charles?"

"I guess it's the decipher specific code, Skip! DAESY is connected to KEDAS at NORAD."

"*What*! You mean those grounded jet-jockey's at Cheyenne Mountain are receiving this information?

"But you took her off-line, Charles…"

"Yeah, but KEDAS and DAESY have a special marriage; a decipher specific program."

Chuck watched Skip's face flush red. "Don't go spastic on me, Skip. Neither one of us knew what was on that tape."

It took Skip seventy seconds to collect his anger and regain control of himself. "Charles, how many analysts operate DAESY?"

"Three, two MI types and myself. Why"

"Contact them on the QT. All of you get out of Dodge with your families. I don't know who else is involved with this conspiracy, but you can be sure Secretary Kelly isn't acting alone.

"The Secret Service must be controlled in some way. It's impossible to guess how many of them may be involved."

Skip ripped the printout from DAESY's printer, folded the paper, unbuttoned four buttons of his shirt, and tucked the printout under his shirt refastening the buttons.

Charles handed Skip the canister containing the tape. "I don't understand, Skip!"

"I think it's time to Dede-mau, Charles. Like right now.

"The President is leaving for Camp David this morning. I'm going back to Washington. I will get on the chopper with him. Once we are at Camp David, I will get the President aside and explain the situation.

"I will give you three phones when we get out to our vehicles. They're my emergency stash. I will contact you when it is safe for you guys to return, so keep your ear to the listening post," Skip warned Charles as they exited NSA.

Cheyenne Mountain Facility
Colorado Springs, Colorado
Saturday—0255 hours EST

It was quiet inside the mountain facility; too quiet to suite Air Force Master Sergeant Chad Milan. "You know something?" he shared with his analysis partner, Sergeant Brenda Murray, "this atmosphere is stifling. All Hell has broken loose in the past nine years when things were this quiet!"

Sgt Murray wheeled on him, "Maybe you should…"

Her warning came too late. KEDAS, Cheyenne Mountains main analytic computer system activated automatically by a remote source. Sergeant Murray glared at Master Sergeant Milan as he approached KEDAS' printer. He read the decoded message, swore, ripped off the printout, typed in a few codes, then headed for the Commander's office at the double quick.

MSG Milan did not use the customary knock. He burst through the wooden door gasping for air.

"Sir, you, you better take, take a look at this," MSG Milan stammered as he handed Colonel Ambroser the printout.

"What the *hell* is this," shouted Colonel Ambroser after browsing the document, "where'd you get *this*?"

"From KEDAS, Sir. Someone at NSA activated DAESY's in-house system to decode a message. Since the message was encrypted specific, KEDAS is automatically alerted. What you have is a copy of the encrypted message decoded by DAESY.

"Sir, I accessed NSA's card reader access system to determine who had entered the facility in the past two hours."

The two men focused on a low hum coming from the ventilation system as MSG Milan caught his breath.

"There were two entries made at the same time: MI Agent Skip Daggard and GS-14 Charles Demois. Demois is one of three analysts assigned to the DAESY system, Sir. He's also a close friend of Agent Daggard."

Colonel Ambroser rose from his chair behind his desk. "What the hell is…are you sure it was Daggard?"

"Yes, Sir. I checked the access reader system three time."

Colonel Ambroser paced the blue carpet floor behind his desk studying the printout. MSG Milan stood at the position of "AT EASE" in front of the colonel's desk watching his commander.

After reading the message for the sixth time, Colonel Ambroser turned to face his sergeant, "What is Daggard doing at the Agency at this hour?" he asked the question not expecting an answer, "shit! He must have come from the White House."

The colonel fell back into his chair. He held the printout before his face and read it three more times while MSG Milan waited patiently at his position in front of the desk.

The tic-toc of the second hand on the white-faced, brown-rimmed, standard issue wall clock echoed loud in the twelve by twelve square room.

Milan stole a glance at the seven pictures of fighter jets strategically placed on the walls in the colonel's office. He studied the colonel's face—indecision. The colonel had no idea what to do. MSG Chad Milan entertained the idea of making a suggestion, then he checked himself.

Colonel Ambroser pushed a button on his intercom box.

Staff Sergeant Mary Marks responded, "Yes, Sir?"

"Mary, would you please get me General Stone on the horn?"

"Yes, Sir."

A minute later SSG Marks spoke through the bitch box, "Colonel, General Stone!"

She made the connection without further instructions.

"This better be good, Sam, waking me up at 0'dark thirty hours!"

"Sir," Colonel Ambroser said, "you needed to be here fifteen minutes ago!"

Ambroser could hear quiet, rapid breathing at the distant end. "I'm on my way, Sam."

Chapter Three
No One to Trust

NSA North Parking Lot
Fort Meade, Maryland
Saturday—0305 hours

Skip Daggard watched Charles drive out of the parking lot. He recalled the shocked horror in Charles' eyes.

"Why should the other analysts and I go into hiding, Skip?"

"Because all of you may now be in danger, Charles. I don't know who to trust. And those grounded Zoomies at Cheyenne Mountain have this info," Skip explained as he shook the printout inches from Charles' face.

"Look, Charles," Skip tried to soften his tone, "You've never been in the trenches. You have no concept of what we are capable of doing to each other."

Charles stood by his vehicle listening and staring at Daggard. Skip tried to soften his facial features and tone some more, but to do so meant Skip had to possess the ability to soften his inner self, a capability that he did not possess.

Skip reached over placing his left hand on his friend's right shoulder. Daggard's eyes went blank as he began, "Old friend, in your wildest imagined horrors you could not conceive the atrocities I have seen or have committed.

"If I was coming after you guys, I'd start with the army analyst, but I would put his wife on the rack, not him. Once I was convinced he didn't know anything, or I obtained the desired information, I would terminate his family, making him watch. Then I would kill him. I'd go after the rest of you and your families until I was satisfied that I had retrieved all the information I sought."

Charles stood riveted to the asphalt. "*Who* and *what* the hell are you?"

Skip turned his head away from his friend's burning eyes. Daggard sucked in the damp night air and slowly turned back towards Charles.

They stared at each other for a few seconds, then Skip said, "I'm one of those animals our government trained and groomed, yet denies exists."

Once Charles' headlights disappeared into the early morning darkness, Skip slid into his vehicle. He sat still all alone. Alone, that's how he lived and that's how he believed his life would end…all alone.

Argonne Hills
US Military Base Housing
Fort Meade, Maryland
Saturday—0320 hours

Charles Demois stood in the driveway of Army Staff Sergeant Neville Butts with Air Force Tech Sergeant Marty Herring.

"What's up, Mr. Demois," asked SSG Butts.

"I've just come from the Agency. I can't give you the details because it's classified top-secret sensitive. But the two of you and I have to put in leave requests immediately for no more than seven days and no fewer than five days."

The two sergeants looked at each other then back at Demois and said, "*Leave requests*!"

"Yes. We will submit our forms simultaneously at 0700 hours. That way the system won't kick our leaves back because the computer recognized a potential problem with all of us being off-sight at the same time.

"We need to take our families and disappear. That's the crucial statement—disappear. Do not disclose this to any one, or your destination.

"You will know when it is safe to return," Demois handed each man a code specific receiving device Daggard had given Demois earlier, "when these beep three times."

The two sergeants stood there bathed in the waning moonlight, staring at Mr. Demois, processing the weight of his words, and wondering what "proverbial shit" had hit the fan.

"All right, Sir," both sergeants said and disappeared into their respective quarters.

Sara Butts and Toni Herring were waiting by their front doors for their husbands.

Neville and Sara had been married for twenty years. She understood the grave look on Neville's face when he entered their home. Sara also understood the importance of a meeting like this one, especially at this hour. So when her husband told her to roust the kids and pack, she gave him no argument.

However, at SSG Herring's quarters the scene was drastically different. "I'm not going anywhere," Toni argued, "and who was that guy anyhow? And why did he come here at this hour of the morning?"

Marty and Toni had been married for three years. He had met her four years ago while home on Christmas leave in Queens, New York. They had corresponded and courted, then married on June 12th 2002.

"Toni, just help me pack a couple of bags and get the baby ready. We'll be leaving in a few hours."

Mrs. Herring was about to continue her fussing when Marty grabbed her, shook her by her shoulders, and said, "I never told you about my work, Toni. I guess now's the time! I'm a Military Intelligence Analyst. I work at NSA. Mr. Demois is a civilian analyst…we work together. Something has happened, and Mr. Demois believes our lives are in jeopardy so Neville and I have to put in for leave. Then all of us: Mr. Demois, the Butts', and us have to go into hiding."

Toni stared at him for a few seconds. "Marty, I thought midnight meetings like this only happened in the movies. You know, elements of fiction."

Marty squeezed Toni's right hand and kissed her. They began to pack.

General Stone's Office
Cheyenne Mountain Facility
Colorado Spring, Colorado
Saturday—0330 EST

General Stone sat in his thick-cushioned executive chair staring at the document Colonel Ambroser had stamped TOP-SECRET—on a need to know basis. Stone hadn't touched his coffee SSG Mary Nettles had placed before him. "Sir, your coffee is getting cold," Nettles said.

"Thank you, Sergeant," Stone said.

He took his coffee cup in his right hand and began sipping on the black, hot brew while he glared at the words on the printout.

MSG Milan ushered SSG Nettles out of the room and locked the door.

General Stone leaned back in his chair feeling very old. He had graduated from the US Air Force Academy in Colorado Springs, Colorado in April of 1965. He sipped more coffee. "Forty years..."

"Sir," both Ambroser and Milan responded.

"I've been on active duty for forty yeas. Maybe I will put in my retirement papers tomorrow. I'm getting too old for this *shit*. Who else has seen this?"

"No one, Sir. At least no one we're aware of," answered MSG Milan.

General Stone snapped his head up.

Milan said, "We're the only site linked to DAESY, Sir."

"At least that's what *we* believe, aye Master Sergeant?"

Silence filled the tiny ten-by-ten room. Milan studied the plastic models of an F-15, a B-29, and a B-117 Stealth decorating the General's desk The models had been given to him as presents by his fourteen year-old grandson, James.

"Let me see if I understand correctly, this message wasn't sent to us, yet we received it?"

"Yes, Sir," MSG Milan said, "it wasn't a transmission, Sir. DAESY at NSA decoded an input request. Because it was an encryption specific performance, KEDAS was automatically alerted through a special fail-safe program.

"Once DAESY completed her task, KEDAS activated her on-line system connecting her to him. He probed her memory, retrieved the data, then printed out a hard copy of the information while storing the data onto his hard drive, simultaneously."

General Stone studied the document for the fifth time. His mind seemed to revolt as if what he was reading could not be true. How could Secretary Kelly be involved in such a scheme?

He could sense the uneasiness in his subordinates as Ambroser and Milan shifted their weight from one leg to the other.

Stone laid the document on his desk while he finished his coffee. "Forty years" he thought. "I gave the Air Force my hair, my youth, and I've acquired midriff-bulge." He rubbed his grizzled hamster like face and said, "What do you make of this, Sam?"

Colonel Ambroser studied the message again before replying, "Sir, Chief Daggard must have intercepted this at the White House. Then he took it to NSA to be decoded. I say let him handle it for now. We put this printout in a sealed envelope in my safe and wait to see what develops."

MSG Chad Milan nodded his head in agreement to Colonel Ambroser's suggestion as General stone rose to his feet. Stone sighed heavily then said, "All right. Let me know immediately if anything happens. I'm going home."

"Yes, Sir," Colonel Ambroser said.

Colonel Sam Ambroser's office
Cheyenne Mountain Facility
Colorado Springs, Colorado
Saturday—0400 hours EST

Colonel Ambroser sat at his oak desk reviewing Ship Daggard's personnel file that he had MSG Milan retrieve from the MI microfiche data bank. He wasn't quite sure why he was scrutinizing Daggard's file. Perhaps it was the nagging throbbing in the back of his head. A warning that danger was imminent.

Ambroser believed Skip was in deep waters and was going to need help. He couldn't put his finger on the source causing his uneasy feeling. But as Ambroser stood to stretch, a realization assaulted his senses; Daggard was going to go after Secretary of State Kelly. There was no other alternative. Skip Daggard had to eliminate the threat. And when he did, all hell was going to break loose, causing a rift in the Intelligence Community.

Colonel Sam Ambroser stepped away from his desk, his face perspiring. He understood his uneasy feeling. Skip Daggard would give his life protecting the President.

Sam stole a look at himself in the mirror attached to his cloakroom door. His blonde hair was cropped short, but styled into a flat top. Three weeks ago he had turned fifty. The only present he received came from his wife, Sally—divorce papers. No way was he narcissistic, yet there was no question about it, he was handsome. Joining the "dating pool" would be no problem.

Ambroser stood six feet two inches tall. He lifted weights three days a week and ran five miles every day. The divorce wasn't a surprise, but he was sorry that twenty years of his life had just been shot to hell.

Sam Ambroser walked back to his desk and sat down. Once he was comfortable, he began to study Skip Daggard's file beginning with the Awards and Decorations section: Army Achievement Medal, Good Conduct Medal with ten oak leaf clusters, Bronze Star with four oak leaf clusters, Silver Star with three oak leaf clusters, one Purple Heart with seven awards. "Jesus Christ," thought Ambroser, "this bastard should be dead."

The ARCOM with two awards, the US Army Meritorious Service Medal, the Navy Cross. "How the *hell* did he win that?"

Next, came the Congressional Medal of Honor with two awards—a real...hero. Then there were his schooling ribbons, twelve in all, Vietnam Campaign ribbons with clusters, a Vietnam Cross of Gallantry, a Unit Vietnam Cross of Gallantry, and an Air Force Vietnam Cross of Gallantry.

"No wonder Daggard never wears his uniform; he can't fit all of the damn awards and decorations on the thing, or else he'd be too weighted down to move," Ambroser said out loud.

Colonel Ambroser leaned back in his executive's chair. He swiveled his chair around focusing his attention on a black framed picture of a clear blue sky dotted by a profile of a US war plane called "Puff the Magic Dragon."

"Puff the Magic Dragon" was a C130 cargo plane transformed into an awesome fire breather with twin .50 caliber machineguns mounted in port windows of both sides of the plane. The rear cargo door could be lowered, when the plane received enemy fire from the rear, and return fire from the rear mounted quad fifties. "Puff" could shoot out every blade of grass on a football sized-battlefield in thirty seconds due to its concentration of firepower. "Puff" had seen service in Vietnam.

Next, Ambroser scanned Daggard's Assignments section. His first assignment was two years in Vietnam with the 1st Signal Brigade, STRATCOM, 29th Signal Group, and 325th Signal Battalion, Thailand. Ambroser studied this assignment for several minutes. Skip's assignment after Nam in February 1970 was to Ent Air Force Base and NORAD in Colorado Springs, Colorado. This was where Daggard and Ambroser first met. Sam Ambroser was a First Lieutenant then and Daggard was a Staff Sergeant. Remembering the encounter sent a shiver up and down Ambroser's spine. He could see Daggard's cold, penetrating eyes as if Daggard was there in his office right now. And Daggard's words, 'I kill "Leftenants" for sport, Lt. so don't fuck with me or get in my business, or I'll blow your head off.'

Ambroser Stared at Daggard's file. He gripped several forms in his hands and thought back to Daggard's third trip to the Mountain. Daggard was conversing with a MI Air Force Sergeant. 'Yeah, two damn years. My tour cost me a fiancée and my sanity. But I guess the army liked my work so much they gave me six addition months to show their appreciation.' Daggard had laughed, but Ambroser remembered the hatred in those sky blue eyes…hatred and death.

Colonel Sam Ambroser closed Skip's file. He had had enough of reminiscence. Agent Skip Daggard was part of them; he belonged to the Military Intelligence Community. Daggard was one of the best the US had, and the past was best left in the past. If Daggard needed help, then the MI Community would back him up… "If we can," Ambroser said out loud.

White House Comcenter
White House, Washington, D.C.
Saturday—0410 hours

SFC Anderson looked at the wall clock for what she felt must be the hundredth time in the past hour, 0910Z. She prepared the day's activities for the on-coming shift seventeen times, rearranging and delegating the workload.

Kristine Anderson took out her compact and stared at her image in the tiny mirror. She touched up her cheeks with a dab of rouge. Pretty! Yes, she was pretty she believed. Not beautiful, but pretty enough to turn heads when she passed by.

Kristine could not understand why Skip was so infatuated with her freckle line that dotted her face from one cheek to the other across the bridge of her nose. She combed her shoulder length ash blonde hair, which was her natural color, then glanced at the clock again. 0911Z.

"Skip Daggard," Kristine said, "I am going to beat you severely across your head and shoulders for keeping me in the dark. *Where are you?*"

Anderson jumped drawing her weapon as the steel door swung open.

Skip raised his hands in mock surrender. "Going to shoot me *again?*"

"Skip! You startled me. And yes! I should shoot you. Where the hell have you been? Why didn't you call me like you promised...?"

Skip allowed the door to close then he hung up his coat. "Slow down, honey. Catch your breath."

"Were you able to get the message decoded?"

As they closed for a hug, Skip took Kristine's weapon from her trembling hand. He looked over her right shoulder taking in the view of the comcenter. There were workstations for the operators to log and catalogue messages, several racks of multiplex systems connected to computers and these systems were connected to distant ends through an intricate maze of cryptic equipment. Teletype systems were located in one corner for both on-line and in-house use.

Skip's sigh of hot breath sent an exotic shiver through Kristine as Skip pulled her in as if he was trying to create one body out of his and hers.

"Which question do you want me to answer first?"

Kristine shrugged her shoulders.

"I didn't call you because I was coming back here," Skip said as he separated from their hug, "I was at the Agency, sweetheart. And I think I just lost a good friend. And I don't have enough of them that I can afford to lose any."

Skip studied her bewildered face. "I'll explain later."

Daggard took the printout from its hiding place in his shirt and handed it to her. As Kristine read, Skip once again scrutinized her facial expressions. "What's wrong with this picture," he asked himself. Then he realized—no emotion. Her expression was devoid of surprise. As if what she was reading was expected.

Kristine handed the printout back to Skip. "What are you going to do, darling? You must at least inform the Secret Service."

"No!"

Skip started walking towards his office holding the printout in his right hand. He stopped and turned to Kristine. "Honey, this is *shit*," Daggard said loudly shaking the printout in the air.

"President Mantle had to pick up the gauntlet of a world depression when he took office in January. But this…this is treason. And I should go to Kelly's quarters, drag him from his bed and through the streets. Drag him into the President's bedroom, force Kelly to his knees, jam my weapon in his mouth, and have him ask the President for forgiveness, then blow the bastard's brains out."

Daggard went to his office with Kristine right behind him.

"S-k-i-p!" he gave her his undivided attention.

"I strongly believe you should turn this over to the Secret Service. Let them handle it. After all that's their job, protecting the President."

Kristine watched his face change; saw the emptiness in his eyes— gone. *How does he do that*? Where does he go? "Skip! Skip, come back, Skip."

She watched the life return to his eyes. "Skip, give it to the Secret Service."

"No. I'm going to warn the President. I am not going to alert anyone else because I don't know who can be trusted or who's involved. Hell, Kristine half the Secret Service could be involved in this plot.

"Besides, what do I tell them? Oh by the way guys, Secretary Kelly is going to assassinate the President. No! I'll get on the chopper with the President and that traitorous son of a bitch at 0800, and fly up to Camp David with them. After I check in with SSG Hoboken, I will get the President aside and tell him.

"I'll let President Mantle deal with Kelly. After all, he's the one who selected Kelly for the position. Then I'll start my leave and go home as planned."

Skip dropped into his Captain's chair, "I'm getting old, sweetheart."

Kristine sat on Skip's lap and planted a juicy kiss on his lips.

"Inappropriate behavior for the office, honey, but give me another one."

"You must be super special, Skip Daggard," Kristine said, "every one from generals down has to be on duty because the President will be at Camp David this weekend, but you get to go on leave."

"Well, honey I am. *You* caught me. Don't you have some work to finish up?"

Skip sat at his desk feeling home was getting farther away, and thinking of a safe place to hide the printout and canister containing the tape. He felt that uneasy premonition again that something was about to happen.

White Marsh, Maryland
Charles Demois' home
Saturday—0425 hours

Charles entered his house and fixed a pot of coffee. He went upstairs. Claudette was sitting up when he entered their bedroom. "Did you get the problem fixed?"

"No, Claudette. It's led to a worse situation. Get up and get dressed. We have to pack and be back at Fort Meade before seven so I can submit a vacation request."

Claudette saw the dark shadows around his eyes. "What has *happened*, Charles?"

"All I can tell you, honey is that all hell is about to break loose. When it does, we have to be in hiding."

Claudette and Charles had been married since forever. She had never questioned him about his work and she wasn't going to start now. If he said they were in danger then she'd comply with his orders.

Charles had returned from the attic with two suitcases. Claudette had dressed and was laying folded clothes on their bed. Charles took some hanging articles of clothing from their closet. Together, they packed their bags.

Charles carried their suitcases downstairs and placed them by the back door. He entered the kitchen as Claudette was pouring coffee into their cups. "What is it, Chuck?" she probed as they sat down at the kitchen breakfast bar with their coffee.

Claudette gently placed her right hand on his, "Chuck, where are you? I asked you what's wrong?"

Chuck sighed and looked around their kitchen. The oak breakfast bar they were sitting at was built and installed by Chuck and Skip. Skip installed the Formica paneling walls. And Skip had helped Chuck bring in the new flat surfaced stove and reconnect the new wiring for it.

"Chuck, answer me because you are beginning to frighten me."

"You think you know someone, Claudette, especially when you work with him for several years and go hunting with him. How often have we had Skip Daggard over?"

Chuck took a sip of coffee and sighed again. Tears began to form at the corners of his eyes. Claudette rubbed his hand. "What has happened, honey?"

"I just learned that I don't know Skip Daggard at all, Claudette," he reached for her hand taking it gently between his and caressing her smooth ebony skin, "How many times have we had him here? How many times has he played with our children? And yet, just like that," Chuck snapped his fingers, "Skip could kill all of us without a howdyoudo. He's a government assassin, an operative."

"*Chuck*, what is going on?"

"I wish I could share with you, honey but it's best for you not to know…except…by the end of today, Secretary of State Kelly will be dead along with a Russian Secretary, and I am part of their murders."

Claudette felt her heart stop as her breath caught in her throat. "*Charles…*"

"We have to leave, sweetheart."

Colonel Ambroser's Office
Cheyenne Mountain Facility
Colorado Springs, Colorado
Saturday—0432 hours EST

Colonel Ambroser returned to his seat with a fresh cup of hot coffee and reopened Daggard's file. He didn't look at the records right away, but stared at his wife and two sons pictures in the gold double frame on his desk. Ambroser studied her red hair and freckles as if he were seeing them for the first time, while he sipped his coffee.

Once his coffee was finished, Ambroser continued reviewing Daggard's assignment section. Skip served eight months with NORAD, three years with the Third Armored Division Drake/Edwards Kaserne, Frankfurt, Germany, and three months at Fort Devins, Massachusetts. Next, Daggard spent two years with the 9th Infantry Division at Fort Lewis, Washington, three years at Field Station Augsburg, three years at NSA with the 29th MI Group, Fort Meade, Maryland, and three months in Teague, Korea at Camp Carroll.

"Damn," thought Ambroser, Daggard reeked havoc in Korea: Two American colonels demoted and one GS-14 American civilian and two Korean officials assassinated.

Sam Ambroser wasn't privy to the communiqué sent by Daggard to then Colonel Hanalin, but Colonel Stone was, and Stone shared a brief statement of the message with Lt. Ambroser.

'I came. I observed. I listened, and then I cleaned up your mess.' That was in the spring of 1986.

Then there were two years with the Military Police at the 519th MP Battalion at Fort Meade, Maryland, back to NSA with a variety of field assignments not specifically identified in Daggard's files; then Skip was assigned to the White House in the spring of 2002.

Daggard's training courses covered one and one half pages to include his advanced courses at Ft. Gordon, GA, Ft. Devins, MA, Camp Lejeune, NC, Ft. Stewart, GA, a naval camp at the Florida Keys, Alaska and the Mojave Desert. Jump training with the 82nd Airborne, escape and evasion training with the snake eating Green Berets in the swamps of North Carolina and the CIA throughout the world.

Ambroser sat back in his chair formulating an image of a man from what he personally knew of Skip Daggard and what he had just learned in reading Daggard's file. The files were deceiving because much of the story was left out. If a person looking at these files didn't know Daggard, that person wouldn't know to read between the lines because all of Daggard's assignments were cover and concealment positions for a well trained Military Intelligence Operative, whose sole purpose in life was to kill and gather information in the best interest of the United States.

A ping of jealousy began to stir in the heart of Colonel Sam Ambroser, but it was more than jealousy; it was a deep admiration for one of Americas' best. However, he would never acknowledge these glowing emotions because he knew Agent Skip Daggard had given up a normal life for his country.

"Let's see," Ambroser said, "where was I? Oh yes!" He continued reading. Agent Daggard is a Linguistics expert—fluent in seven languages, has had sniper and Seal training, demolitions and explosives training, and is an expert in cryptology and encoding and decoding procedures. Daggard has an Associates Degree in Criminology, a BS in History. He has completed the army's 171 hours of the 95 Delta Criminal Investigations Course (CID), 170 hours of the Precommissioned Officer's Course, and MI's advanced Technical Listening Device's usage and repair courses. The list continued but Ambroser had had enough.

Sam Ambroser leaned back in his chair again. He placed his elbows on the armrests and his chin between his fingers after he had closed Daggard's file. "Why hadn't Daggard excepted an Officer's Commission? And why am I wasting time on Daggard's file?"

Colonel Ambroser leaned to his left. He placed his left elbow on the armrest of his chair and his chin in the palm of his left hand and closed his eyes. Sam thought about his beautiful redheaded wife and the birthday present she had just given him, yet forced himself to think about the current situation.

"Why am I wasting time on Daggard's file? Because of that damniable message and Daggard's involvement, which means at some point in time I will be involved along with the entire MI Community; therefore, somebody better know something about the man we're about to put our credentials on the line for.

"Hell," Ambroser spat out, "I am already involved. We're all involved now."

White House Comcenter
White House, Washington, D.C.
Saturday—0445 hours

Skip Daggard gave up thinking about the events that were unfolding which may have an impact on his homecoming. Instead, he diverted his thoughts back to the evidence and where to stash them. He observed Kristine at her communications station through his small office window. Skip waited for five minutes after she had placed her headset on before he approached her. Stealth-like, he hid the canister and printout in a secret compartment at the base of her handbag. His face was devoid of any expression as he performed his task. Daggard didn't even crack a smirk as to his cleverness. "After all," he thought, "giving Kristine this handbag was simply a precautionary measure. One never knows what information one will have to smuggle out of where."

Once Skip was finished, he backed up slowly then approached Kristine so he was visible in her peripheral vision. She removed her headset, stood up and kissed him. "Skip, I am sorry, but I'm worried."

"Honey, there is nothing to worry about. I've been doing subversive work for over thirty years. The only time I was caught was by the Soviets, and that was in 1975. They had me for two long days until my boys came and rescued me.

"You *do* realize that kissing is another infraction, and inappropriate behavior while you're on duty!"

"Shut up and kiss me again."

"Yes, Ma'am."

After a long, wet kiss, Skip said, "I'm going to lie down for awhile. Please roust me out at 0715."

"All right, honey. Sleep well, and try not to have any nightmares."

White House Comcenter
White House, Washington, D.C.
Saturday—0750 hours

Skip Daggard finished with his grooming then checked the clock, 1250Z. Inside he felt calm. A calm that comes after the adrenaline rush just before he killed someone. The same calm he had gotten waiting on a "demarcation line" prior to jumping off on a mission.

His senses were acute. Kristine's perfume was burning his nostrils. The oil in the commo equipment smelled like hot gun solvent. Skip could hear all of the intricate, silent devices on the computers. He looked everything over, as he stepped out of his office, wondering if this would be the last time he would see this place.

The avenue he was about to approach was cast in deep shadows. Skip had no idea who could be trusted. "Strange," he thought, "just how secretive and elusive his world really is." The President was about to be assassinated; he couldn't go to anyone to set up a trap to take out the suspected perpetrators for fear of his own life.

Skip knew he couldn't go to the Secret Service, or the FBI, or his own people. Maybe he should do what Kristine suggested, 'turn it over to the proper authorities.' No!

He knew that was not an option.

As Skip approached the coat rack, Kristine came to him. They hugged then Skip said, "When you're relieved, honey I want you to go directly to Mr. Bloom's cabin. Don't go near our place or call anyone. Simply go to the cabin and remain silent until I arrive. Do you understand?"

Kristine nodded her head. She saw that the blood had drained from Skip's face, and his eyes were cold and calculating. When they parted from their kiss, she felt a ripple shiver her spine. "Skip, I have to report back for duty this afternoon."

There were thirty seconds of silence as Skip paused in the doorway of the comcenter. He stepped back inside while he held the door open, "Kristine, we may never be returning to duty after today." Then Skip closed the door behind him.

As Skip walked up the corridor passed the Secret Service Desk Officer, he broke stride. "Maybe I should...," Skip thought as he turned his head to speak, then he continued on.

Chapter Four
The Traitor

White House
Washinton, D.C.
Saturday - 0800 hours

Skip left the White House through the garden exit under the surveillance of a security camera. He stepped out into a bright, sunny morning with blue skies and raced across the rear, freshly mowed lawn. As he neared the waiting helicopter, he fell in with the President who was in a stand-down dress code. President Mantle wore a pale tan polo shirt, white Dockers slacks, and dark brown Dockers deck-hand loafers. He carried a light tan sports jacket and a brief case. "I thought you were on leave, Skip!" declared the President.

"I want to check on communications at Camp David before I go, Sir." Skip replied taking notice of Secretary of State Kelly who was all business-like in his gray cotton three piece suit and tie with black Cockrens.

As the helicopter lifted off, the whoop, whoop, whooping sounds of the blades reminded Skip of another time...another place...Vietnam.

No matter how hard he tried to avoid a transformation Skip couldn't because he had spent too many days...too many months and countless hours hearing the whirling sounds of chopper blades from Huey Gunships and Chinooks as they arrived and departed from LZ's. He had been on too many of them. The whirling sounds of chopper blades *always* affected him. The images and sounds of a world gone insane always flashed through his mind. Young soldiers moaning as their blood shot up from wounds and splattered against the ceiling of Huey's. The rapid fire...Rat-a-tat-tat explosions of .50 cal. machine guns mounted in side doors. And the last, soft, gentle whispers of breath of a young man saying goodbye to his loved-ones.

Skip tried to limit his contact with the Secretary of State because he felt the rage building up inside of him—the demon testing the restraints and trying to bust loose fighting for control. At times, it

43

frightened him because he was out of control. The demon force made grave demands upon him: kill, smash, pulverize, and destroy. The only way to release the pressure was to obey.

Skip felt himself leaning forward towards the traitor. He felt his right arm stretch out across the small space of the helicopter and his hand fastening around the scumbucket's throat while his left hand opened the door. He could hear Secretary Kelly screaming as he was yanked from his seat and went airborne at seven hundred feet.

Skip shook his head realizing it was only in his mind. He fought the urgency of the rage and averted his eyes from Secretary Kelly.

Chief Daggard thought back to another time in Vietnam when he had been ordered to acquire information at any cost. "We need that information, Sergeant Daggard. You're the man to get it," explained Lieutenant Hanalin, "now get it any way you can. Memorize these six photos. They're the VC that has the information we need. They're in Phenomphen. Be back here twenty-one hundred hours tomorrow."

"Phenomphen? Last night President Nixon told the American people we weren't fighting in Cambodia!"

Lieutenant Hanalin glared at Skip.

"Ooh," responded Skip, "one of those little white lies it's Okay. for a President to tell."

"Just do it, Daggard. Now get going."

On that particular excursion, Skip threw two VC out of the chopper at six hundred feet, making their comrades watch as the bodies of their friends splattered on the hilltop. When he reached for the third VC they gave him all the information he wanted, plus some extra. Satisfied they were telling him the truth, Skip kicked them out as well. His mission didn't call for prisoners.

Right now, at this moment, Skip wanted to do that to the Secretary of State, yank him up and kick him out while the chopper was at eight hundred feet over the Catoctin Mountains.

Skip sat back, maintaining a distant coherence to the conversation between the President and the Secretary. He surveyed the terrain below trying to locate the lines of march of Lee and Meade's forces on their way to Gettysburg.

Daggard thought, as he continued his search, how strange are the events of war. Lee's intention was to capture Harrisburg to draw the Army of the Potomac away from Washington, then drive south to capture the capital. However, two things happened: Lee didn't have the eyes of Stuart's Calvary, and his men desperately needed footwear. So Lee gave in to demands from his officers, and allowed for a small force to travel a short distance southeast into Gettysburg to acquire all of the boots and shoes available. It was this decision which led to one of the most famous battles in world history, which is still studied today by many domestic and foreign leaders.

But no matter how hard Skip tried to avoid the Secretary, he realized he couldn't, "I may have to kill you before the week is over," Skip whispered to himself.

An Exxon gas station
Washington, D.C.
Saturday - 0820 hours

SFC Kristine Anderson sat in her blue Mercedes convertible remembering the deafening sound of the code lock securing as Skip had closed the door behind him. She had turned to SSG Parker, "Ceres, I have outlined the duties for the day. SSG Hoboken's team is on-site. We changed the sandwiches at 1255Z. Camp David will complete a commo check with you every thirty minutes until the President returns to the White House."

Kristine felt a chill ripple up and down her spine in the eighty-degree heat of the bright Saturday morning as she swung her legs out of her vehicle. She stood up and gently closed her car door, then straightened her Garrison Cap on her head. She left her Greens jacket draped across the back of the passenger seat. Her stockings made a rustling sound as she walked across the asphalt close to the two rows of three gas pumps toward the telephone. She stood inside an outside telephone booth near the rear of a faded white building of the Exxon station wiping sweat from her brow trying to determine if the temperature or what she was about to do caused her perspiration. The underarms of her green blouse were stained with sweat.

People were using the pumps and going into and out of the convenience store of the gas station. Jackhammers were pounding against the concrete as chisels smashed the cement into small pieces two hundred yards from where she was standing. Pedestrians were choking on the gray dust from the work even though they held handkerchiefs to their noses and mouths.

Kristine was dressed in her proper military attire. She stood erect, fumbling with the encryption telephone transmission device and dial pad as she connected the devices to the handset and the black telephone box. She felt a cold shiver again as Skip's words, "Don't call anyone," echoed in her ears as she began pushing buttons on the dial pad.

The phone rang three times before someone answered. SFC Anderson responded in a soft voice in Russian. "The dog is on the scent."

"Guide him as needed. In twenty-four hours you will be the only agent remaining in Amerika."

She paused for a moment, "I will figure out a way," and hung up. Carefully, she removed her devices. She lingered in the phone booth thinking about what she had to do. Finally, she opened the glass door and walked back to her car.

Standing by her vehicle, Kristine thought back to her eight years with MI and how she had prayed for the day she would finally get to work with the infamous Military Intelligence operative, Army Staff Sergeant Skip Daggard. She had dreamed of it since she was twelve.

"Papa, she said to the man in the brown uniform with red markings, "who is this Daggard you speak of in anger an awe? I think I will marry him!"

Kristine watched the men working with their jackhammers. Her Papa's voice, she remembered, sounded similar to those jackhammers.

Papa grabbed her by her left arm. He bent down as he yanked her into his scolding face, "You will *never* marry this man, Putchka. He is our enemy."

Now she watched seven years of training and preparation pass before her eyes. The years she spent in "Little America" in Georgia, Russia.

She heard the admiration in her countrymen's voices for Skip Daggard as they planned and plotted to kill him. Yet, week after week he lived and her love for him grew.

Kristine Anderson gazed upon Washington and the Capitol Building listening to the workmen tearing up the sidewalk. She recalled more memories as she watched people move along the street. How much fun she and Skip would have spy jumping around the world! The taste of his lips on hers, and how she would jump into his arms shouting 'yes, yes, yes' when he asked her to marry him. She sighed getting into her car because she knew the future she had just set in motion was going to change her dreams. She also knew beyond any reason or doubt that when she gave her beloved the information she had, pertinent information he needed, he would kill her.

As Kristine drove out of Washington she shivered again because she had come to know Skip Daggard, know him as much as he allowed. His beliefs were simple: Defend the American people and the Constitution against all foreign and domestic enemies even if the enemy was the American Government.

He grew up at the beginning of and during the cold war. She knew he detested communism and fought them with a vengeance even though the Iron Curtain had come crumbling down. "Yes, fighting does make sense," he told her one night, "because communism hasn't been defeated," and as he put it, "I hate all Commies."

It's this belief of his which frightens her the most because if and when he finds out her secret, Skip may shoot her without giving her a chance to explain. But she *must*, at whatever cost to herself, tell him who his true target is.

"How strange life is," she thought, as she steered her car over the Potomac River into Virginia past Arlington Cemetery. Her dreams had come true only to be foiled by an outside variable. "To arrive at my station, the fiancée of my childhood sweetheart, only to be killed by him," she said to the tombstones as she drove by.

Camp David
Fort Ritchie, Maryland
Saturday - 0930 hours

The Presidential Marine helicopter landed at the LZ at Camp David without incident. "I will speak with you before I head out," Skip said to President Mantle as they disembarked from the chopper.

The President nodded his head in acknowledgement as a second helicopter touched down with the Joint Chiefs of Staff. In this time of terrorism, the US was taking precautions by not putting all of its leaders together.

Daggard completed a visual on the transmitter towers as he crossed the green to the tree line west of the LZ pads. He unlocked the repeater substation steel door at the base of one antenna tower to check the inside temperature and to insure all LED's were functioning. He stood just inside the door feeling the cool breeze from the AC unit with his black coat over his shoulder. The rain had ceased and the sun was shining.

The temperatures on the East Coast had been hovering around 70 degrees for the passed month. When Skip stepped into the bunker type building's cool air, a flash from the past brought a smile to his face.

The comcenter at Bang Pla was kept at a constant 60 degrees, but the outside daytime temperatures ranged from 110-130 degrees. Because it was his first day on duty, Skip had to work the day shift for OJT, which usually lasted about two weeks. He finally got to go for chow at 1230 hours. As he approached the outer two steel doors of the comcenter and began to pull open the left side door, the duty MP said, "You better open that door slowly!"

"Why?"

"Because of the head," the MP said.

Skip started chuckling remembering what had happened next. He had yanked open the door against the MP's advice, and was sucker punched in the face and chest and sent flying back inside across the floor.

"What the hell happened?"

Tony, the on-duty MP had laughed then said, "I tried to warn you, but all of you newbies are the same, you think you know it all. So let me explain "the laws of physics." Our inside temperature is sixty. The outside temp is fifty to seventy degrees hotter so when you yanked open the door you created an updraft. It's that updraft that hit you."

As he closed and locked the door to the substation, Skip was still smiling over the fact that he had been twenty years old and had to learn how to open doors again. But Skip became solemn because he remembered Americans had to learn how to do many things different in Nam—often a soldier never got a second chance.

Skip checked in with the Sergeant-in-Charge of communications at Camp David, "Is everything okay here, Paul?"

Daggard took in the commo station in one quick glance. Sergeant Knead was performing a commo check with the White House comcenter.

"Yes, Sir. What's wrong that brings you off of your leave?"

Skip ignored SSG Paul Hoboken's question as he looked things over and checked written instructions. Once he was satisfied, Chief Daggard responded, "I opted to do a final check before I went to visit my mother so I wouldn't have to worry about getting a phone call," Skip lied. He spent twenty-five minutes with his Ops Sergeant shooting-the-breeze so the President would have time to settle in.

The President was sitting at a glass table on the rear patio sipping coffee and reading the newspaper all alone when Skip found him. "Mr. President, walk out with me please."

President Mantle looked up as he lowered his newspaper, "*What?*"

"I need to speak with you, Sir," Skip said, "so please walk out with me."

President Mantle trusted this operative, but didn't like him because Skip Daggard was too headstrong and a lone wolf. However, he put down his newspaper and drank down the last of his coffee. "All right, Skip!"

When they had walked about forty yards, Skip wrote on a piece of paper, 'Remove your jacket lay it on the grass. Empty all of your pockets. Leave nothing in them; no change, bills, wallets, pens or pencils.'

As the President began to speak, Skip placed his finger to his own lips.

The thick green lawn had been freshly mowed. Mist rose from the ground in swirls as a gentle breeze blew across the top of the hill.

President Mantle removed his tan sports jacket staring at Daggard. "Is this really necessary, Skip?"

Skip stared at the President.

After the President did as directed, they walked out another ten yards, "What's with the Cloak and Dagger routine, Skip?"

"Sir, you have to swear to secrecy of what I am about to tell you. Swear!"

President Mantle had known of Daggard's irrational, unorthodox behavior because as a Senator and a member of the Military Appropriations Committee, he had signed funding for Daggard's exploits.

Mantle had learned in the few short months he had been President to trust this loner with high standards and values. He swore.

"Mr. President, Secretary Kelly is plotting against you. I intercepted an encrypted message this morning between Kelly and Schmirnoff in the Russian Embassy here in Washington."

Skip told him what he had discovered about the Secretary's plot to assassinate him, and that some Russians were involved.

President Mantle listened quietly focusing on Skip's eyes while Skip explained the situation.

"Are you sure, Skip?"

"Yes, Sir. I have the conversation on tape."

"Where is the tape, *on you*?"

Skip had not survived twenty-five years as a field agent and covert operative because of luck. No! It was his sixth sense, his warning device that kept him alive. Now it was ringing off the hook. The President's question was what people in the business called, a fishing expedition.

Skip turned his back to the President for two seconds, "What's wrong with this picture, Skip Daggard?" he asked himself. The thought raced through his mind, what's wrong is the lack of shock or surprise on the President's face; just flushed anger. Skip felt the President's response was all wrong.

"Skip, where is the tape? I want to listen to the conversation *now*," President Mantle demanded.

"That made sense," Skip thought, but something was out of kilter and Skip found himself wondering how to proceed.

He turned back to the President. He was not going to inform him about the printout. "I have it in a safe place, Sir. I will bring it to you Tuesday as soon as I return from leave. That was my intention," Skip lied again.

Skip watched the President's cheeks go rosy, "I think you better cancel your vacation. I want that tape immediately," the President shouted, "I'm ordering you to bring it to me within the hour."

Skip stared at the President as his warning signals shouted, "Danger, danger! Warning, warning! Something's not right here, Skip Daggard!"

"No, Sir."

"What?"

"Sir, I haven't been home in about thirty-five years. My mom is expecting me today because I had given her a ring-down five days ago. And quite frankly, Mr. President, your reaction puzzles me."

Skip stealthily stole a glance at the house. He faced President Mantle again. "I think we should terminate this meeting, Mr. President. Secretary Kelly may be getting suspicious. You are having a dinner party on Tuesday. I'll bring you the tape then, and no one will be the wiser."

President Mantle was not happy as he sighed and argued with himself whether he should force the issue with Daggard. But he didn't want to alienate Daggard or make Skip suspicious, "All right, Skip. The dinner begins at seven. I *want* to see you with the tape before six."

"Yes, Sir. I believe that's a better plan. You can listen undisturbed and without the Secretary. I'll bring a small recorder to the Oval Office at 1800, I mean 6 p.m."

As they walked back, the President retrieved his sports jacket, wallet, and pen. Skip helped President Mantle into his jacket. "All right, Skip, 6 p.m. Tuesday night."

When they reached the steps leading up to the patio, Skip saw Secretary Kelly standing by the French glass doors, which opened onto the multicolored stoned veranda.

Skip stepped inside as the Secretary slipped out and began conversing with the President. Skip located Special Agent Ben Brookes and asked if he could take him to the Ft. Ritchie motor pool.

The President's facial expression stayed with him toying with his conscience while Agent Brookes drove the black Chevy Yukon down the mountain to Fort Ritchie. "Oldies" were blaring from the surround sound system. "You got to know how to hold them. Know when to fold them." Words to "The Gambler" by Kenny Rodgers, "Is there a meaning here, Skip Daggard?" he asked himself.

Fort Ritchie motor pool
Ft. Ritchie, Maryland
Saturday -1030 hours

Agent Brookes dropped Skip off at the Fort Ritchie motor pool where he intended to acquire a vehicle to drive to his mom's place in Morristown, New Jersey.

"Hey Skip," said Master Sergeant Harkman.

"Hey Hark, how goes the war?"

"Not so bad since you've been here last. I've got some good mechanics who care about the quality of their work."

"When I was here last year you had a group of deadbeats! What happened?"

Daggard watched mechanics working on various types of military vehicles. Two Pfc.'s were in their green T-shirts rebuilding an engine for a Deuce and a half truck. One female mechanic was in the pit changing the oil on a jeep, and two generator mechs were rebuilding a fuel line on a Mod. D-68, dual generators for a mobile communications center.

"Remember I told you I had jumped up and down, yelling and screaming about better help?"

"I remember."

"But that wasn't the cause for the change; no Sir! When the rear wheel came off of the General's vehicle sending his car into a ditch with him and his girlfriend in it, that brought immediate transfers."

Both men laughed.

"I remember the traffic on the commo circuits regarding that incident. The powers to be were kicking around the idea of retiring your general."

"Yup. It's water under the bridge except the sucker received his second star four months later."

The eight bay doors were open to allow a gentle breeze to blow through the motor pool.

"You need a vehicle, Skip?"

"Yeah. Give me a good one, Hark. Log it out to "Personal Use," and I'll pay up when I return it."

"That's what I admire about you, Skip!"

"What's that?"

"You're the only one I know who pays for using a government vehicle for his own personal use. Most of 'em sign a vehicle out to government business, but not you."

The Motor Sergeant assigned Skip a 1997 Dodge sedan, blue with all the upgraded options: AC, CD, PS, PW, and power brakes.

While MSG Harkman was inspecting the vehicle and checking to make sure it was topped off, Skip was surveying the outer perimeter of the motor pool. He spotted the standard issue secret service black sedan parked along the curb a quarter mile down the street.

"Amateurs" he thought, "unprofessional amateurs." He began to entertain the idea of running towards them drawing his weapon, but MSG Harkman broke into his world, "She's ready, Skip."

"Thanks Hark. I'll get it back to you in about three days. Going over to Jersey to see my Mom." Skip's heart stopped and a lump formed in his throat as he stared at the Motor Sergeant. "I'm going *home*, Hark!"

Tears began to form at the corners of Daggard's eyes as he placed his right hand on Harkman's right shoulder. "I'm finally going home."

As Skip drove out of the motor pool gate, he looked up the street. The vehicle was still there. "I wonder what his malfunction is?" Skip said to himself. "Maybe Kelly managed to overhear his conversation with the President after all."

Thurmont, Maryland
Saturday - 1045 hours

Skip drove east from Fort Ritchie along route 550 down the mountain towards Thurmont. It was a gorgeous spring day. Trees were alive with new buds after their dormant winter sleep. Lawns were receiving their first manicures of the season while robins were dive-bombing for insects and sparrows were remodeling their summerhouses.

Observing these indicators of spring, Daggard began a methodical mental playback of the conversation he had with the President as he checked his rearview mirror—no vehicle. The undertone was not sitting well with him. His sixth sense was still at work warning him something was wrong. Skip wasn't sure what had activated his alert system, but he had learned a long time ago to listen and react to his warning system.

Skip kept looking in his rearview mirror, but the twists and turns of route 550 made it difficult for him to see if he was being followed. It wasn't until he pulled out onto route 15 at Thurmont heading North that he realized he had a tail.

Skip had taken the route fifteen-north exit and guided his vehicle into the flow of traffic.

The sedan he had seen from the motor pool fell in four cars behind him. "Skip, you are too paranoid," he said to himself, "you've been in this business too damn long."

"Seems it's the same thing Kristine had said," he thought.

He drove through Gettysburg looking at the historic monuments on either side of the road. Skip was traveling the same road that divided the battlefield one hundred and forty-two years ago. General Picket's men crossed this road, led by General Lewis Armistead, on their ill-fated charge against General Meade's center position.

Revisiting Gettysburg evoked Skip's memory of the one hundred and twenty-fifth anniversary of the battle of Gettysburg. He had been a Civil War reenactor with A Company, First Maryland Volunteer Infantry, a Union unit from Baltimore. The combined forces of reennactors were estimated at seventeen thousand men and three hundred cannons.

As the Rebs marched towards the Union line, they were shoulder to shoulder with their battle flags waiving in the slight July breeze. Their gray ranks appeared to stretch across the field a half-mile long and a mile deep. A Union officer on horseback stood up in his stirrups waving his hat in the air shouting, "Passad," a cheer honoring the bravery of the oncoming Rebs. The chant was taken up by the entire Union ranks eleven lines deep and numbering about forty-five hundred troops.

We stood waving our Kempi's and yelling, "Passad," while tears began filling our eyes for the courage and bravado of these Americans in gray.

When they started charging we discovered that the first three ranks of our lines were the only troops that could fire. An officer had the first rank lie down, the second rank kneel, and the third rank stand while the remaining eight ranks loaded and passed muskets forward. The result was a continuous volley of fire by twenty-five hundred men for twenty minutes.

Once the carnage had ended, Skip had stood looking about wondering if what they had just done was the same thing that happened during the original battle. The Rebs didn't have a chance. They charged into a continuous hale of bullets. During the real battle, the left and right flanks of the Army of the Potomac swung in on the attacking confederates.

During the twenty-minute fray of the reenactment, it was estimated that the three union ranks had fired 75,000 rounds.

Skip continued through Gettysburg towards Carlisle and I-81. He turned east on I-81. At this stage in his journey, Skip was three hours from home.

His plan was set in his mind. He would drive until I-81 intersected with east I-78, follow I-81 north until it intersected with east 80, and travel east 80 until he crossed into New Jersey at the Delaware River. From that point, he would continue on Jersey route 80 until the Netcong exit to his sister's place.

However, the Fates were mobile on this bright spring day and had other plans for Skip Daggard.

Director Rickard's Office
CIA Headquarters
Federal Building, Washington, D.C.
Saturday - 1046 hours

Director Rickard paced behind his desk. He glanced across the Potomac as he passed his office's huge bay window and cussed the President. The winter had been long and harsh.

Director Jim Richard had made plans to take his son Bill and Bill's two boys deep sea fishing this weekend, but he had to be here instead because the President decided, on Wednesday, to have a social working weekend with the Joint Chiefs of Staff at Camp David.

Rickard sat down at his large oak desk twiddling his thumbs when his Bat Line rang. "Director Rickard here, Mr. President."

"Jim, I want you take some of your men and secure the White House Communications Center. Remove all Military Intelligence personnel, take control and then call me here at Camp David. Use my cell phone number and secure procedures."

Before Director Rickard could inform President Mantle that was mission impossible, his line went dead.

"Shit!" He considered contacting General Pete Sarenson the Director of Defense. "After all," Rickard thought, MI and NSA come under his office. "Besides! Why didn't the President contact Sarenson in the first place?" Rickard spoke to the picture of his son, Bill and his two grandchildren.

Jim Rickard was a thirty-five year veteran. He had started his career in the Navy as a Gunner's Mate. Next, he went into communications as a linguist. Then he worked his way up through MI to NSA as a field operative. From NSA, he went into the Secret Service, then the CIA. Now he was its director.

During his career, Jim Rickard had been shot four times, divorced twice, and held prisoner in a Soviet complex in Georgia, Russia for one year before the US could affect his release. He had butted heads with Skip Daggard on several occasions over whose organization should take out a certain Cuban leader, which led to animosity between the two men.

Now the President had put him in a paradoxical position. Either do as he had been ordered or face charges of disobeying his Commander-in-Chief, or, he could follow his orders and face the consequences of his actions by Military Intelligence and NSA, which meant Skip Daggard because Daggard was the White House Commo Chief.

The President had hung up without giving him a chance to dispute his demand, which meant *comply immediately*. But maybe he should still give his friend Sarenson a heads-up. No!

White House basement
Washington D.C.
Saturday - 1130 hours

The sky was clear—an endless light blue sea as Director Rickard and three of his most trusted field agents drove through the east gate, entered the White House through the front entrance, showed their credentials to the Marine guard, and proceeded through a hidden doorway to the basement.

When they arrived at the Secret Service desk and were in the process of identifying themselves, the duty agent stood up, pointed to the comcenter door, and left his post.

The CIA agents looked at each other, "I guess he received his orders, too," explained Rickard.

Staff Sergeant Parker slid back the steel plate window when the buzzer rang and peered out through the six bars. "Sergeant, I am Director Rickard, CIA. The President has ordered me to secure the communications center. You are to open the door, collect your personal belonging, and you and your personnel are to leave."

She wasn't sure if this was a drill, a test, or *what*. She decided to follow procedures.

"Sir, I don't know who you are, therefore, I cannot allow you access to a secured area of NSA. And I cannot leave my post at the request of a civilian."

"Open the door, Sergeant Parker or I'll be forced to blow it open!"

"Sir, if you do that I will shoot you."

Parker closed and secured the steel plate. Rickard could hear the metallic sounds of the locking and loading of several M-16s.

"We're not going through that door without a fight," he told his men.

SSG Parker spoke from the inner side of the steel plate. "Sir, can you hear me?"

"I hear you, Sergeant Parker."

"If you will stand by, I will contact NSA to see if they will honor the President's request, but I am sure it will have to be in writing."

She went to an on-line Teletype machine and began to type. ///November Sierra Alpha this is Whiskey-Hotel Charlie; Charlie

India Alpha requests occupation this station-flash response requested//////

The response was immediate. ///Whiskey-Hotel Charlie this is November Sierra Alpha; Sierra Charlie ur lc-Gulf-Hotel being advised////

///November Sierra Alpha, Roger—M-16s loct and loaded—stndg by////

> *NSA, this is White House Communications*
> *CIA wants to occupy comcenter*
> *White House Communications, this is NSA, Secure your location;*
> *General Hanalin is being advised.*
> NSA, *Roger, M-16s are locked and loaded—standing-by*

SSG Parker stood with her back to one of the few Mod-90 teletypewriters still in use. For her, time seemed to have stopped. Seconds became hours. The AC unit was functional, yet beads of sweat oozed from her pores. She waited wondering what insanity was shaping the world beyond her doors.

Director of NSA General Hanalin's Office
NSA, Ft. Meade, Maryland
Saturday-1135 hours

General Mac Arthur Hanalin was practicing his golf putts with his new putting iron and ball catcher his wife, Nancy had given him for Christmas. He could practice when he had to be on duty while the President was at Camp David because it was one of the few times when there was nothing for him to do.

"Sir," Army Military Intelligence Staff Sergeant Sara Heath's voice boomed over the intercom as General Hanalin was about to make a putt shot. He jumped. "Why does she have to do that all the time?" he asked himself. "Yes, Sergeant?"

"Sir, Captain Tobias is here to see you."

"Send him in, thank you."

Captain Taylor Tobias was new to MI. He had been a tank Commander, was tenth in a class of one hundred-fifty at the Point, and had served during the Gulf War of 1991. He knocked, but did not wait for the customary, "Come in."

"Sir, there is a major breach in progress at the White House Comcenter. Staff Sergeant Parker, one of our MI operators, is waiting for orders."

Captain Tobias handed General Hanalin the printout from Parker. Hanalin's response was decisive and immediate. "Goddamnit, what is CIA trying to prove?"

"Where is Chief Daggard? He should be handling this!"

"He signed out on leave this morning, Sir. He is in New Jersey."

"Where is his second-in-command, Sergeant Anderson?"

"She's not answering our calls, Sir. CIA may have taken her into custody. I've sent three agents to her residence in Georgetown."

"Good! Keep me appraised."

"Yes, Sir."

General Hanalin sat down at his desk and scribbled his response. He handed the orders to Captain Tobias, "Get this to Sergeant Parker and stand-by outside my office."

"Yes, Sir."

As Captain Tobias retreated, General Hanalin had his secretary call Colonel Heather Hempden who was commanding the 704th Military Intelligence Brigade at Ft. Meade.

White House Comcenter
Washington, D.C.
Saturday - 1140 hours

Staff Sergeant Parker turned back to her Teletype when bells began to clang on the machine indicating a flash message in progress.

///Whiskey-Hotel Charlie this is November Sierra Alpha—Gulf-Hotel respnds—Sierra-Charlie your lc—Seirra-Hotel-Oscar-Oscar-Tango-India-Frank-Lima-Charlie-Bravo-Romeo-Echo-Alpha-Charlie-Hotel-Echo-Delta///

///Tango-Mike, Gulf Alpha Charlie—understood/////

//Whiskey-Hotel Charlie this is November Sierra Alpha—Gulf-Hotel respnds—Hotel-Echo-Lima-Papa—Echo-November-Romeo-Oscar-Uniform-Tango////

///Copy, Tango-Mike////

> *White House Comcenter this NSA, General Hanalin responds—Secure your Location—Shoot If Location Breached.*
>
> *Thanks Much! Understood.*
>
> *White House Comcenter this is NSA, General Hanalin responds—Help in-route.*
>
> *Understood! Thanks much.*

After transmitting her reply, SSG Parker positioned her team, and went back to the steel plated window. "Sir?"

"I'm still here, Sergeant Parker. I have passed on your message to the President," he lied.

"I have another one for you, Sir! It's from General Hanalin, NSA. If my position is breached I am to shoot to kill. If you and your men are outside this location within one hour you won't have to worry about me…"

"Why is that, Sergeant Parker?"

"General Hanalin is sending troops. If you're still out there when *they* get here…well, I guess you can imagine what *their* orders will be."

Agent Rickard thought about this new development as one of his men was placing two explosive C-4 charges at the upper and lower hinges of the twelve-inch thick steel door. His demolition agent looked over at him for orders. He was given the index finger across the throat sign and removed the C-4 packages.

"Damn," Rickard thought, I wondered what they'd do. "I'll contact President Mantle. You three stay here until I come back"

His agents looked at each other, "Sir, what if you don't come back," asked Agent Harding, the demolition officer. There was no reply.

Director Rickard walked passed the Marine guard and looked at the tall Marine wondering if he was MI. He stepped off of the veranda and away from the building. Jim was facing the Washington monument, but had the Marine guard in view while he dialed up the President. "Mr. President, we have a problem…"

"Do not try selling me that line, Jim. All I want to hear is that you have control of the center."

Rickard felt his retirement slapping him in the face. "Sir, General Hanalin is sending MI troops from Ft. Meade to secure the comcenter"

"He can't do that. He hasn't the authority," President Mantle shouted in his phone.

"According to the sergeant inside the center, Sir, the troops are already in-route.

"She's led me to believe that if we are still on the premises when they arrive we will be shot."

Agent Rickard heard deep breathing from the President followed by a long string of profanity.

"I will contact the Director of Defense. You stand by the comcenter. I do not want anyone in there. Do you understand? No one."

Director Jim Rickard thought, "Mr. President, you should have contacted General Sarenson in the first place."

"Mr. President, I will need more soldiers. Would you please order the Secret Service in?"

"No! Get some of your men."

"I do not have any available right now."

"I will contact the Director of the FBI to get you help and the Director of Central Intelligence to stop General Hanalin."

"Sir, do you realize that you are about to start a war within the Intelligence Community? When MI troops arrive they will be locked and loaded.

"Sir, the comcenter belongs to NSA and MI. If I try to hinder their access in any way the situation will escalate into a shoot-out."

"The Joint Chiefs of Staff are here with me; I will have them intercede and stop General Hanalin's aggressive operation. But I want you to carry out my order—do you understand?"

"Yes, Sir."

Director Rickard turned off his cell phone. He looked out over the serene landscape surrounding the monuments and the White House. As he turned to reenter the building, he thought, "I hope he stops

Hanalin or the White House basement will become a battlefield, and for what?"

Chapter Five
No Going Home

General Hanalin's Office
NSA, Ft. Meade, Maryland
Saturday - 1156 hours

"Sir," Sergeant Heath spoke into the bitch box, "Colonel Hempden is on line one."

"Heather, I want you to put an eighty troop company together immediately for an assault on the White House."

There was a short pause followed by some hysterical laughter.

"*Colonel*! This is a serious situation."

"Yes, Sir!"

General Hanalin could imagine the colonel sitting to a position of attention.

"I want them aboard helicopters at the airfield in forty-five minutes."

"Sir..."

"The target is the White House Comcenter. I will have an update for you prior to lift-off. Divide them into two platoons. You will lead the assault, Colonel." Click.

Colonel Heather Hempden sat in her chair strait-backed. "What the *hell* is going on?" she thought. "Assault the White House! Has the general gone crazy? Who gave such an order, or is this some kind of a drill to see how fast they could isolate and secure the White House from a terrorist attack?"

Cheyenne Mountain Facility
Colorado Springs, Colorado
Saturday - 1203 hours EST

Colonel Ambroser stood near the coffeepot in the break room. "Sir!"

"Yes, Sergeant Milan?"

"Sorry to bother you, Sir!"

"Is it my appearance, or are you sincere about bothering me? Do I look that bad?"

"Drawn and quartered, Sir."

"It has been a long day. Coffee, Sergeant?"

"Yes, Sir. Thank you, but it is going to get longer, Sir"

Milan accepted the steaming brew and was grateful for it. He sipped at his coffee for a minute enjoying the peace of the break room. At the age of fifty-four, he was still full of piss and vinegar and figured he'd give the Air Force another four or five years.

Milan was third generation Italian-American, and still had a head of thick black hair. He stood five-six in his stocking feet and was a burly chested fellow, but was beginning to put on some weight around his middle.

"What is it now, Sergeant?" Colonel Ambroser asked taking a sip of his black coffee.

"You better put down your coffee cup, Sir!"

The Colonel placed his cup on the counter while Chad Milan closed and locked the break room doors. Ambroser stared at MSG Milan. He didn't like the grave look on the Sergeant's face. A claustrophobic feeling assaulted Ambroser—all of a sudden he felt the need to escape.

"We've intercepted a breach of security from the White House Comcenter to NSA and two from NSA back to the White House."

MSG Milan handed the colonel both communiqués.

Ambroser felt old as he began reading the printouts. He retrieved his coffee cup, and began taking small sips—thoroughly enjoying his drink. Therefore, what he was reading was not penetrating passed his eyes for several seconds. Then, he dropped his coffee cup, grabbing both edges of the printouts, "*Good God Almighty has someone gone crazy?* Do you think this is a drill, Sergeant?"

"No, Sir. If it were a drill, the infiltrators would be Secret Service or a Marine Rifle Company. Someone wants something they perceive to be in the comcenter; therefore, the CIA was ordered in.

"Sir, the only person who could do that is the President."

"Or the Secretary of State," replied the colonel.

"Yes, Sir. That's who I'm thinking of, but he'd have to pull some strings because he doesn't have any authority for such an act."

"Unless…"

"Unless, Sir, members in authority are working with the secretary regarding his plot."

The colonel took another cup from the cupboard while the sergeant cleaned up the mess. They both sipped coffee for a few minutes weighing the repercussions of the events unfolding in Washington. "I better call the Ole' Man."

FBI Center, Federal Building
Washington, D.C.
Saturday - 1205 hours

Special Agent Dan Boulder, Agent-in-Charge of the Clarksburg, West Virginia office, sat in a dingy and ancient Washington Bureau office sipping coffee and reading the Washington Post when the phone rang. He didn't want to answer it, but the other agents in the room weren't making a move so he picked up the receiver, "FBI, Agent Boulder may I help you?" There was a touch of disgust in his voice; he'd rather be in his new plush office at the Clarksburg Center playing with his secretary. Boulder wished she'd hurry up and decide to marry him instead of keeping him hanging.

"Agent Boulder, this is President Mantle," with a snap of his fingers, Boulder alerted the six agents in the communications room. Two agents put on headsets and began recording. "I want you to get as many agents as you can. Report to the White House Communications Center and meet with CIA Director Rickard.

"Report in tactical gear because you will help Agent Rickard repel an assault by members of MI-TAC in-route from Fort Meade."

One agent removed his headset giving the thumbs up. "He's calling from Camp David. Maybe this is a drill to see how fast we can respond to a real world threat at the White House."

"Yes, Sir. I can have thirty agents there in twenty minutes."

"You will need one hundred there in fifteen."

Agent Boulder was a twenty-five year veteran. He knew there was no way possible he could obtain that many agents on such short notice. He would first have to contact the director for final approval.

"Mr. President, I can get ten there in ten minutes, but I have to contact Director Higgin's for conformation."

Just then FBI Director Higgins entered the office. Agent Boulder handed him the phone explaining in a soft voice what the President wanted.

"Mr. President, this is Director Higgins..."

"Bill, I gave orders to Agent Boulder-carry them out." The phone went dead.

Director Higgins looked at Agent Boulder, "What's going on, Dan?"

"The President wants one hundred agents to marry-up with the CIA at the White House Comcenter in fifteen minutes. Something about MI-TAC troops from Ft. Meade assaulting the White House."

The director thought about this situation. He knew that the Joint Chiefs of Staff are at Camp David with the President and decided this must be a drill. "All right call them in. Issue the appropriate gear with blank ammunition. I will review and tape the drill from the security room in the White House."

"Yes, Sir." The agents began a recall.

Fort Devens, Massachusetts
Saturday - 1211 hours

General Timothy Toomey had been the Director of MI for three years. He was a young buck-private during the Korean War when he distinguished himself at Inchon. He was battlefield commissioned and had advanced to three stars.

He could have retired fifteen years ago, "To do what?" he had asked himself and his wife Madge. He had found a home in the army, one he never had living on the streets of Brooklyn, New York.

At the age of sixteen, he was given a choice by the court system, "Go in the army or go to prison."

There was no choice. At least he'd get paid for fighting in the army; besides, there was a war on and he could get all the fighting he wanted.

He was about to tee-off at the Fort Devens golf course when his driver approached. "Sir, you have a call," and handed him a cell phone.

"Damn the inventor of these things," he thought. "General Toomey here."

"General Toomey this is Army Joint Chief of Staff Mandville. General Hanalin has MI troops preparing to assault the White House. I want you to stop him immediately." The phone went dead.

Toomey chomped down on his cigar. The burning end fell to the turf. He spit the other end out, grumbling, "What the Hell!"

He punched in Hanalin's number at NSA. "General Hanalin's office. Yes, Sir. I will connect you immediately."

"Mac, what in Good God's name is going on down there. I just received a call from Mandville."

"I was going to call you myself, Tim. I think you better rendezvous with me down here. Something's going on and it's getting out of control."

"What's this you're sending troops to the White House?"

"Yes, Sir. The CIA is trying to access our facility there."

"By whose orders?"

"Director Rickard says the President."

"Why didn't you contact me? He can't do that! Only you or I have that authority."

"I don't have to contact you. However, I already explained, I was just about to call you."

General Toomey's reply was slow in coming, "Yes! Proceed. Keep me apprised. Use my cell number. Damn these things anyway," he said, handing his cell phone to his driver. He took out a cigar tin from his back pocket and placed a cigar in his mouth, then replaced the tin back into his pocket. Toomey bent over and placed another ball on the tee, straightened up, then threw his iron on the green. "Damn," he blurted out as he walked towards his vehicle, "CIA in the White House. MI troops in-route. And the terrorists are probably laughing their asses off."

Fort Meade Airfield
Ft. Meade, Maryland
Saturday—1245 hours

Colonel Heather Hempden was performing an inspection of her troops with Platoon Leader Lt. Raven and Platoon Sergeant First Class Keno as two Chinooks stood waiting for their human cargo, with blades turning and engines whining.

The inspection took ten minutes. Lieutenant Raven gave the order to lock and load and to begin boarding. As the soldiers began to embark, General Hanalin arrived. Colonel Hempden thought the general had aged one hundred years since she had seen him yesterday as he emerged from the OD green vehicle.

"This operation has General Toomey's blessing, Heather. Does each troop have sufficient ammunition?"

"Yes, Sir, two hundred rounds each plus every third soldier is carrying an ammo box."

"Your mission is to secure the White House Communications Center, Colonel. We know you will be confronted by CIA and God knows, who else"

Mac Hanalin looked off towards the horizon in the direction of D.C. The colonel waited, watching him.

"It's going to be a long day, Heather," he sighed.

"Sir, we have live ammo. I am..."

"Your mission is to secure the comcenter. *Do* you understand?"

"Yes, Sir."

"Heaven help us Heather! You better psych up your soldiers during your flight because they will be engaging our own."

General Hanalin watched the last soldier board and remembered other times and other places, too many. That was war, but this was entirely different. Now, he was sending troops in to face family members—members of the United States Intelligence Community. They were going up against Americans and for what?

The general studied the colonel's face as she turned back and saluted. A line had been drawn, but who the hell had defined it? And who had dictated what sides each organization should take?

As he watched the colonel board, the ramp close, and the choppers begin to lift-off, another scenario was unfolding in Pennsylvania.

I-81 rest area, Pennsylvania
Saturday—1300 hours

Skip Daggard drove his vehicle into a rest area thirty minutes before he would reach the intersection of I-81 north and Penn-78 east. Skip sat in his vehicle low in the seat. The dark colored Cavalier found a parking spot near the entrance into the rest area. Skip smiled, "Gotcha!"

He stepped out of his vehicle without looking towards the Cavalier and went into the building and rest room. While he relieved himself, Skip devised a plan. When he came out of the building the two men were still sitting in their vehicle. Skip walked towards his vehicle, then ran to the Cavalier pulling his weapon. Before the occupants realized what was happening, Skip was beside them, smashing the driver's window with his weapon, and putting the muzzle of his 9mm in the crotch of the driver. "Hi, Bill! Weren't you at Camp David with the President?"

"Skip, would you please remove that thing!"

Daggard slapped Bill's hand away as he tried to lift the gun from his crotch. "Answer me!"

Bill had learned about Skip's temper during the Granada incident in 1982. He had witnessed the killing rampage Skip had engaged in. He knew the trouble he and his partner were in. "Yes, we were there," Bill declared.

Skip's hand started to tremble, his face turning red, his eyes changing from blue to glowing embers, "You should have stayed there! Who sent you?

"Don't look at your partner, asshole, I'm talking to you! Who sent you? What're your orders?"

Bill Baker was a nineteen-year veteran. He had started out in Military Intelligence in the navy, moved over to NSA as a civilian, then CIA, and now worked as a Secret Service Agent. He had been twenty-nine years behind the footsteps of Skip Daggard, but would never be half the agent Skip was. Bill knew he had been a good soldier, but now he was going to die and didn't understand why.

Here was the legend of the elite. The top gun of all the subversive agents in the world with his gun pressing into Bill's crotch with the hammer cocked. Baker didn't doubt for a minute that Skip would not shoot so he gave over the information, "Secretary Kelly. Our-our—orders—orders—were to-t-take—y-you out," he stammered.

Skip looked into their eyes measuring the validity of Baker's words. Baker saw the blank expression, "Skip, for Godsake, please don't!"

"But it's all right for you to shoot me, hey? Where was the President when the secretary gave the orders?"

"President?"

As Skip lifted his pistol Baker's world became animated. "Strange," he thought, "how things slow down at the moment of death—everything. People, the sky, life." He heard all the noises, the conversations of passerby's, the revving of the different types of vehicle engines—gas and diesel.

He could hear the raspy voice of a trainer he had years ago. "Don't get married while your in this business—it's a liability."

But he *was* married with three kids and one grandchild.

He heard a car door open, turned his head and felt the muzzle flash burn his face as he watched his partner roll out of their vehicle onto the ground. It was the last thing he saw. People started screaming as they fell to the ground or took cover behind their vehicles as two shots exploded.

A Penn State patrol car was entering the rest area. The officer slammed on his brakes jammed the transmission into park, rolled out of his cruiser drawing his weapon. Skip stood up, placed his Browning 9mm on the roof of Baker's car, and started walking towards the officer with his credentials in view. "I'm Military Intelligence Chief Warrant Officer Skip Daggard, with A Group Military Intelligence. Those two men were Russian Secret Service Agents who had been sent here to kill me. They had killed two of our Secret Service Agents and stolen their credentials and weapons."

The ten-year police veteran stood there looking at Skip with his mouth open studying Skips' identification.

"Call it in. Have your supervisor respond to this location. Are you listening?"

"Yes, Sir. I'm sorry, but nothing like this has ever happened to me before."

"Understood. I'm going to make you a hero, son. Once your supervisor arrives, tell him the bodies must be transported to Washington immediately, to Secretary of State Kelly, who must be appraised of this incident, and that the bodies are in-route to him. Understand?"

"Yes, Sir," answered the trooper puffing out his chest.

Skip chuckled to himself regarding the officer, and how that traitorous son of a bitch was going to interpret this incident. "Well Skip, you stepped into the shit this time," he said to himself as he turned from the trooper heading back to his own vehicle.

Daggard knew he was in trouble. However, he was confused. He had spoken with the President, yet Baker stated it was the secretary who sent them. How did Kelly hear the conversation between him and the President? Then Skip remembered the warning signals as he retrieved his weapon from the roof of Bakers vehicle. "*Shit*, what the hell is going on?"

Skip Daggard fell against his sedan with his knees jammed into the driver's door. He slammed his hands down on the roof of the car and swore to himself. He observed the officer run the police crime-scene yellow tape around Baker's Cavalier while an old cruiser pulled in next to the trooper.

A fat Sergeant exited the patrol car and began conversing with his subordinate who pointed towards Skip several times.

Daggard took in everything. Several people, in shorts and jeans wearing various styles of tops, gathered around the crime-scene to see the two dead men. Truck drivers were standing on the running boards of their eighteen wheeler's keeping far back, yet close enough to watch. Skip scrutinized the fat sergeant's approach with contempt for the man's obesity and bullying swagger.

The sergeant got in Skip's face violating Daggard's personal space spewing spittle as he blurted out in a loud voice, "I'm Sergeant Hope and I don't give a damn who you are. You killed people within my jurisdiction. I'm gonna take you in and the homicide…"

Skip's reaction to the sergeant's violation was swift and powerful. The fat officer was on his back with a foot on his throat. "Don't *ever* get that close to me again, asshole!

"As far as going with you, I don't think so. And if you try to push the issue I'll kill you! Now, go help your trooper."

Sergeant Hope had been in the Marines. He had seen the faces of many men who had gone over the edge from too much killing. He saw that detached look on Daggard's face and knew it for the danger it was. He hated to backwater, but if he didn't his supper table would be short one tonight—permanently.

The sergeant went to help his subordinate as Daggard drove out of the rest area. Skip stopped at the exit of the rest area before entering the highway. "Now which way, Skip?" he asked in a low tone. He looked east towards home and the tears welled up in his eyes.

Agent Daggard gripped the steering wheel as he tried to yank it from the column. He smashed his right fist on the dashboard several times and punched the console until all of the glass was broken. Skip Daggard ignored the blood oozing out of the cuts on his right hand. He pulled out onto the highway-heading east for one hundred yards, then turned off the road onto an emergency pull-off in the center of the highway, and repositioned his vehicle onto the roadway-heading west towards Thurmont and Camp David.

Skip looked into his rearview mirror as New Jersey, his home, his family, his mom disappeared. "I'm sorry, Mom," he said allowing himself five seconds of tears and grief. Then he sucked in the pain. It was over. He wiped the teardrops from his face as his skin tightened around muscle and bone. His eyes closed to vertical slits. He was a warrior again. "Now," he pledged, "Now, Mr. Secretary, you're going to die."

Fort Meade Airfield
Ft. Meade, Maryland
Saturday - 1327 hours

As the Chinooks disappeared into the horizon, General Hanalin saluted. He stood near his sedan chewing on the stem of his corncob pipe wondering about the next hour and the immediate future. Never, since its conception in 1952, has the National Security Agency taken such drastic measures to secure its operations. Who could have guessed it would be against its own community?

"I wish I knew what was so damn important," General Hanalin said to Captain Tobias, his driver, "and what makes the President think it's in the White House Comcenter."

Once the choppers were insignificant dots in the sky, General Hanalin slipped into the back seat of his sedan. Captain Tobias steered the vehicle towards NSA.

Five minutes into flight Colonel Heather Hempden rose from her seat and began pacing within the confines of the steel box attached to the belly of the Chinook. She observed her team members checking each other, fastening their new-style kevlar flack jackets and re-adjusting packs.

She was in the lead helicopter with assistant Platoon Staff Sergeant Martha Trapp. SSG Sergeant Trapp was a 27 year-old black soldier from Alabama—a linguist fluent in Russian and Korean.

Lieutenant Raven was the team leader of the second group with Platoon Sergeant Keno. Lt. Raven was of Cherokee and Irish blood. He was thirty-six, fluent in six languages, but chose a leadership position over linguistics.

Platoon Sergeant First Class Max Keno was born in Texas. His mother was Mexican and his father Anglo-Saxon. He had joined the army fifteen years ago at the age of seventeen to get away from street gangs. He was with Colonel Hempden during the Gulf War.

Colonel Hempden had been in the Gulf War. She had been sent behind enemy lines to set-up an observation/listening post with twenty MI cryptic specialists. Some were civilian, but most of her command were Military Intel people. Somehow her platoon got sloppy and they came under attack. The civilians bailed, leaving her with twelve soldiers, Airman, and Marines to fight it out.

Her troops were in the process of destroying their equipment with incinerator grenades when a voice bellowed out from behind the Iraqi forces, "Hello the camp," and the desert erupted in an explosion blotting out the sun with a massive ceiling of sand. When the sand settled, Skip Daggard was standing before her grinning. The fifty Iraqi soldiers lay about in several pieces. "Who are you?"

"Agent Daggard. You did a fine job, Ma'am. Fine job!"

She saw five other troops standing by, grinning and conversing with her soldiers. "Where did you come from," she asked wiping sweat and sand from her face. She followed his finger with her eyes towards the sky, and saw the helicopter for the first time.

"We were on another mission when we received your distress call. Guess Hussein will have to wait; although the President is going to be one pissed-off puppy!"

As she continued her pacing, she realized it was the warble of the blades of the Chinook, which brought back that rescue, and how Agent Daggard had held her in the darkness of a similar box attached to another Chinook.

She could still hear his words, "You did mighty fine, Leftenant, mighty fine. Going to put you in for a medal and a promotion."

"Why do you call me Leftenant; that's a Brit pronunciation?"

"Two reasons. One, yes it's Brit lingo, which I like and two, I've never met a Right tenant until today-Lieutenant."

Perhaps it was being in the box again, which evoked the memory, or perhaps it was something else and she couldn't quite put her finger on it.

White House basement
Washington, DC
Saturday—1330 hours

Dan Boulder arrived at the White House with eighty-five agents He was late, but thought, "Hey we're here," and proceeded to the basement. Director Higgins went to the security room.

"Hi, Rick! Your back-up is here."

"Hey, Dan! This is the situation," he began as the two men shook hands. "The President wants us to secure the comcenter or, at the minimum, not let MI have access to it."

"Roger that! When do you think the troops from Meade will make their ill-fated attempt?"

"I'm not sure. Within the next forty-five minutes, maybe. Depends on when they went airborne."

"Well, we brought some extra rounds. I might as well hand some out to you and your crew."

Director Rickard stared at the cartridges Agent Boulder had placed in his hands. "What the *hell* are these?"

"Blank ammo," replied Agent Boulder, "why?"

Special Agent Rickard grabbed Dan by the arm dragging him to the comcenter door and banged on it. "Sergeant Parker!"

"Yes, Sir?'

"What kind of ammo do you have locked and loaded?"

"Sir?"

"Blank or live?"

"Live, Sir."

"And what kind of ammo will your reinforcements be using?"

"Live, Sir."

The two senior agents stared at each other for a few seconds before Agent Boulder responded, "This...This isn't an exercise-*a drill*?"

"What the hell ever made you perceive this to be a drill, Dan? When those MI troops arrive, it's going to be a bloodbath here."

"Shit, Rick! We can't shoot our own people!"

Upstairs in the security room Director Higgins was going ballistic. "Get me the President on the horn, now," he lashed out to a Secret Service Agent.

"Sir, it's ringing."

"Mr. Secretary, this is Director Higgins. I need to speak to the President."

It took the President a few minutes to come to the phone, "What is it Higgins?"

"Mr. President, what the hell is going on here," he demanded.

"Follow orders, Higgins," the President shouted into the receiver and hung up.

Cheyenne Mountain Facility
Colorado Springs, Colorado
Saturday - 1332 hours EST

As General Stone entered his office he found MSG Milan at the Reception's desk.

Milan came to attention and offered the general coffee.

"Bring it into my office, Sergeant, Thank you. Where is Sergeant Tamara? Isn't she supposed to be on duty?"

"Yes, Sir. I assigned her to another office."

General Stone stopped as he was opening the door to his office and looked back at Milan's blank face.

Colonel Ambroser rose to his feet as the general entered. "All right Sam, what happened?"

"A fray is in progress at the White House. General Hanalin is sending in a company of MI troops to secure the comcenter, Sir.

"*What!*"

"We intercepted three communiqués: One from the comcenter to NSA, and two responses from NSA back to SSG Parker at the White House."

Colonel Ambroser handed the printouts to General Stone as the general fell into his plush captains' chair. MSG Milan entered with a cup of coffee and placed it on the desk before the general.

It was a silent atmosphere as the general read the printouts. When he was finished, General Stone lay them on his desk, picked up his coffee cup and began to sip at the hot beverage.

"Where's Chief Daggard?"

"We have no idea, Sir. Perhaps that's why General Hanalin has stepped in."

"Hell, Sam, Sergeant Anderson is second-in-command! Hasn't she been notified?"

"No, Sir," answered MSG Milan, "NSA has sent agents to her residents. My section received a commo check from Agent Halbrooke. He used a specific code indicating his location at SFC Anderson's, and that she was not present."

"Sam, ring-up General Hanalin, please."

Colonel Ambroser went to the outer office to access the line. "Sir, General Hanalin."

"General Hanalin here."

"Mac, this is Stone."

"Hello, Ralph what prompts this call?"

"Agent Daggard was at your store this morning."

"Yes, I know. I saw the sign-in sheet when I arrived this morning. I've also received a call from the President at 1030 to allow three CIA Agents into my comcenter, but I have taken action to prevent that."

"I know. We intercepted your transmissions. Do you know what Daggard was doing there?"

"No! But he had an analyst fire-up DAESY. The on-duty officer informed me shortly after I had arrived."

"So you don't have a copy of the decoded request…a copy of the printout?"

"What request? What printout?"

General Stone paused for a few seconds staring at Colonel Ambroser. "You better contact your analyst, Mac."

MSG Milan, who had stepped out to relieve himself, came storming into the general's office, "Sir, you have to read this," handing colonel Ambroser an AP Teletype printout.

"Hold on, Mac. What is it, Sam?"

Colonel Ambroser handed him the paper. He browsed it quickly, "God All Mighty!"

"Ralph! Ralph, what the hell's going on?"

"Mac, Daggard's in deep Kimchi. I am reading from an AP report. 'At approximately 1330 hours today, it has been reported to the Secretary of State and the President at Camp David, US Military Intelligence Special Agent Chief Warrant Officer Skip Daggard, assigned to the White House Communications Center, shot and killed two Presidential Secret Service officers in a rest area off of route I-81 in Pennsylvania. The President, Secretary, and Joint Chiefs of Staff are in-route from Camp David back to Washington.'

"Mac, we have to meet. I will contact Tim Toomey. You call your group leaders, and we'll marry-up this afternoon at your AO."

"Roger that! See you when you get here, Ralph. What was it Skip had analyzed?"

"I will bring it with me, Mac. It's too sensitive to discuss over the airwaves. One thing I can tell you, Mac, MI will have to stick together on this one."

When General Stone hung up the receiver his BAT line rang.

"Oh, General Toomey! I was just about to call you."

"What's up, Ralph? I am at my comcenter and there's a series of alarms. My goddamn War Room looks like a Christmas tree."

"Tim, Agent Daggard is involved in something. I don't want to disclose it over *any* landlines or airwaves-it's that sensitive."

"How can Skip be involved with anything? He's at the White House."

"Tim, I just got off the phone with Mac. I informed him we have to meet. I am leaving here as soon as possible. I suggest you march feet down to NSA so we can analyze this situation and develop a game plan."

"Three bags full!"

"Damn ground-pounders," thought Stone. "Three bags full of what? S*hit*!"

Stone looked up at his two subordinates while hanging-up his receiver, "All right," General Stone said, "we've got to put this into perspective. Milan, take notes. What do we know so far?"

"Well Sir, we know Chief Daggard intercepted a communiqué between the Secretary of State and Schmirnoff, the Ambassador's secretary, at the Russian embassy in D.C. He went to NSA to decode the message. The process was accomplished by one of the three analysts. We received the info DAESY decoded for Agent Daggard. Three top CIA Agents arrived at the White House by order of the President, and Chief Daggard killed two Secret Service Agents."

General Stone took out a cigar and lit it. "How do we know it was Schmirnoff?"

He reclined back in his expensive leather chair, releasing ringlets of smoke into the atmosphere.

"I checked the ID Code on the printout. The code wasn't ours. I assumed it was Russian so I used our Russia system to access the KGB files. I found the code, Sir, plus a red flag on Schmirnoff's file."

The general concentrated on enjoying his cigar allowing scenario images to invade his thoughts. He was satisfied with Tech Master Sergeant Milan's explanation. "There is one other thing," General Stone said, "General Hanalin has troops in-route to the White House where CIA and FBI agents are waiting."

Stone studied the situation, as MSG Milan spoke, wondering where these events were going to take them. One thing was certain— the White House Comcenter belonged to NSA and Military Intelligence, therefore, it and the equipment would have to be secured by MI immediately and troops were in-route.

"Sam, according to the AP release, the President, Secretary, and Chiefs of Staff are in-route to Washington. That means that the Commo team is still at Camp David."

"That's correct, Sir."

"I want them to stay there. See to it. And now we also know Daggard's location"

Colonel Ambroser and MSG Milan stared at him.

"Does Camp David have SIV's capabilities?"

"Yes, Sir," responded MSG Milan. "The team has Secure Imagery and Voice because Agent Daggard is in charge."

"Good."

"I'll take care of it right now, Sir," MSG Milan said and left the room.

"Sam! What do you think Skip's next move will be?"

Colonel Sam Ambroser looked at his general. Both men's eyes were locked like two huge bulls glaring at a red flag. Sam Ambroser smiled, which caught Stone off guard. He could answer that question because he had taken the time to review Daggard's file. "Daggard will go after Secretary Kelly. He will try to protect the President by killing the Secretary of State."

General Stone nodded his head. He had reached the same conclusion; however, one question tugged at Stone's conscience. Where was SFC Anderson?

"Sam, would you contact General Bains at the Academy. I'll need a plane ready to depart in two hours. There will be one passenger, and I'll pilot the jet. I need you to stay here and mind the store."

"Yes, Sir. You and Milan will go to Ft. Meade?"

"Yes. Have Bains make it an F-15E. I need my combat flight hours. Guess this is as good a time to accumulate them as any."

Both officers looked up as Master Sergeant Milan entered, "Sir, we cannot access our system at Ritchie. They are in a lock down mode."

"All right. You are going with me to Fort Meade. Once we are situated, try their system again."

"Yes, Sir!"

White House
Washington, D.C.
Saturday -1350 hours

Visitors at the Mall, and monuments, who were enjoying a pleasant day, were unaware of events at the White House until the arrival of the two army Chinooks. Their warbling sounds drowned out the street noise.

Hundreds of people watched the sky as the Chinooks began to hover over the front and rear lawns of the White House.

A CIA agent, who had been standing on the front porch of the White House, went down into the basement. "They're here, Chief," he said to Director Rickard.

"How many are there? And have they landed?"

"There's two Chinooks. They're just hovering. One's behind the White House, and one is in the front. They haven't landed, or deployed any troops yet."

"All right, Boulder send one of your men to the rear lawn. Jacobs, you go back out to the front. Let us know as soon as the helicopters land, or troops are deployed."

"I don't like this at all," said Boulder, "no, sir, not one bit."

"Nor do I, Dan. But they're here so we have to deal with it."

News media personnel began setting up along the black iron fence in front of the White House. Curious on-lookers began gathering across the street as the chopper behind the White House set down. A Channel 2-news helicopter was forced out of the zone by one of the Apache Attack helicopters that patrol the Potomac.

Troops began to repel from the Chinook onto the front lawn. Many people began to cheer the military demonstration.

News cameras were now broadcasting the descent of the troops. Traffic was backed-up. Washington was a gridlock. Five hundred feet above the Washington monument, the President's helicopter hovered as the occupants watched. "Mr. President," said the pilot, "Secret Service in the White House states we can not approach until the Chinooks depart."

President Mantle nodded his head glaring at the scenes unfolding on his front lawn. "Is that an Apache helicopter?"

"Yes Sir," replied the pilot."

"Why doesn't he do something to stop the assault?"

"They're on a different frequency, Mr. President. The pilot is probably contacting his base in Virginia to get further orders."

President Mantle shouted back at the pilot, "Isn't the purpose of that Apache to protect the White House?' The pilot nodded his head. "Then why doesn't he engage?"

Captain Fuller turned in his seat. "For the same reason, Mr. President they didn't shoot down the civilian plane that hit the Pentagon in 2001. They're ours!"

The soldiers from Ft. Meade began to set up a base perimeter, and take control of access to and from the front doors of the White House. One squad of twenty troops was sent to within forty yards of the iron gate at intervals of fifteen yards.

Once all of the troops had deployed, the Chinook moved out. The lead chopper landed at the rear of the White House, and dropped its gate for the troops to disembark. Colonel Hempden deployed her troops in a defensive posture in a semicircle thirty yards from the rear of the White House. She used her TAC-12 to contact home base at the 704ths S-2. "Whiskey Hotel Leader to base, we have taken up our positions. I am waiting for further orders."

"This is Base Leader to Whiskey Hotel Leader; Roger, Mission Leader being advised. Base out."

"Whiskey Hotel Leader out."

Colonel Heather Hempden stood in the center of the defensive arc of her soldiers. She removed her helmet and adjusted her headset and mouthpiece, then placed her helmet back on her head.

Three beeps rang in her TAC-12 headset.

"This is Whiskey Hotel Leader!"

"Whiskey Hotel Leader, this is Base. Mission Leader advises you to relieve the FP on the East Gate ASAP."

"Base, this is Whiskey Hotel Leader, roger that…I am to relieve the FP on the East Gate. Lt. Raven, did you copy that transmission?"

"Roger, Ma'am! Platoon Sergeant Keno is assigning Sergeant Beorn and Corporal Mapp to the task."

"Roger, Lt. Raven. Tango-Mike! Advise me when the mission is accomplished. Whiskey Hotel Leader, clear."

Lt. Raven responded, "Whiskey Hotel Papa, clear."

The Lt. and his troops watched as Sergeant Beorn and Corporal Mapp marched across the green, front lawn of the White House towards the East Gate.

Chapter Six
NSA Takes Control

White House
Washington, D.C.
Saturday - 1400 hours

Thomas Treowe watched the two soldiers approach his post at the East Gate of the White House. He had spent twenty years as a Marine Military Police Officer. Once he had retired three years ago, he had joined the Federal Police Force and had been assigned to the White House after graduating from the academy.

Treowe wasn't sure exactly what was happening, nor did he like the situation, or the fact he was now being approached by two armed troops. He had witnessed the arrival of the soldiers and wondered what had happened to cause this type of protection. No information had been transmitted to the six FP's on duty, nor had the on-duty Secret Service Agents appeared to marry-up with the arriving troops.

Thomas Treowe stood six-foot-three and weighed in at two hundred pounds of solid muscle. He kept his blonde hair short, and maintained his military bearing, but he was puzzled regarding the events unfolding before him and the approaching soldiers.

Sergeant Beorn said, as the two soldiers reached Treowe's post, "Sir, you are to take your personal belongings and leave your post. The army is now in control of the White House."

Officer Treowe wasn't sure what to do. He knew CIA and FBI agents were in the White House as well as the White House Secret Service staff so he opted to try and make contact with the Secret Service. Treowe also knew the Vice President was in his office, but he could not, for the life of him, figure out why the presidential helicopter was not landing. He rang the Secret Service, Chief Agent Whitcomb.

"Sergeant," Treowe said, waiting for someone to answer his call, "I don't know what is going on, but I am not abandoning my post. I am trying to contact the Secret Service Chief for my instructions."

The two soldiers waited near the door of the guard booth while Treowe made his call.

"Director Higgins, FBI."

"Sir, this is Officer Treowe at the East Gate. I have been informed by an army sergeant to leave my post. He says that they are taking control of this post. I need to speak with Chief Agent Whitcomb"

Higgins swore viciously. "Have they told you where to go?"

"To leave the compound, Sir."

"Go home, Officer Treowe."

"Sir?"

"Go home, Treowe."

"Yes, Sir."

Thomas Treowe closed out his daily log, "Relieved of post by orders of Director Higgins, FBI to Sergeant Beorn, US Army." He handed over the handheld walkie-talkie, keys, and log to Sergeant Beorn and departed. As Treowe drove away, he looked back as soldiers improved their defensive lines and wondered what in the hell was goin' down.

Five minutes after the army took control of the East Gate; a dark blue Chevy Sedan approached. The three occupants showed their credentials to Sergeant Beorn. Beorn checked his access roster, then he waved the vehicle through.

The Apache helicopter hovered 100 feet above the Vietnam Memorial observing the activities and was reporting the information to the Flight Officer-in-charge at their Virginia base.

The presidential helicopter maintained its position over the Washington Monument, while the Joint Chief's were in their respective offices issuing orders. However, the only responses any leader was getting were that any troop-movement orders had to be authorized by General Hanalin.

Seana Sine Siusan stood close to the iron fence smiling a pleasant Irish grin at a soldier in camouflaged battle dress. The sergeant glared at her, but did not order her to move back. Seana wore a spring-blue dress, navy pumps, and her fiery shoulder length red hair flamed more brilliantly due to the sun's reflection. "Are we on?" she asked her cameraman. He gave her a thumbs-up.

"This is Seana Siusan with Channel-2 News. We are live at the Iron Gate in front of the White House witnessing a precision military

84

exercise of the protection of the White House in case of a terrorist attack.

"Two huge helicopters landed troops just a short time ago. I've been informed that these helicopters are Chinooks. An Apache Attack helicopter is hovering behind us, it appears, to lend air support to the ground troops who have now deployed into defensive positions.

"The Presidential Marine helicopter is hovering over the Washington Monument. We have learned the President is aboard evidently observing the exercise from the air. When we have more, Channel-2 News will bring it to you immediately. This is Seana Siusan Channel-2 News outside the White House Iron Gate."

Once all of the troops had repelled down to the front lawn, the Chinook gained altitude, flew over the White House, and the pilot landed his craft forty yards from the other chopper on the back lawn.

Special Agent Halbrooke observed the Chinook lift-off as he and his comrades stepped out of their vehicle in front of the White House. Hurlee Halbrooke was a rogue like Daggard because he wore his own style of clothing; not the standard black or dark suits that agents were expected to wear. He was dressed in a tan tweed sports jacket and Dockers light tan dress slacks. His semi-tan complexion and thick brown hair weren't any indication of his ancestry, but his first name was Gaelic and his last name was a corrupt form of an English name.

Halbrooke felt exhilarated as he and his team walked passed the Secret Service Agent in the corridor and came in contact with CIA Agent Rickard and FBI Agent Boulder, who were standing near the door to the communications center. Halbrooke had wondered why MI was taking over this way, and how many laws they were breaking and what the *hell* was going to happen when this was over and just what the mission was. Halbrooke knew Agent Daggard was at the forefront of the operation, but had no idea what that operation was. He was following an order, which was his loophole at the conclusion of this operational mess. And that order was to search the comcenter for anything out of the ordinary, retrieve it, and bring the information back to NSA.

"Director Rickard," Halbrooke demanded, "you have CIA and FBI agents deployed in a defensive posture trying to take control of our comcenter. I have troops outside. Do we stand-down or fight?"

Agent Rickard knew too well the consequences if he took an aggressive stance. He decided to leave the decision up to the President. "I'm taking out my cell phone, Halbrooke," Director Rickard declared as he reached into his left inside pocket of his dark blue suit jacket.

"If anything else appears, you're a dead man."

Agent Halbrooke knew no one had ever imprisoned the President in the White House. Even when the British invaded and burned Washington during the War of 1812, President Madison and the Congress managed to escape through the underground tunnel system George Washington had constructed in 1797.

Hurlee Halbrooke new Generals Toomey and Hanalin had taken charge of the military, and virtually stripped the Commander in Chief of all powers over the US forces. Then, to top it off, they ordered him here with two assassin agents to take charge of the White House communications center. And to insure those orders were carried out and the comcenter protected, they had the audacity to send in TAC troops from Fort Meade to secure the outer perimeters. And upstairs, the Vice President was confined to his office guarded by two White House Marines, who were MI troops.

"The Bahamas," Halbrooke thought, "that's where I'm going to be before the ax falls once this mess is over."

There were now one hundred and thirty-three agents of the FBI, CIA, and NSA crammed together in that long corridor in the basement of the White House just outside the steel door of the communications center.

Outside, in a defensive posture, were eighty MI soldiers ready to attack if shots rang-out from the basement, or if CIA tried to force the issue of entering the comcenter.

Director Rickard moved slowly and deliberately so as not to trigger a shootout. Rickard dialed the President's cell number. "Mr. President this is Rickard. What's your location?"

"I am hovering over the Washington Monument, Rick. I hope you've secured your objective. I have been in contact with Vice President Ferchar. He informed me that two Marines are guarding his door, and he's not allowed to leave his office, is that correct?"

Director Rickard surveyed his surroundings. Men and women on the same side were now lined up on opposite sides and ready to shoot it out. This situation boggled his mind, but worse, he had not secured his objective. Now he had to shoot or give it up. And now the President wants him to rescue the Vice President! "No, Mr. President I have not secured the objective. I am waiting for your orders to either shoot or withdraw to the Oval Office. And as far as the Vice President is concerned, I have been informed he is locked-in until this is over"

"*Can we land?*" President Mantle shouted into his cell phone.

"Hal, the President wants to know if he can land."

"Absolutely. Then he can go straight to the Oval Office."

"Yes Sir, you can land. I will meet you on the front lawn."

"Christ, heads are going to roll when this is over," Halbrooke said to his two agents as he depressed the black button near the comcenter window.

"Who is it?"

"Staff Sergeant Parker, I am NSA Special Agent Halbrooke. You were supposed to receive notification of my arrival. TAC forces have secured the perimeters."

Staff Sergeant Parker slid the steel plate along its track, but did not show herself. "Drop your weapons and credentials in through the bars."

"Agent Daggard trained you well," responded Halbrooke.

The three agents complied. Parker closed the window. Halbrooke moved to the door. He was staring at something he saw on the door near the hinges. He rubbed his right palm over the marks on the door as the other two agents bent forward to get a better look. Halbrooke removed his hand. The three agents looked at each other. "The bastards were going to blow down the door," Halbrooke declared, then he glared at Director Rickard. Rickard glared back without saying a word.

Inside the comcenter, SSG Parker picked up the three 9mm semi-auto handguns placing them on the message counter next to the window. She instructed her four-member team to continue their work. Next, she retrieved the agents' credentials verifying the pictures with those that had been faxed to her an hour earlier from NSA along with instructions. Satisfied, she opened the door holding her M-16, finger on the trigger, sling over her neck and shoulder the way Skip had showed her so she could go into immediate action without having her weapon yanked from her.

Agent Halbrooke went to the BT Line and dialed NSA. "Yes, Sir we're in," Halbrooke spoke to General Hanalin, "I will contact you when we've completed our search. Sir, be advised SFC Anderson is not at her abode. We checked the interior. It appears she hasn't been there in the last 24 hours nor Daggard. There are two CIA Agents posted outside their residents.

"Yes, Sir, they saw us because we waved and smiled at them."

He hung up the red receiver. "Sergeant Parker, have you noticed anything different when you reported for duty this morning?"

"Sergeant Anderson seemed to be on edge about something. She was in a hurry to leave."

"How about anything within the perimeters of the comcenter?"

"No, Sir."

Staff Sergeant Parker was baffled. She never had, in her wildest dreams, imagined that one-day she'd be solely responsible for securing the White House Comcenter. She remembered the day she had been offered the assignment. That was the only way MI personnel were attached to this prestigious post.

As an E-4, Parker had demonstrated to her superiors during the Gulf War how devoted she was to NSA and America by remaining at her listening post when other MI personnel were engaged in battle two hundred yards from their eavesdropping position. She alone kept up the circuits of communication at the risk of her life. She was the one that beaconed in the rescue forces. Although that incident was never reported to the media, she was awarded the Silver Star. "Sir, what the hell is going on? It seems like the world has gone insane beyond my doors."

Halbrooke looked at Parker wondering how much if anything he should tell her. Hell, he was just as much in the dark as she was. Her comment played again in his head; "*it seemed like the world has gone insane.*"

"Indeed," he thought. "Indeed." Their eyes held each other over five seconds of time. How much...maybe he shouldn't tell her anything. Then how was he going to explain their search? Did he have to explain?

Staff Sergeant Parker was dressed in her dress greens skirt, and white blouse with black tie, but was not wearing her greens' jacket. Her black hair was cut just above her slender ebony neckline. Halbrooke noticed she was in strict military bearing. She was part of the agency. She was family, but should he share info with her? Does she have a need to know? What the hell he thought. She's proven herself. "Parker, all I can tell you is that Daggard is involved with some serious shit, and now the entire internal and external security community is at war with each other. The Military Intel Officers have decided to support Skip and we've secured the White House. It is in a lockdown mode."

Halbrooke watched Parker's black cheeks flush rosy-red. Her brown eyes widen as she fell back into a chair, allowing her weapon to fall into her lap.

"We're in control of the military," Halbrooke continued.

"My God," Parker muttered, "our world *has* gone insane! Does anyone know what Chief Daggard is involved in?"

"I don't know," responded Agent Halbrooke, "but I believe the generals know. At least I hope they do."

"There's coffee and it's fresh," she said in a soft whisper.

"Thank you!"

Halbrooke filled a cup for himself and SSG Parker, but Agents Tenny and Furgeson turned down the offer.

"Now we have to conduct a search, Sergeant Parker, to determine why the CIA were determined to gain access," Halbrooke explained as he handed Parker her cup.

At that moment, Director Rickard was meeting with President Mantle on the rear lawn as the President disembarked from his helicopter.

White House Oval Office
Washington, D.C.
Saturday—1425 hours

President Mantle sat at his oak desk lost in thought. His emerald eyes were blank as he stared at his OPS Plan. First Lady, Martha

Mantle sat quietly on a chair close to her husband's desk, sipping her coffee.

FBI Director Higgins, Agent Boulder, and Secret Service Director Teddy Talbort sat on the sofa looking at the President. Director of CIA Rickard sat in a chair close to the First Lady. Next to him, sat Secretary of State, Marshall Kelly. MI Agents Halbrooke, Furgeson, and Tenny were in the comcenter with Staff Sergeant Parker.

Colonel Hempden was stationed in a GP small army tent, which she had set-up as her CP. Lt. Raven stood behind his men on the front lawn with his back to the White House.

Martha Mantle studied her husband as she sipped her coffee. She noticed the scowl on Manty's tanned and weathered face. His furrow lines stretched across his forehead.

President Mantle was trying to figure out what had gone wrong. How could one man—one damn MI agent so disrupt his world and ruin his plans for immortality? He sighed deeply.

"Manty?"

He looked at his wife. "How beautiful she is," he thought, "with her long brown hair and deep brown eyes."

"Yes, Martha?"

"I do not comprehend this situation. Agents running through the White House. Troops landing on our lawns."

"This is government business, Martha. I do not expect you to understand."

"I cannot express my feeling of dread and fear as those troops began dropping onto the lawn. Soldiers in BDU's sliding down ropes past my window."

"Martha, Daggard informed me this morning that he is going to kill the Secretary of State simply because he believes the Secretary is a spy. You and I both know that isn't so. And I have just told you too much. Don't you have "tea-time' somewhere?"

"Do we, Manty?"

President Mantle looked at his wife as he shuffled papers on his desk. "Do we what?"

"Do we know Marshall is not a spy?"

Secretary of State Kelly spoke up, "Excuse me, Madam!"

"I had enough of this conversation, Martha. Go to your room!"

"Excuse me! How dare you. I am not one of your flunkies, Manty, nor am I a child for you to dismiss. No! I will not go to my room."

President Mantle sprang up from his chair causing everyone in the room to lean back in their chairs. He walked over to the window overlooking the front lawn. He saw the TAC troops preparing their defensive positions. "How did things get so out of my control?" he wondered, "and do I have a retaliatory course of action I can take once this thing is over? Can I get the Defense Department to intervene? After all, they are in charge of NSA. Damn, can I even leave the White House?"

"Manty, look at it," Martha said, "Skippy is a veteran of what—thirty something years? He doesn't go off half cocked."

As the President turned back to the room, he spoke to Martha, "That's why I had the CIA try to retrieve any evidence from the communications center, Martha. NSA took offense. I think you should leave now, Martha."

Martha rose gracefully and poured a cup of coffee. She took it to Manty. "In all of our thirty-five years of marriage, Manty, have I ever left your side when there was trouble?"

His eyes misted over. "No!"

"So, drink your coffee and be quiet," she said taking her seat.

Everyone in the Oval Office smiled at her as the President took a sip of his coffee.

"I can't profess to understand the situation, Manty, but Skippy wouldn't—no offense Marshall—attack the secretary without cause."

President Mantle rose and walked over to his television set, and turned on the TV to see what the news people were broadcasting from outside of the gates. One thing was apparent, all the news stations were speculating about the events. Neither he nor his public relations officer was offering any information. That's because they weren't allowed.

Sam Gear, the PR chief came in just then. "Mr. President," Gear said, "we're shut down. Could someone please tell me what's going on?"

"Sit down, Sam! We have a serious situation here, and I purposely kept you out of the loop. But now I suppose it's time to bring you up to date.

"Agent Daggard informed me this morning that he is going to kill the Secretary of State."

"Is that why we are being protected by MI Intel troops?"

"No! We're not being protected, Sam. We are...a captive audience," President Mantle declared as he shook a fist at the air.

"Here Sam," said Martha, "have some coffee."

White House Communications Center
Washington, D.C.
Saturday—1437 hours

During their search, Halbrooke found a safe hidden in a bottom cabinet in Agent Daggard's office. "Sergeant Parker," SSG Parker came to the office door," do you know anything about this safe?"

"No, Sir. This is the Chief's office."

Tenny went through file cabinets while Halbrooke tried to gain access to the safe. Furgeson rifled through desk draws then went to the communications console. He studied the take-up reel for several seconds, then scrutinized the counter numbers. Furgeson looked at the Zulu clock before he spoke. "Hal, get permission from Echo-Bravo Group at NSA to turn off the on-line recorder. Something isn't right."

Agent Furgeson studied the ribbon on the take-up reel while Agent Halbrooke contacted Echo-Bravo Group.

Agent Halbrooke came out of Chief Daggard's office. "Okay, Furggy, we got permission to shut her down. What's up?"

Furgeson turned off the recording device. "I'm not sure, but there appears to be an irregularity on two separate edges of a strip of ribbon.

"See," Furggy showed Halbrooke.

"Yeah, but what does it mean?'

"If I miss my guess, Hal," Furgeson took a deep breath then exhaled slowly, "I'd say that is a splice."

SSG Parker's team went about their daily activities of cataloguing messages and commo checks with Camp David. SSG Parker stood-by near Agent Furgeson in case the agents needed her help.

Halbrooke was staring at the irregularities Furgeson was pointing at, trying to determine the significance of the splices, if that's what they were.

The clanging of the Teletype keys against the paper and the platen rollers, the small talk between the soldiers, and the voice-noise of commo checks seemed loud to the agents, but the commcenter activity noises were subtle sounds to the on-duty personnel.

"Sergeant Parker," Furgeson explained, "I need replacement tape and reels, please."

While SSG Parker walked to a gray metal cabinet in the right back corner of the comcenter to retrieve the requested items, Agent Furgeson wrote down the stop-time and counter numbers of the recorder on a daily log attached to a clear plastic envelope taped to the left side of the recording device.

"Here you are, Sir," SSG Parker said as she handed Furgeson a sixteen-inch take-up reel and a full sixteen-inch reel of magnetic tape.

Furgeson removed the reels of the on-line operations tape from their spindles. He attached the reels SSG Parker had given him, then fed a leader section of tape through the slit on the take-up reel. Next, Furgeson rotated the take-up reel clock-wise one full turn to make sure the leader was fastened to the reel. Once he was satisfied, he laced the ribbon through the recording mechanism, turned the take-up reel again until the beginning of the tape was one inch past the recording mechanism, and then turned the recording device on and reset the counter numbers. He wrote the change and six zeros counter numbers on the log.

Halbrooke stood at Furgeson's left elbow as Furggy laid the reels flat on the console counter in front of the recording device. "See, Hal," Furgeson said pointing to the irregularities.

"How did you detect those?"

Furgeson pointed to his right eye, "A trained eye, son. And explicit training from the master, Chief Daggard."

The secure line from NSA rang-Halbrooke answered it. "Agent Halbrooke, this is a secure line."

General Hanalin was on the distant end.

"Yes Sir, Agent Furgeson seems to have discovered something, but we are still in the analyzing stage to determine its significance."

Furggy took the reels to a hand-crank system on a gray metal table outside of Chief Daggard office. He placed the reels on the spindles, and then he began to rewind the tape back onto the main reel. When Furggy got to the place on the ribbon where he thought he detected an irregularity, he took out a can of powder from his briefcase. Furgeson tapped a blue powdery solution on the tape. He waved to Halbrooke.

"Sir, hold on. It seems that Furggy has found something."

Halbrooke stepped to Furggy's left side again as Furgeson took a small pocket sized black lamp from his briefcase, plugged it in and moved the bulb, under the extended magnetic tape, back and forth several times. As Halbrooke, Tenny, and SSG Parker looked on, a flash of light melted a minute segment of the blue powder that lay on top of the tape. Everyone except SSG Parker understood the significance of the chemical reaction—the tape had been spliced. Furggy performed the same procedure at the irregularity on the far left of the magnetic tape.

"Whew, Sergeant Anderson is *good*," said Furgeson.

"How do you know it was Anderson?"

"Because if Skip had done it, Hal I would not be able to detect the splices. But the question is…"

Halbrooke finished the sentence, "Why was the tape spliced in the first place?"

"Exactly!"

"General Hanalin, this is Halbrooke, sorry to keep you holding, Sir. We found a spliced section of tape on the operations reel.

"Yes, Sir.

"No Sir, there is nothing else. We're leaving now. We should be at your AO within an hour."

"What did he say?"

"He wants us to bring him the tape immediately, and not to surrender it to anyone but him."

Furgeson took the reels and placed them in a bubble wrap taping the wrap tight, then put the prize into a metal container, then placed the container into his briefcase. Furgeson affixed handcuffs to his right wrist and the handle of his briefcase. "Now what do we do, Hal," asked Furgeson.

"Follow the general's orders. I wish we could get into that safe. But knowing Skip, it's probably booby trapped."

Agent Halbrooke took out an MFCPTAC-33, multi-functional tactical communications system. It was a cell phone, walkie-talkie, compact computer, receiver, recorder, and listening device. He dialed up a code-specific number.

"Colonel Hempden, this is Agent Halbrooke. I am in the White House Comcenter and need an escort to one of your choppers."

"I'm coming in with five men. Standby."

White House Oval Office
Washington, D.C.
Saturday—1505 hours

The President was watching Secretary of State Kelly, who was glaring at Martha regarding her remark about him being a spy. Martha sat straight backed on the edge of her chair, sipping her coffee, and looking over her cup at the secretary when the phone rang. Everyone jumped. The President answered, "What is it?"

"Sir, there are five MI troops standing by the comcenter. They just came in," a Secret Service Agent said.

President Mantle thanked him, then turned to Director Rickard, "MI troops are at the comcenter door. Go down there and find out what's going on."

Rickard rose and left the room. FBI Agent Boulder went with him.

Silence prevailed. President Mantle was back at the window. "Marshall!"

"Yes, Sir."

"Get the Secretary of Defense on the phone."

SOS Marshall Kelly laid the receiver in its cradle. "Sir, his secretary stated that the Secretary and Assistant Secretary of Defense are in-route to NSA."

President Mantle sighed in disgust. "I have this deep-seated feeling, Marshall that we're in trouble."

The Secretary nodded. Martha began to voice a question then stopped. Marshall leaned close to Mantle, "Sir, we should have heard from Rickard by now on the situation at the communications center."

White House Basement
Washington, D.C.
Saturday—1512 hours

Rickard and Boulder approached the comcenter, observing five troops and a colonel as the comcenter door opened. The troops formed two files on either side of the door with the colonel positioned against the far wall inside the formation. The three NSA agents appeared and closed the door behind them. "Hey, Dan."

"Hi, Hal."

"Hello, Director Rickard."

"Halbrooke!"

Rickard and Boulder noticed the briefcase and handcuffs. Tension sucked the air out of the small confinement. No one moved, but everyone studied each other. Adrenaline began to pump. It seemed as if each person was afraid to move. Tense seconds ticked off the wall mounted brown clock, which hung above the Secret Service Officer's desk.

One stupid move and it would all be over. The bloodbath would begin. "Dan," Halbrooke broke the tension, "we're leaving, but I'll be back."

"Agent Halbrooke, you need to come upstairs to see the President," Director Rickard said.

"Director Rickard, when it comes to national security, NSA decides whom sees who and what. And my orders are to return to NSA, not stop off to visit with the President."

FBI and CIA agents began to shift in place behind their directors. This shifting caused a response from the MI troops. They formed one line and hip-leveled their M-16A2s. Colonel Hempden took up a leadership position center and two feet behind her troops facing Director Rickard with her Browning 9mm clasped in her right hand pointing towards the floor.

Sweat shone on everyone's faces. The clock's ticking pounded against their eardrums. Here it was; that which had been avoided earlier was now going to blow up and people were going to die. "All right, Director Rickard," Halbrooke said defusing the situation, "we'll go up to speak with the President. But I warn you, any attempt to imprison us, or to acquire this briefcase Agent Furgeson is holding will be catastrophic."

White House Oval Office
Washington, D.C.
Saturday—1520 hours

Agent Halbrooke stood before the President, who was sitting behind his desk. The First Lady sat near the President's right side. Secretary of State Kelly was standing left oblique of the President's desk and three feet to the right of Halbrooke. Director Higgins stood right oblique of the President and two feet to the left of Halbrooke. Director Talbort stood to the right of the President while Rickard and Boulder were positioned at the right front corner of the President's desk. Agents' Furgeson and Tenny stood two feet behind Agent Halbrooke.

"Mr. President," Agent Halbrooke said, "We didn't find anything in the comcenter. However, you nor no one else is authorized to enter that facility per orders of Generals' Toomey, Stone, and Hanalin."

"Really! As soon as I contact the Secretary of Defense, that situation will be remedied.

"Why is that briefcase handcuffed to your agent?"

"It was handcuffed to Agent Furgeson when we arrived, Sir. So it's handcuffed to his wrist now."

"Agent Daggard informed me there was a tape in his desk draw; I want that tape Agent Halbrooke."

"Mr. President, there wasn't a tape in Daggard's desk, nor in his safe, or his file cabinet. Now we are leaving. Any attempt to stop us will bring in the MI troops. I do not believe you want that, Mr. President. Any how, what is so damn important about this tape you mentioned?"

President Mantle threw his cup of coffee. The cup shattered as it hit the wall spilling pieces of china and liquid on the carpet. "I want that briefcase, Halbrooke. I want it now."

This comment created a shifting of all personnel in the room. Agent Halbrooke produced a hand grenade. "I think not Mr. President. We are leaving."

On that note, the three MI agents moved to the door. "Mr. President," Halbrooke spoke over his left shoulder, "I am sure General Hanalin will be in touch."

"Am I *not* in control any more, Agent Halbrooke, or am I simply a prisoner?" asked President Mantle.

"That's not my call, Mr. President," Halbrooke said as he closed the door behind him.

The President and directors watched from the window as the troops began to board the choppers. In five minutes the troops were gone.

Chapter Seven
General Hanalin makes a Command Decision

US Air Force Academy
Colorado Springs, Colorado
Saturday - 1530 Hours EST

Colorado Springs stretched out lazily under the warm, late spring sun. The ghosts of The Garden of the Gods whispered peaceful welcomes to the tourists on the gentle wind that glided softly through the canyons.

General Bill Bains, the squadron commander at the academy, met General Stone and Master Sergeant Milan at the airfield parking lot. "Nothing like waiting until the last minute, Ralph!"

"*What?*"

"The last minute to take out a jet in order to maintain your flight status. What did you think I was talking about?"

"Right. You know how crazy it can get in MI."

General Bains stared at General Stone for a minute. "How the hell would I know how things can get in MI? I am not, thank God, one of you damn spooks!

"I have your destination down as Andrews Air force Base, Clinton, Maryland. You will have to contact the 916th Air Refueling Wing at Seymour-Johnson Airbase, North Carolina one hour into your flight. I have taken the liberty of alerting them of your flight pattern and destination so they will have a refueling craft standing by.

"I have also taken the liberty to lay-on a helicopter for you at Andrews to fly you to Fort Meade."

"Thanks Bill," Stone said as he shook hands with General Bains. "I am not sure how long we will be at Fort Meade."

"If I need my jet, I'll come and get it. I suppose your flight-mission has something to do with the situation in Washington?"

General Stone glared at his old hometown friend, "What do you mean, Bill?"

"All of the military academies received a Teletype directive from the Assistant Secretary of Defense at NSA to stand-down unless orders come directly from him. Besides, it's all over the wires and TV and radio."

The three men stood in close proximity to each other. General Bains was studying his friend's facial expression, while Sergeant Milan looked off towards the flight line.

"So there it is," General Stone thought, "NSA has taken control of the military. Heaven help us when this is over!"

Stone looked at his friend. "Something's happened…"

"No, shit, Ralph!"

"Hmmm! There isn't much I can tell you, Bill. And it's probably best that way."

Both generals stared at each other for a few seconds before General Stone said, "I will take good care of your 'bird,' Bill." Then Stone turned towards the flight line and walked with MSG Milan to an F-15E fighter jet.

As Stone and Milan were performing pre-flight checks of their aircraft, Skip Daggard was driving into Thurmont, Maryland.

Thurmont, Maryland
Saturday—1535 hours

Skip Daggard had adopted a policy during his campaign years in Vietnam never to use the same route in or out of an area if at all possible. Today was no exception. Many people would think he was crazy, but to Skip's way of thinking it was a fight for survival. So instead of taking the most direct and sane route back to Thurmont, Skip drove the brief distance back along Route 78 to the I-81 and I-83 loop and headed south on I-83 towards Baltimore. When he reached Route 695, the Baltimore Beltway, he headed west around the loop until he reached the I-70 west exit. Then he headed west on I-70 until he reached Frederick. From there, Skip picked up 15 north towards Gettysburg and Thurmont.

MI Agent Chief Skip Daggard allowed a smirk to crack his somber face as he drove into the small, sleepy community of Thurmont, which sprawled out at the base of the Catoctin Mountains. Nestled in the mountain peaks were Fort Ritchie and Camp David. He knew that Secret Service Agents would be hunting for him, so he devised Plans-B and C to deal with the situation. Plan A had been his long drive around back to Thurmont. His devious attitude to maneuver, never doing the expected, was the cause of his smirky smile.

Skip had learned many lessons during his career. The hardest lesson he learned was that he couldn't trust the military for support. When he was on a mission, he was alone. Another hard lesson learned was that he could not trust his backup, or people in leadership positions to be there when they were needed. Both of these deficiencies almost cost him his life on several occasions.

One mishap had taken place in Thailand where the US troops were not allowed to be armed, except in extreme situations, but the VC came a-callin' one night and caught him out in the middle of the compound. The other had been in Frankfurt, Germany, when the CIA interfered, and the Russians had held him captive. It was these types of breech of protocol which caused Daggard to operate completely independent of all support, and rely solely on his own capabilities. So he devised a MO which allowed for his own support and escape and evasive actions. His arrival in Thurmont was no accident. It was from this hamlet that he was going to launch his attack on the Secretary of State. But first, he would have to ditch his government vehicle and acquire another one.

Daggard drove slowly on his approach towards an abandoned farmhouse at the north end of town. He made one pass east passed the house, and then he drove two hundred yards before he turned around. Next, he drove west for two hundred yards. Satisfied, Skip drove into the driveway one hundred feet then stopped his vehicle in front of the old barn. He waited about five minutes before he exited his car.

Skip stretched slowly, looking over the terrain, and then he went to the barn and opened the doors by sliding them along a metal track. Although the garage was newer, he used the old barn because he could use bails of hay to hide the vehicle.

Once he was pleased with his work, Skip started walking the quarter mile into town. Twenty minutes later, he entered a country cafe. But before he took a seat, Skip stood just inside of the door and observed the street and sidewalks for three minutes.

Skip moved over to a table against the far wall where he had an unobstructed view of the entire room and doors and windows. He had already chosen his escape route; he would charge over the enemy coming through the front door taking them out, and any one who waited outside. He felt this was his only course of action, take out his opponents as they appeared.

He reached for the menu that was resting in between the sugar dispenser and the napkin holder as he studied the approach of the tall, smooth-faced, tanned, bleach-blonde, thin woman with large breasts, who would be his waitress.

"My name is Linda. I will be your waitress this afternoon," she said taking out her order pad from her sheer-lace apron, which was fastened around her waist. "So, did I pass your inspection?"

Skip looked into her gray eyes noticing the light touch of mascara on her eyelashes and rogue circles on both her checks. "You seem safe enough!"

"Well now, isn't than damn generous of you! You want anything to drink while you're deciding?"

"A small glass of milk, but I'm ready to order." He ordered two grilled cheese sandwiches and a bowl of homemade vegetable soup.

While Skip waited for his meal, he reminisced about another cafe in Morristown, New Jersey. It was situated on Washington Street between the library and Madison Street.

Skip had lived on Madison Street for two years, thirteen and fourteen. He had visited the diner every Saturday at noon because they had the best-grilled cheese sandwiches and homemade tomato soup. Now he couldn't eat tomato soup because it gave him heartburn. "Old age, go figure," he thought.

The cafe was quiet. A middle-aged, brunette waitress sat on a red-leathered stool at the far right end of the counter reading a newspaper. An older couple sat at a table near the front left corner of the café looking out on the street, enjoying a pleasant conversation. Four ceiling fans made small humming sounds as they slowly rotated clock-wise. The atmosphere was cool inside the café, but Skip Daggard was beginning to boil inside.

It was alone times like these that evoked memories of his childhood days, and the countless days and nights he had spent all alone growing up. A deep sigh, some wishful thinking, but Skip had come to realize a person could never go back, or go home. The only constant thing in life is change.

Skip began to playback events as he ate. But his first thought was of his mom. He had stayed away for thirty-five or so years in order to protect her, now he had placed her in harm's way.

He felt his anger building. "Skip," he chastised himself, "maintain! You can't afford to loose it now." He regrouped inside himself fighting the monster for control. After a forty-second battle, he harnessed his PTSD. Now, he had to do something that violated his philosophy; he had to trust in General Hanalin to protect his family because no matter which way he sliced it, Skip could not get to his mom.

If it hadn't been for the exploding thunder and crashing lightening of the storm, he wouldn't have been in the comcenter and intercepted that damn conversation, killed two Secret Service Agents, and placed his mom and countless others in danger. However, the President would have been, and was still in grave danger. "So Skip," he declared to the last bite of his grilled cheese sandwich, "it's all up to you to take out the traitor and save the day."

While he devoured a piece of apple pie-a la mode, Skip devised a plan of action.

Once outside the cafe, he laid his overnight bag on a bench in a small park, opened it, shifted his clothes, and exposed a secret compartment. "Let's see! Who do I want to be? Off course! All right, Jeff Bloom, you're the man of the hour," Skip spoke softly at the identification card.

Daggard took out a driver's license, a social security card, and two credit cards: a Master Card and a Debit bank card. Once he had all of the cards and some money in a wallet secured in the vest pocket of his coat, he walked one half mile west to the first automobile dealership and began checking out used vehicles. He was going to purchase a vehicle to drive up to Camp David and terminate the traitor.

White House Oval Office
Washington, D.C.
Saturday - 1540 hours

While Skip Daggard was in the café in Thurmont, the President sat at his desk reviewing his Ops Plan. He was also scanning the War Clauses of the President of the United States. These were the war clauses written for President Lincoln by Ann Carroll of Kent County, Maryland in the spring of 1861. Until that time, it was Congress and the military that dealt with such affairs. The clauses shifted certain powers over to the President, like declaring war.

It was a somber atmosphere inside the Oval Office as a hard rain began to fall on Washington. "Begging your pardon, Sir." Agent Rickard spoke to the President, "but would you mind terribly sharing with us why we just declared war on NSA?"

President Mantle glared at Rickard over the tops of the papers he clenched in his hands, then he laid the papers down as he slowly rose from his chair, and walked to the Rose Garden doors.

President Mantle looked out on the garden watching the pounding rain beating down the flowers. He clasped his hands behind his back. He sighed deeply, feeling that this situation was a pounding rain beating against him. The rain clouds had hidden the late afternoon sun. The dark and damp atmosphere caused the President to shiver. "Marshall, contact the Secretary of Defense, I want him here immediately."

"Mr. President," FBI Director Higgins spoke up," the Secretary of Defense is at the underground Pentagon at Fort Ritchie. The Assistant Secretary is either on his way there, or is at NSA."

President Mantle continued to stare out onto the Rose Garden. The rain had subsided to a gentle but steady shower. He asked himself out loud, "How did things get so out of control?"

"I believe if you had followed protocol, Sir," Director Higgins said, "this situation could have been avoided."

President Mantle spun around glaring into Higgin's eyes. "When I want your advice Mike, I will ask for it!"

"I thought you were, Mr. President," Director Higgins responded with sarcasm, "but you haven't answered Agent Rickard's question yet."

"Go back to your respective agencies. I want Daggard before me by 9 am tomorrow."

NSA third floor Conference Room
Fort Meade, Maryland
Saturday - 1545 hours

The walls were decorated with pictures of the old building, a part of which they were in now, and portraits of officers who have served as directors of NSA. Although a modern and technologically advanced conference room had been constructed in the new section, which was added onto the old building in the eighties, General Hanilan preferred the old conference room.

Hanalin was studying President Truman's picture. It had been Truman, who on January 22, 1946, took the necessary steps and created what is now called the "Intelligence Community." His Executive Letter established the Central Intelligence Group, which became the Central Intelligence Agency (CIA), and created a National Intelligence Agency (NIA) headed by the Secretaries of State, War, Navy, and a representative of the President. It was the National Security Act of 1947, which enabled President Truman to establish these two organizations. At the end of World War II, the military intelligence branches were unified and transferred briefly to the War Department. The Defense Department created the Armed Forces Security Agency in 1949, which became the National Security Agency (NSA) on November 4, 1952. This centralized and intelligence element reported directly to the Defense Department.

Seated at the huge oak table were Assistant Secretary of Defense Albert Collins, Colonels' Hampden of the Army's 704th MI Battalion, Payton Clay of the Air Force Security Squadron, and Captain Samuel Harding of the Naval Security Group on Fort Meade.

"I hope you realize the position you're in, Mac. You have sidestepped procedures and regulations, not to mention certain protocol."

"Mr. Secretary," General Hanilan turned to face Collins, "the issue was never in my hands. Besides, we have a larger crisis facing us. The Military Intelligence Community has been split apart by the President."

"Yes Mac, and your assaulting the White House with troops did not help this situation any. Perhaps..."

"Perhaps, Albert, you have to decide which side you are on," General Hanalin stated as he took his seat at the head of the table, "I do not have a hypothesis regarding the President's action, but I do have procedures regarding mine. Besides, where the hell is the Secretary of Defense? I haven't been able to contact him."

Secretary Collins stiffly rose to his feet glaring at General Hanilan. Collins undid the knot in his black tie, and pulled it off. He slipped off his brown sports jacket, then unfastened the top button of his Van-Heusen white shirt.

"We come directly under the Department of Defense, Albert," General Hanalin began, "however, when one of my groups or sections is attacked, I have authority to act under Defense Department Orders established in accordance with the National Security Act of 1947. And I did follow certain protocol by contacting you.

"Now, Mr. Secretary, you can stay, or you can take your leave because what is about to happen in this room is strictly top secret. General Stone and General Toomey are on their way. Once they arrive, NSA goes into a lock-down mode. That, Sir includes Cheyenne Mountain, Ft. Ritchie, NORAD, and the White House Communications system-to include Camp David.

"Also," General Hanalin continued, "Agent Halbrooke is on his way back here. He and the other two agents found something in the comcenter. Are you staying, Albert?"

"Mac..."

"Albert, one of our top agents, Skip Daggard, has stumbled onto a catastrophic plot. He's MI, Albert."

Secretary Collins rose from his seat not liking the tone of this conversation. He strolled over to the coffee cart, which had been brought up earlier from the cafeteria. He filled his cup and places two Jelly doughnuts on a small plate. He turned and faced General Hanalin. "What is this plot, Mac?"

"I won't know until Ralph Stone arrives, Sir."

"All right Mac! I guess I am staying. But to address the issue of the Defense Secretary's whereabouts, he's at the underground Pentagon at Fort Ritchie."

Mac Hanilan looked at his old friend with a warm smile. "That's an ideal location for him. When was that procedure conceived?"

"This morning," ASOD Collins responded with a curt smile on his face.

Both men chuckled and shook hands.

Oddly enough, Collins felt good for his sixty-three years. He had joined the army from the streets of Harlem, put in thirty-five years and retired as a general. Then he went into politics. Now he was the Assistant Secretary of Defense. Not bad for a young and wild black man, who was on his way to prison. "What do we do now, Mac?"

"Now, Albert, we wait."

**Federal Building
Washington, D.C.
Saturday - 1550 hours**

FBI Director Higgins sat at his desk reviewing policies and procedures while Deputy Director Boulder was writing a list of the day's events. "Ok Dan, the law states that the FBI is the principal organization responsible for internal security. In part, it 'provides: that the CIA shall not have any law-enforcement powers, or internal security functions.' So my question is, under what authority is the President giving such powers to the CIA?"

"I've been wondering that same thing, Sir! Isn't there a clause that gives the DCI responsibility for protecting intelligence sources and methods from unauthorized disclosure?"

"Yes, here it is, but in my opinion the President has violated certain protocol policies and procedures."

"You want to call him up and advise him of his rights?" Dan said handing the receiver to his boss.

Director Higgins glared at Agent Boulder. "He did contact the Secretary of Defense," Higgins said.

Agent Boulder waved the gesture off. "No, Sir he did not. If you remember, the Secretary made like a mole and took to a hole when he saw the shit slinging from the ceiling fans, and it was about to splatter all over his person. Even the President can't reach him. Totally unacceptable behavior for a leader of his caliber."

Higgins took the receiver from Boulder and placed it back in its carriage. He gave his agent a severe crossed look.

"What do we do now, Sir?"

"I suppose that depends on the President."

"Yes, Sir! But in accordance with the 1947 National Security Act, we could corral and arrest the CIA for improper Law Enforcement violations! Boy, wouldn't that ruffle some feathers."

Higgins dropped the conversation when he saw his agent began scribbling on a note pad. He got up and leaned forward to get a close look, and realized Agent Boulder was creating a list of the past events.

CIA Headquarters
Washington, D.C.
Saturday -1555 hours

Director Rickard stood behind his desk staring out on Washington and the top of the Washington Monument. The ancient Egyptian style structure rose 169.29 meters. Its walls, covered with white marble from Maryland, are 4.6 meters thick at the base, and 46 centimeters thick at the top. The inner walls are set with 193 carved memorial stones donated by individuals, societies, cities, and other countries. Robert Mills designed the monument, and the cornerstone was laid on July 4, 1848 using the same trowel George Washington used to lay the cornerstone for the Capital in 1793.

Agent Rickard was somber. He knew that the agencies had overstepped their boundaries. The only redeeming factor, he felt, was the fact that the President had given the orders. Procedures and protocols had been thrown out the window. Why hadn't the Secretary of Defense been contacted? In the overall scheme of this nightmare, why hadn't the Assistant Secretary of Defense taken charge?

Rickard rubbed his stubbled jaw. "Mr. President," he spoke to his reflection in his office window, "I hope you know what you are doing!"

Director Rickard went to an easel, which was situated near the rear conference table in his office, and began to brainstorm, write down events.

Once he finished, Rickard began to list the proper authorities that should have been present, or should have given the orders.

One thought kept pulling at his brain, what was NSA and Military Intelligence going to do next? They were the eyes and ears of the United States Military. Their ranks number one third of the entire military force. And where in the hell were Daggard and Anderson?

He moved back to his window. A light rain was falling. He wished he could sneak out of Washington, and take up residence in the subterranean section of Langly where he could hibernate until this was over. And it would be over soon. Skip Daggard was a shaker. No matter how many people the President sent against him, Daggard would accomplish his mission. Rickard decided to call his son.

Used Car lot
Thurmont, Maryland
Saturday - 1600 hours

"May I help you?" Skip was on his knees inspecting the undercarriage of a 1995 Cherry-red, four door, four-wheel drive Chevy Blazer. The first things he saw turning his head were a pair of nylon covered legs and white pumps. When he moved his head from under the vehicle he found himself lost in a plaid skirt. Looking up those slender legs, he could see her pink panties. "Two years ago you could have helped me," Skip mumbled under the ladies skit, "but not now; unless you're talking about selling this vehicle," he said standing up.

The saleswoman displayed an arrogant smile. "Yes! That's exactly what I am referring too…the vehicle."

"Your sticker price is too high." Skip took out Mr. Bloom's checkbook from his blue blazer and wrote down the sum of twelve thousand dollars, handed her the check and said. "Shall we go into your office and sign the papers?"

NSA Central Meeting Room
Fort Meade, Maryland
Saturday -1615 hours

General Hanalin was sitting at the far end of the huge dark, brown executive table. He had just ended his conversation with his staff and the Assistant Secretary of Defense when Agents' Halbrooke, Furgeson, and Tenny where let into the room. "Sir," Halbrooke said, "we have a spliced tape."

Agent Furgeson placed the briefcase on the table near General Hanalin and removed the handcuffs. Furgy slid the black leather case to his commander. Hanalin opened it and took out the case containing the reels. Furgy helped Hanalin to remove the reels from the container.

Once the reels were on the table, Halbrooke stepped forward to help Furgeson unwind the tape to the spliced spots. "You see, Sir," Furgeson said, "A neat job. However, this was done by SFC Anderson, most likely under Skip's direction or assistance."

"How do you know it was Anderson and not Daggard," asked the ASOD.

"If Daggard had done the splice, Sir, I would not have been able to detect it. But the question I've been working on during our flight is why did Skip have Anderson do the splices?"

"And that is significant, Agent Furgeson?"

"Yes Sir, Mr. Secretary. It's very significant. Skip covers his back trail. I believe he had Anderson do the splice so we would find it. Skip wanted us to know something was wrong. I believe Skip knew NSA would protect the comcenter against unauthorized access. And according to SSG Parker, Skip had given them all explicit instructions not to allow any one access except NSA personnel. Not even the President, unless he, Daggard authorized it."

"I do not understand, Agent Furgeson, what do you mean, Skip covers his back trail?"

"Mr. Secretary, Skip is a perfectionist. He always checks his work. Skip would not have left this unless he wanted the splices to be found."

"Do you think this is what the President was looking for, Mac?"

"No, Sir. The splices simply indicate that Skip took some information from the reel. I believe the President is looking for the information on that reel. But I don't know how the President figured any information was in the White House Comcenter."

"Now what?"

"Now we wait for the rest of the players to arrive, Albert, because Ralph Stone is the one holding the key. He has some kind of a printout."

Agent Halbrooke went to the coffee cart. He filled his cup, then went around the table refilling everyone else's cups as well. His hand trembled as he poured coffee into General Hanalin's and the Assistant Secretary's cups. Halbrooke accepted the involuntary movement as an omen...*it's going to be a long weekend.* But where in the hell were Daggard and Anderson?

Bloom's Cabin, Virginia
Saturday - 1630 hours

Skip Daggard was driving off the car lot as Sergeant First Class Anderson awoke to the ringing of her alarm clock. She rolled over, stretched out her left arm, found the clock with her hand, pushed in the plunger, and peered through half closed eyes to the illuminated green digits.

She sat up wrapping her arms around her knees and looked at the time again. Kristine began thinking about the phone call she had made and what Skip had told her, "Go to our rendezvous point at the end of your shift. Don't go home. Disappear, and don't call anyone. I'll get there as soon as I can."

Kristine rose, put on her black silk robe, and went into the kitchen. As she fixed coffee, she watched two yearlings frolic in the front yard. The Lincoln Log cabin sat near a half-acre pond. She had no idea who owned it, but when queried, Skip referred to a Mr. Bloom.

The cabin was completely self-contained. Power was supplied by a generator housed in a soundproof pantry connected to the south corner of the cabin. There were no telephones.

Her only link to the outside world was a vintage WWII short wave radio. She was scanning the channels while sipping her first cup of coffee when she stopped the dial. The radio had picked up CNN news. "The top story of the hour, President Mantle has issued and arrest order for Military Intelligence Officer Skip Daggard to the CIA and FBI Agents. The President issued the order from the Oval Office thirty minutes ago just two hours after Agent Daggard had murdered two Secret Service Agents in a Pennsylvania rest stop on Highway I-81. Please stay tuned to CNN for further developments."

Kristine collapsed. Her coffee cup crashed and shattered on the hardwood floor. "Skip. Skip, where are you?" she cried out.

Thurmont, Maryland
Route 550
Saturday - 1635 hours

Skip Daggard had heard the same announcement on his vehicle radio as he began the drive up route 550 towards Fort Ritchie and his appointment with Secretary Kelly. "What the hell? Damn, the President believes I'm a rogue. That goddamn traitorous Secretary son of a bitch!"

Skip turned his vehicle around and began the drive to Bloom's cabin. He began a mental review of the events, as he knew them. He intercepted an encrypted message from Kelly to Schmirnoff. Next, he had Charles decode the tape at NSA, and NORAD received the info due to a special program between DAESY and KEDAS. He went to Camp David with the President. Informed him of the Secretary's plot, then he took-out two Secret Service Agents who Kelly had sent to kill him.

As far as Skip was concerned, the facts were not adding up. Something was out of sync. Skip decided he wasn't going to agonize over the situation until he could relax at Bloom's cabin. But he tried to second-guess what was transpiring in Washington and NSA.

By the time Skip had driven into Frederick and turned west on I-70, he knew precisely what course of action he was going to take. He was going to protect President Mantle at all costs.

Chapter Eight
The Game of Cat and Mouse

FBI Headquarters
Washington, D.C.
Saturday—1640 hours

A gentle drizzle began to fall on Washington and the surrounding areas. The rain mixed with the warm air to create a transparent mist.

Dan Boulder was sitting at a desk he used when he was in Washington. He was dressed in a dark blue suit typical of the normal attire for agents, but had his suit jacket hanging over the back of his chair.

There were twenty other desks assigned to agents in the large room. Most of the desks were now manned. Dan leaned back in his black leather executive series office chair with his arms resting on the cushioned arm rests. The sleeves of his white shirt were rolled up above his elbows.

He was studying the expressions on some of the other agents' faces. One apparent thing seemed to be clear: there were no happy campers here. Most of the men and women in the room had been with him at the White House.

Dan rose from his chair. He went to a chalkboard and wrote down a header in large bold letters:

PRESIDENT USING CIA, FBI, AND NOW BATF AGENTS TO HUNT DOWN MI/WH COMMO CHIEF DAGGARD—NOT SECRET SERVICE.

By the time Dan had finished, other agents had gathered around him. He turned to them, "I think we have to put this situation into perspective…"

Agent Ken Kitchen spoke out, "What do you mean, Dan?"

"I was sitting here studying all of your faces, and it seems that the feeling is universal, something is not right."

The twenty agents nodded their heads and voiced their agreement.

"Now that we have been ordered to regroup and prepare to locate and take out Daggard, I think we should try to put this situation into some semblance of order. At least that's my feelings."

Agent Dan Boulder moved six feet to the right down the chalkboard. He stood near an easel with a black marker in his left hand staring at his fellow agents.

Agent Ken Kitchen and the other agents agreed. "Dan!" Kitchen spoke up, "I served some with Skip in Nam. Back then, we gave him a nickname, Snoopy."

"What's the relevance of that, Ken?"

"To alleviate a long exposition, Dan, if Skip doesn't want to be found, we are not going to find him. If we do find him, it's because he wants us to.

"You don't know him, Dan. You've never met, nor have you ever served with him. When he's on the hunt, or being hunted, Skip Daggard is a very, very dangerous adversary.

"Snoopy, the Peanut's character was like an icon to many of us during that fucked up abortion in Nam; patriotic and all that. Skip's values reminded us of that dog. He doesn't believe in governments, but he does believe in our Constitution, and he'll fight to the end of time for the American people.

"If we find Skip, we're dead meat. But I agree with you Dan, something is wrong with this picture. So let's review what we know."

The agents began to brainstorm. First they decided to start with procedure. The Secretary of Defense should have been the first one contacted. That didn't happen. The next in the chain was the Assistant Secretary of Defense. He was not contacted either.

"What we do know is that someone contacted General Hanalin, Director of NSA. We also know that the Joint Chiefs of Staff were at Camp David with the President, but we do not know if they contacted anyone in the chain of command."

Agent Kitchen spoke up. "DIA has contacted us that the respective senior officers of MI are in-route to NSA. But why did they contact us? We also know that the President has pressed us into service, but the CIA and BATF have no business being involved, let alone the CIA heading this operation since their sole mission is external security."

"But why hadn't the President contacted the DIA to take control?"

"That's a damn good question, Dan," Kitchen spoke out, "but my question is, why is Skip hell-bent on taking out the Secretary of State?"

A mummer rose from the FBI agents in the room. They had formed a semi-circle around the easel to help with ideas. Now, a curious picture was beginning to take shape.

"The President seems reluctant to answer that question, Ken. Director Rickard asked him that a few hours ago. The President's response was, 'Do your duty.' So there isn't any satisfactory answer I can give you."

As they continued to brainstorm, the FBI agents began to realize they were being used. But on a more serious note, just who the hell was in charge?

Agent Kitchen summed it up, "This is fucked up!"

White House Oval Office
Washington, D.C.
Saturday - 1645 hours

President Mantle used his fork to poke at his food. He sat on the couch directly across from the left corner of his desk. Director Teddy Talbort, of the Presidential Secret Service sat across from the President. "Teddy, I apologize for not speaking to you earlier about the goings on here, but I didn't, nor do I want your people involved in the search for Agent Daggard. I need you and your personnel here."

"Mr. President, I am somewhat confused over these events. But our mission is to protect you, and follow your orders. Now that the MI troops have gone, the FPO's are back at their posts. I have two agents with each Federal Police Officer."

"Thank you, Teddy!"

President Mantle continued to poke at his supper. The gentle rain increased in intensity as the gray sky darkened over Washington. "Teddy, our main concern is to protect the Secretary of State. From my understanding, Secretary Kelly is Daggard's target. I want three of your best people with Kelly at all times."

"Yes, Sir, and I am going to put three extra agents with you as well!"

The President smiled, "All right, Teddy."

Director Talbort left to issue the President's orders, and oversee the placement of his officers. President Mantle, alone in the Oval Office, began to eat his supper.

"Manty?" Martha interrupted.

"Come in, Martha!"

"I am frightened," she said sitting down on the couch across from her husband, "Skippy is the best we have. If he wants Kelly, do you think all the President's men will stop him?"

President Mantle cocked his head as he stared over at his wife. "What do you mean, Martha?"

"Manty, he had kept himself out of reach of the best enemy agents in the world, and always managed to perform his duties. If Skippy wants Kelly, he will get him no matter how hard you try to stop him. But what I am having great difficulties with is why does Skippy think Kelly is a spy."

President Mantle rose from his seat in a smooth liquid motion. He went to his wife. Martha stood up. He pulled her to him. He began to speak, then caught himself. He had almost given away his secret.

NSA Conference Room
Fort Meade, Maryland
Saturday - 1730 hours

General Toomey entered the conference room. "Mac, Sam, everybody! What's our situation?"

"Tim. We still do not have a location on Daggard or Anderson. The last known location for Daggard was at 1300 hours in Pennsylvania. Albert is in contact with the Secretary of Defense at Fort Ritchie.

"I was in the process of issuing a recall of MI troops to Colonel Hempden, Colonel Good, and Captain Seward."

"Good, Mac. Continue."

General Toomey shook hands with everyone, then found a seat. "We will go on a twelve and twelve/twenty-four/seven until this situation is cleared up. Begin your recalls," General Hanalin ordered.

General Hanalin took his seat as the respective commanders left the room to return to their groups and start the recall leaving himself, General Toomey, and the Assistant Secretary of Defense in the conference room.

"Tim," Hanalin began, "Ralph should be here by nineteen-thirty hours. He's bringing a printout that should explain what this crisis is all about."

"I hope so, Mac. Have all of our satellite stations been contacted yet?"

"No. We are in the process of sending out cryptic messages explaining that we are going into a crisis specific situation, and further information would be forthcoming."

"So at least they know there is a crisis? Good!"

General Toomey turned to the Assistant Secretary of Defense, "Why isn't the Secretary of Defense here, Albert?"

"He wanted to direct things from the Safe House at Ritchie, Tim. We have a direct secure line to him via the SODLP (Secretary of Defense Little Pentagon) circuit."

General Toomey nodded his head.

The Little Pentagon was one of those well-kept secrets, like so many others. There's an archival vault somewhere just to keep account of all those secret places and what type of business is conducted at those places. Not to mention the top-top secret circuits that are connected to nowhere. And what individual knows of all those hidden places? None because one person can not be trusted with all of that knowledge, but many personnel know of many specific locations.

"So, the SOD has taken himself out of the loop, hey?"

"Yes," answered the ASOD.

General Toomey sat down at the far end of the huge mahogany table looking down its twelve-foot length at Hanalin.

Bloom's Cabin
Virginia
Saturday - 1800 hours

Kristine was cleaning her dishes when she heard the distant hum of a vehicle. She went to the black, thick metal gun cabinet and took out an AR-10. The rifle was a semi-automatic in .223 caliber with a fiberglass-reinforced black synthetic stock. Kristine raised the front window two inches, crouched in a shooting position, then locked and loaded one of the three thirty round magazines she had removed from an ammo can located close to her position. She laid the other two clips on the floor near her right knee.

Skip Daggard had turned off the Georgetown Pike onto a dirt access road into the Dranesville District Park. He followed the road north until it intersected with a ghost of a road overgrown with grass. He drove slowly for about one hundred yards. Skip parked his vehicle, turned it off, got out and went to a predesignated spot and observed his back trail for ten minutes. Satisfied, he went back to his vehicle and continued along the straight overgrown road.

Bloom's cabin sat in the center of one hundred acres in the northeastern right corner of the park. The cabin had been built in eighteen eighty-two by Issa Bloom. Skip had seen the advertisement in the Baltimore Sun in March of nineteen ninety, and purchased the estate from the last descendant of Bloom. Skip had learned to follow his instincts. When he saw the ad and it appeared to jump off the page at him, Skip didn't question the logic or reason. He simply made a call to view the property.

Skip had asked Miss Bloom if he could spend a few weekends on the property. He gave her a small compensation so there wasn't a problem with his request. Skip fell in love with the rustic cabin and its serene surroundings on the first day. But it was his discovery of the tunnel on the second Sunday, which brought a smile to his face.

The entrance to the tunnel was in the far right corner of the property bordering the Potomac River.

He had found the grate when he was picking juicy black berries. It took him four hours to free the rusted grate. He greased it, then replaced the iron barred grate.

On Monday, he and Miss Bloom had closed the sale. The following Saturday, Skip was exploring the ancient tunnel. He could hear the Potomac River overhead. When his walking counter read five miles, he noticed sunlight. He discovered a ladder and climbed it. The grate was partially covered with bushes. Skip couldn't move the rusted bars. He made an indication of the grate on a map he was constructing.

Skip followed the tunnel for thirty miles. He found grates at variations of miles increments, and added them to his map. The tunnel ended near Constitution Avenue between the Roosevelt and Arlington Memorial Bridges.

The following Sunday, Skip had crossed the Potomac using the Capital Beltway. He found a parking area near the C&O Canal. The canal berm was now a hiking and biking trail so Skip took out his black Mongoose twenty-one speed mountain bike, and began to follow the canal trail.

He found the locations of the grates near the small town of Barton, near Clara Barton's Historic House. The second one was situated one mile from the junction of Mac Arthur Boulevard and Sanganore Road, just south of the Dolly Madison Chain Bridge. A third grate was concealed one and a half miles from the junction of Mac Arthur Boulevard and Reservoir University Hospital Road, at the end of Foxhall Road and Potomac College. He discovered the last one to be near Constitution Avenue hidden in a grove of bushes just two hundred yards from the Washington Monument, and about two and a half miles from the White House.

Skip had sat on the lawn near the Washington Monument, and deduced that this was the escape route President Monroe and Congress used when the Brits burned Washington during the War of 1812. He rationalized this fact due to the type of stone used in the tunnels' construction.

As Skip drove the last mile towards Bloom's cabin, he noticed there weren't any lights. He gave a cracked smile because he figured out Kristine must have heard his vehicle. He could imagine her hiding somewhere ready to shoot the intruder.

When he parked the car close to the front door, he saw the muzzle of a rifle disappear. Kristine was in his arms before he had time to stretch when he exited his vehicle.

She smothered him with kisses hugging him tightly, then stepped back and clobbered him with a quick roundhouse. This time, her fist connected, but only glanced off of his chin because Skip was quick enough to begin stepping back in an evasive posture.

"What the hell was that for?"

"One of these days, you will learn to keep me informed."

Skip rubbed his chin as they entered the cabin when Kristine spoke out, "*What* is going on, Skip?"

"Honey, I have no clue to what is going on," Skip said as he removed his jacket, and hung it on the wooden coat rack inside and to the right of the great room door.

Kristine led the way into the kitchen and began fixing supper. She placed a small chuck roast into a black roasting pot. Next she added about an inch of water, shook salt and pepper on the meat and two shakes of garlic salt for good measure. She added five potatoes and a small pack of bay carrots, and then she placed the covered pot in the preheated oven.

Skip had poured them cups of coffee. He placed her cup before her at the kitchen table, and then he sat down across from her.

"Dinner will be ready in forty minutes, Skip. Did you really shoot those two Secret Service Agents?"

Skip placed his left arm on the armrest of his chair. He placed his thumb from his left hand under his lower lip between his lip and chin.

At first, Kristine thought he was lost in thought until he blurted out his answer.

"Yeah!" He sighed. He took a sip of coffee after lifting his head from his thumb, and looked down the table at Kristine. "They had been sent by Kelly to kill me, Kristine. But I can't figure out Kelly's involvement. I was on my way back to Camp David to shoot the son of a bitch when I heard the announcement over the car radio that the whole bunch were in-route back to Washington."

Skip had noticed Kristine's attire as they had walked from his vehicle to the cabin. Her sheer silk black robe was open revealing her silk sheer black panties. He stood up and began his approach.

Kristine saw the lust in his eyes. "Oh know, you don't!" she said standing up to repel his advance.

"Oh yes, I do!" he said as he closed on her.

"I suppose you want me on the table?"

"Yeah!"

"Skip Daggard, you're incorrigible," Kristine purred as she let Skip lift her onto the table and slide down her panties, "how can you speak of killing and love-making all in the same breath?"

"Welcome to my world, Kristine," he whispered as he showered her with kisses.

Thirty-five minutes later, Kristine was fixing their plates while Skip cleaned off the table.

"That was a mighty fine meal, honey. Thanks!"

Kristine was still furious with him because he had left her in an anxious state of worry. She glared at him as she placed a bowl of French Vanilla ice cream in front of him. Kristine was standing at the table across from Skip so he received the full force of her stare. "Gee, ice cream too?"

"Do not try to change the subject, lover!"

It was dark in the woods around the cabin. The rain was an on-again-off-again plague all day. Now it was raining hard. The windows and doors had been open to let in some comfort from the cool breeze, but now Skip had to leave the table to batten down the hatches.

The pounding of rain drops on the leaves and tin roof was loud in the silence of the forest.

When Skip returned to the table, he declared, "I'm going to change that damn roof one of these days."

It wasn't a gentle rain or drizzle, which bothered him, but torrential downpours such as now, which created uncontrollable anxiety within him. The poundings of the heavy raindrops were like exploding incoming rounds to his ears as water spattered on the tin.

Kristine sat down across the table studying him. She would not be put off. "We'll sit here all night!"

"I'm confused, honey," Skip declared, "I saw the President, leased a vehicle from the motor pool, and started for New Jersey. Next thing I know, I have a tail. I stopped at the rest area and so did the Secret Service Agents. It doesn't make sense!"

"What doesn't, Skip?"

"They told me that Kelly had sent them to terminate me."

Kristine studied Skip's eyes. She knew he was lost in his thoughts, probably trying to analyze recent events. She waited patiently.

The rain slowed to a steady cadence. Yet, raindrops continued to pepper the tin roof and leaves. Kristine lit a cigarette. She rarely smoked because Skip disliked the smell of stinking smoke. She inhaled deeply of the smoke blowing it out of the left side of her mouth.

Kristine was leaning back in her chair when Skip spoke, "I'm going to kill the Secretary of State, Kristine. I am going to do it tomorrow. I'm going to sneak into the White House, grab the traitorous son of a bitch, drag him in front of the President and blow out his fucking worthless brains all over the Oval Office."

So matter of fact was his statement that she almost fell over backwards. The front legs of her chair crashed down on the floor. Skip began to laugh.

"Glad you find my mishap so amusing," she shot out at him.

"My mother, aunt, and grandmother used to yell at me for sitting back like that. One day Nanny came into her kitchen where I was sitting back devouring a bowl of her homemade custard. She had surprised me. Needless to say, I fell backwards hitting the floor. 'I told you so' is all she said." Kristine and Skip laughed.

"How do you plan on pulling off this marvelous feat of yours? Especially since Washington is crawling with people who want to kill you!"

She said this leaning her arms on the table. They measured each other as the battery operated kitchen clock's second hand clicked off several seconds.

Skip broke the amiable trance, "Isn't it bedtime?"

"I suppose you want an encore on the kitchen table?"

She saw merriment dance in his blue eyes. "Yes Ma'am. I'm ready for a second dessert."

They rose and she led him off into the bedroom.

Potomac River
Northwest of Washington
Saturday - 1910 hours

The two Apache helicopters were flying at treetop level. Why he had ordered them to "run silent," Chief Warrant Office Hedgerow could not imagine, but he had. They were flying in a zigzag pattern over ground left and right of the river. They were in constant communications with the tower at Langley. Chief Hedgerow had taken them from Langley over the northwest tip of Washington. When their coordinates indicated the intersection of Military Road and Connecticut Avenue, the pilots turned their birds south. The pilots steered their choppers around the White House following a predetermined flight plan.

They followed Connecticut Avenue west to the Potomac River, then headed northwest following landmass and the George Washington Memorial Parkway. This route took them over the CIA Headquarters and the Federal Highway Administration and the northern section of the Dranesville District Park.

"Hedgerow, I want you to fly with your ears on," said Director Rickard.

He had called the flight line prior to the routine surveillance flight the pilots flew over and around Washington.

In the scheme of things, especially in the protection of the US Government, the lay citizen is unaware of procedure and protocol—those things that happen on a continuous routine basis. One of those twenty-four hour daily routines includes flight surveillance of two Apache attack helicopters, which fly the Potomac and circle the Washington area. However, back to the scheme of things, the helicopter flight patterns always changes, and tonight their AO (area of operation) took in a larger section of landmass.

The four-inch dish attached to Chief Hedgerow's running bars was active. He was picking up conversations from all places. He heard people fighting, making vacation plans, and various other conversations. When he flew over the northeastern tip of Dranesville Park, he heard what Agent Rickard hoped for, "PR surveillance to LG tower."

"LG tower to PR surveillance, go ahead."

"Ten-four; picked up their voices in sector-six. Only way in is a dirt road from the south."

"Ten-four PR surveillance! Understand you have them located in sector-six?"

"Ten-four. We are leaving the AO. Will take up a hovering position over Glen Echo. PR Surveillance out."

CIA Rickard's Office
Langley, Virginia
Saturday - 1915 hours

Agent Rickard leaned back in his chair smoking a Marlboro. He blew smoke rings towards the stucco ceiling when his phone rang. "Agent Rickard!"

"Sir," the tower sergeant said, "the quarry is located in sector six."

Rickard jammed his cigarette out in his brown ashtray. He took out a map and located sector six. "That's in the right hand corner of Dranesville Park."

"Yes, Sir. Chief Hedgerow said you will have to take a dirt road in from the south."

"Roger! I see it on my map. What I don't understand is…"

"Chief Hedgerow stated there is a cabin. Smoke is coming out of the chimney. He explained that because he was in stealth mode he went down for a look."

Damn, Rickard said to himself. Stealth or not, Daggard is no pilgrim.

"Any thing else?"

"Chief Hedgerow stated his team will hover over Glen Echo…"

"Have them return to Langley. I don't want them noticed. It will take me an hour to get my team together."

"Yes, Sir!"

Rickard slammed his phone's receiver down on its cradle. He pushed a button under his desk that was connected to an intercom speaker in James Jorgon's office. Jorgon was Rickard's top agent. He was going to assign James the task of gathering up the troops to make the assault on the cabin in Dranesville Park. But he was upset with the stupidity of Hedgerow for going down too close to the damn cabin.

"How can I soar like an Eagle," Rickard blurted out, "when I am surrounds by shits for brains."

Agent Jorgon entered Rickard's office and heard his comment. "Excuse me?"

Rickard looked up from the map on his desk. "James, I want you to get the team together. We have our pigeons located, here." He pointed to the location on the map.

"Who is shits for brains?"

Rickard started to laugh. Then thought better of it. "That damn Hedgerow. He took his bird down over Daggard's head. He thinks just because he was in stealth mode, Daggard wouldn't be aware of his presence. I have to call the President. We leave in one hour."

Once James left the room, Rickard picked up his telephone receiver. He stood behind his desk holding the handset to his right ear judging his motives regarding his actions against Daggard, then dialed the President's cell phone number.

"Mr. President, this is Agent Rickard. We have our quarry located. I am preparing to move against them. We will begin our assault in one hour."

"Excellent, Rickard. Keep me posted. This is great news. Thank you. Do you need any personnel from this location?"

"No, Sir. I have a team standing by here at Langley."

The President whispered into his receiver, "I want them eliminated, Rickard!"

"Yes, Sir. I understand."

Rickard slowly lowered the receiver to its cradle. He inhaled a deep breath, exhaled and spoke out loud, "That's easier said than done, Mr. President!"

Agent Rickard left his office to oversee operations.

NSA Conference Room
Fort Meade, Maryland
Saturday - 1920 hours

General Stone and Master Sergeant Milan entered the conference room. They found the conference table surrounded by eighteen officers of MI.

"Guess you all are wondering why I called this meeting?" Stone chuckled as they entered the room.

"We're not amused, Ralph."

"Yeah? Skip always got a chuckle from his audience. And since we are here because of him, I thought it appropriate."

Stone and Milan went to the refreshment table. Milan filled their cups, and both men filled small plates with sandwiches.

General Toomey inhaled on his cigar. General Hanalin sat patiently glaring at General Stone, "Any time, Ralph would be fine with us."

The new arrivals found their chairs. "Officers of Military Intelligence, I believe you have been waiting for this!" General Stone produced a one-page document in twenty copies from his black briefcase, and began to pass them to his constituents.

> *This is the ball to the bat! I am at home plate.*
> *I am at first base! Says the bat to the ball.*
> *Please to make all acquaintances...at 1938 Hoppstrausse*
> *and At 13918 Lead Plaza and At...1415 Off-Strausse.*
> *Old acquaintances are hereby met!!.*
> *This is quaint news. The Umpire will be pleased...//*
> *It will be jubilant, when, He retires///*
> *Places will be set. no rudements//10 on the nine, twenty-four the six off drisic.*
> *The ball is in your court...*

General Toomey was the first one to react slamming his chair with the backs of his knees as he jumped to his feet, "What the *hell* is this?" He demanded waving the printout at General Stone.

"Tim," General Stone began, "this is a hard copy of the message Skip had decoded at NSA this morning. It is an encrypted translation.

"Sergeant, if you please!"

Master Sergeant Milan handed the officers another piece of paper. "This, my fellow officers, is the cause of all that has transpired since 0400 this morning. What you are now looking at is the final translation."

This is Kelly! Every thing is ready here.

I understand!

Proceed with plans, Schmirnoff.

The players are in place.

He will be taken out at the Plaza in Munich

At 0950 the eighteenth of September this year.

The Soviets are happy with this arrangement.

The date is confirmed//.

Alert the Soviet Assassin.

"Ladies and Gentlemen, this is an order from the Secretary of State to Schmirnoff the under secretary to the Russian Ambassador in D.C. to assassinate the President of the United States during his European tour. The assassination is to take place when the President is giving his Speech under the Glockenspiel in the Munich Plaza."

The officers stared at the piece of paper in their hands. General Toomey, again, was the first to react. "We should storm the White House and kill that traitorous son of a bitch."

"Tim?"

"*What*!"

"We don't have to," said General Stone, "Skip is going to take care of him."

"What *we* have to do," said General Stone softly, "is cover Skip's back."

"Do we have a fix on his location?"

"No, Ralph. But I believe Skip and Anderson have gone underground-literally."

"Mac…"

At that moment Captain Tobias rushed into the room. "Sir, the Washington Surveillance Choppers went silent. We initiated Operation Stealth One-Ops # 3. We intercepted their surveillance transmission to CIA at Langley. They've located Daggard and

Anderson in the northeast section of Dranesville Park just northwest of Langley.

"We also intercepted a call from Rickard to the President..." Tobias had to stop so he could catch his breath.

"Well, Captain," said Toomey, "are you going to keep us in suspense?"

Captain Tobias stared at the officers. He wasn't sure how to proceed. He remembered something Skip had told him once, 'When in doubt, jump in.' "S-S-Sir," Tobias began to stammer, "the Pr-Pr-Pr-President ordered R-R-R-Rickard to take them out!"

"Take them out? *Kill them*?"

"Yes, Sir."

General Toomey rose in a calm fashion. He walked over to the President's picture, then threw his coffee cup. As glass fragments fell to the floor, he turned to his comrades, "What in the *hell* is going on? Are you mistaken about Daggard speaking with the President at Camp David?"

General Stone spoke up, "Master Sergeant, would you please check that?"

"General Hanalin will have to give Tango-Echo Group the go-ahead, Sir"

"Your group has certain instrumentation that can reconstruct voice and imagery. Master Sergeant Milan knows how to recreate a past conversation in order to identify who said what."

"Proceed, Sergeant. I'll make the call."

Bloom's Cabin
Virginia
Saturday - 2000 hours

Kristine sat straddling Skip on a kitchen chair. Sweat dripped from their bodies. She hummed and smiled at Skip; however, she knew his mind was elsewhere by the far away look in his light blue eyes. Kristine allowed the tremors of their lovemaking to subside before she broke the mood. "A penny for your thoughts!"

It took a few seconds before Kristine's words penetrated his thoughts. Skip looked up at her.

"I was reminiscing, honey about the past thirty-five years of my life. And how, in a single second, a person's world can crash and burn."

She pulled his face gently into her breasts, "Don't think about that now. You will spoil this moment!" She cooed.

Skip nibbled at her, then moved his face. "Sometimes I think too much. I guess it's because of who I have become."

Kristine was going to respond, but saw that her lover was gone again. Skip was lost to her. Lost in that world he goes to where no one can reach him.

She smothered him between her breasts whispering, "I'll hold you until you come back."

It was Skip's sixth sense that was calling to him. Taking him away from Kristine. He didn't want to go, but something was pressing at his conscious. Drawing him to a familiar sound...a familiar place.

Skip lifted Kristine onto the table again. He could see and feel all those wonderful sensations again, but there was something...*what?* His subconscious slowly gave up the information. They were making love. He was looking out the window. What was it that caused him to shift his concentration? He remembered. Skip jumped up and Kristine fell to the floor.

"*What is your problem?*" She screamed at him as she pulled herself from the floor using the table for support.

"We have to get out of here."

"What?"

"We're going to have visitors. While we were engrossed with pleasure, I saw the treetops swaying. There's no wind or breezes, Kristine. The storm has subsided. We can take a quick shower, grab the packs I have prepared, and head out."

Kristine stood naked before him. Her body gleaning in the reflective light, which was shining off her sweat-soaked body. One 60-Watt bulb burned over the center of the table. Kristine wanted to clobber him, but Skip had already clamped down on her left hand and was leading her from the kitchen.

"Where are we going? I don't understand, Skip," was all she could blurt out before she was drawn into the shower stall.

Skip answered her question while they lathered-up. "Washington, via the express tunnel."

"The what? And why do we have to leave?" She managed to exhale as Skip pulled her from the stall still soapy and drenched.

"Because, honey-bun, we have been found."

They must have taken the quickest shower in history because they were dressing within three minutes from the time Skip stated they would have to leave.

They dropped their packs on the kitchen floor. Both Skip and Kristine were dressed in SWAT style black jumpsuits and black canvass jungle boots.

Skip had turned off all the lights in the cabin before returning to the kitchen. He now extinguished the kitchen lights as well.

Kristine called out to him in the dark room, "Skip!"

"Hmm?"

"Are we just going to sit here?"

They sat in the dark looking at each other's shadowy silhouette. "Until the time is right."

Skip and Kristine watched the approaching vehicles' lights appear and disappear through the trees and brush. "Looks like they're here."

"Who is it?"

"Probably Richard and Associates!"

"We just going to sit here?"

"Give the dumb-shits about five more minutes. I mean, how hard is it to follow a road?"

Kristine checked her wrist watch-2015. She studied Skip. How can he be so cool? But of course, this was his game—the cat and the mouse. "Skip?"

"Yes!"

"They're getting closer."

"Yeah, the shit for brains finally figured out the terrain."

"I know you have a plan…"

Skip reached out for, and took her right hand in his giving it a reassuring, gentle squeeze.

"I always have a plan, Kristine. They may not always turn out according to *plan*, but fret not darling, I keep several plans in reserve."

"Skip…"

"I know; they're here. Lets go."

They went out the back door just as Rickard began his announcement for them to surrender. "We have you surrounded, come on out!"

Rickard waited three minutes. "All right, go in and get them."

As the agents approached the cabin slowly, the cabin exploded. The agents took cover behind their vehicles, behind trees, and lying face down in the cool, rain drenched dirt as cabin parts of wood and stones rained down on them.

Once all of the pieces of flying debris settled to earth, the CIA agents rose. "What the hell happened?" asked Rickard.

The agents glared at him. "All right, we know they weren't in there so fan out and find them. That bastard has to be here somewhere!"

The area was illuminated from the fire. Agents began to comb the woods for their quarry using their flashlights to help find their way around.

"Sir, I found something," one agent called out.

"It's a grate!"

"Yes, Sir, and footprints."

Rickard stood over the grate working through possibilities. He wasn't sure if this was part of Lincoln's tunnel system, or one of the newer ones. "Hicks, pull open the grate."

Hicks stared at him. Rickard looked over at him, "Did you hear me? Open the damn grate!"

"Not me, Captain!" Hicks called everyone captain. It was a habit he had picked up in the army.

"What the hell do you mean, not you?"

"Cap', I was a "tunnel rat" in Nam. Daggard was just coming into his own as an operative. He learned every method known to warfare about torture, tunnel evasion, and then he made up some.

"If Daggard went down that hole, this child isn't going after him. No Sir, not this kid. Daggard's crazy. I met him once when he and my team were after the same group of subversive VC's. We came to the hole they had used to evade us. It was my job to go in, but Daggard stopped me by grabbing my arm as I went to my knees to crawl in. 'I'll take it from here. Besides, I haven't eaten yet today.'

"You ever here the term "Snake Eaters"? It was the damnedest thing I had even seen. A bunch of snakes, all poisonous, fell on Daggard's head when he poked it into the opening.

"Daggard must have known what was coming because he struck out with his right hand and grabbed the snakes before they had a chance to strike at his head. Then he had begun to chomp down on the slithering reptiles eating those snakes alive.

"No, Sir! No way am I going into a hole after Skip Daggard."

Director Rickard and the other agents stared at Hicks in total disbelief.

"Smith…"

"Right! The white boy won't go down so send in the black guy?"

"Shit! You know me better than that."

Rickard threw up his arms and stormed away towards his vehicle, "I don't believe this,' he shouted, "thirty-five tough agents afraid of one damn rogue subversive!"

"Not just one subversive, Chief, "Hicks yelled back, "only the best in the whole damn world!"

Rickard keyed his mike on his car radio, "Haggardy, this Rickard, I need the Corps of Engineers."

"On the radio, or do you want them at your location?"

Rickard worried over the question for three minutes, "Have them come here with the schematic maps of all the tunnels out of Washington, D.C."

"Roger."

"Oh yeah, and have them bring a life-size dummy."

There was a pause before Haggardy answered, "Yes, Sir. A life-size dummy! Would that be male or female?" Haggardy began to chuckle.

"Shut up!" Rickard retorted.

His men began to gather around him, "I have the Engineers coming. Once we know where this tunnel leads, half of you are going to follow it. I will take the rest to its end destination. That way we'll flush them through, and I'll take them when they come up."

Hicks studied Director Rickard for a few minutes. "Cap' I think we better do some strategy brainstorming about your plan. In my opinion…"

"I don't give a rats ass about your opinions, Hicks!"

"Sir, it appears that you seem to think we're dealing with a rational human being; we're not. If Daggard and Anderson went down that hole, then he has a plan."

"You have a better idea, Agent Hicks?"

"Unfortunately, no."

"Then we'll go with mine."

Director Rickard sat in his vehicle with the driver door open. He began to survey the surrounding forest wondering if Daggard was sighting in on them now. He shivered. "So where are you now, Skip Daggard?" He asked the question to himself.

Chapter Nine
The Plotters are revealed

Under the Potomac River
Virginia
Saturday—2035 hours

Once Skip and Kristine had left the cabin, he set the detonation timer, and led Kristine to the tunnel entrance just as the cabin exploded. "That ought to hold them for a while! Let's go."

He lifted the grate. "Go down," he said to Kristine.

"What's down there?"

Skip sighed evenly understanding her fears. "Our way to Washington! Move, sweetheart. We don't have time for chit-chat."

Kristine shivered, then began her descent down the slippery iron ladder into the dark unknown.

Skip was right above her, but he had to stop so he could shut and lock the grate. She waited until he started moving again before she finished her descent. "It's about a thirty mile journey," Skip whispered in her ear, "we'll come out near the Washington Monument."

He took the lead. Skip set a quick pace. His stride was forty inches long and he moved at the double quick somewhat faster than a walk but slower than a trot. Kristine was able to maintain the pace due to her physical conditioning, but found she had to run at times in order to keep up with Skip.

The ancient stench of decay and ankle-deep, stagnant water caused them to take short shallow breaths as they moved quickly though the natural rock constructed passageway. "Where are we Skip?"

"Under the Potomac."

"It smells like a septic system backed up!"

Skip ignored her comment. He was using a large stick to knock down recently constructed spider webs. He also used his walking stick to agitate the water in front of them in order to scare-off any creepy crawlers.

Kristine didn't want to know why he was beating the water before them, but she stayed right behind his back just in chase she would have to launch herself onto his shoulders. If anything touched her feet, she was going airborne.

"Do you think they will follow us?" Kristine asked with a hint of anxiety in her voice.

"No doubt, Kristine, once they take a hacksaw to the lock. Rickard will have to contact someone to find out where this tunnel leads. Once he has that info, he will go post-haste to the end location. The only two entrances and exits shown on any of the maps detailing this tunnel are the one we entered through and the one at the end of the line."

Skip produced a small section of tanned deer hide. This is the only map I know which shows all of the grate exits in between. I drew it during my investigation of this tunnel three years ago.

"Rickard's plan, no doubt, will be to send a force through the tunnel to flush us out towards the exit where he will be waiting.

"The only fault with his plan is we're not coming out…"

"*We're not?*"

"No, ma'am, we're not. I know something they don't. When we don't appear and his team does, Rickard's going to have a shit-fit," Skip snickered at this thought, "I wish I could see his startled face when his team leader pops his head out of the hole."

"Where are we going to be, Skip? Do you think they will catch us?"

Skip stopped so suddenly that Kristine ran into him. She wrapped her arms around his waist. He was barely breathing. His chest hardly rose and fell with his inhales and exhales. Skip stood immobile. He had turned off his flashlight. Precious minutes passed. Kristine became frightened.

"Again," he was thinking, "again with the fucking questions!"

"No, Kristine," he hissed, "they won't catch us. As I have just stated, I know something that has been buried for one hundred and forty-five years!"

He started off again. Kristine almost fell trying to release her hold on him. It took her a moment to realize the reason he had stopped so abruptly, her questions. But she couldn't stop the next one from coming out.

"What is this place, Skip?"

"I believe it's one of George Washington's tunnel systems. It leads into another tunnel, which branches off to the White House and the Capitol Building.

"If my archeology and history serves me right, this is the system our government used to flee Washington when the Brits burned our Capital in 1812. Now moove it, Dolly," he said, alluding to Dolly Madison and her escape when she saved the Gilbert Stuart Portrait of George Washington.

NSA Tango-Echo Group
Fort Meade, Maryland
Saturday—2036 hours

MSG Sergeant Milan sat at a computer console swearing. NASA had been using Star Wars for space photography; therefore, Milan could not get a lock on the system. He had entered the access code: Angel Three Tango- - -NSA Purge...Goto 230 longitude, + 200 latitude...Execute   00130Z-goto-Zone,   NE.   execute   ecko-tango*+&*+.

The code was accepted by the system. However, the flashing red LED light indicated NASA still had a lock on the satellite. "Sam, rotate the Microwave dish PD on CATMANDO ten degrees west, six degrees low." Milan gave his request to the duty officer, Captain Sam Wordsmith.

"Milan, the Secretary of Defense has to give that order."

PD is a code name for a hidden huge microwave satellite dish in the Catoctin Mountains. The P equates to the President and the D equals to David, Camp David. The micro dish is approximately three miles southwest from the communications center at Fort Ritchie. The comcenter is the senior operations facility for the satellite system, but NSA can override any US system in the world when it so chooses.

"I have authorization. Do it!"

Captain Wordsmith did not take kindly to such treatment from a sergeant; however, he knew that Milan was working with General Hanalin, so he obeyed.

After Wordsmith punched in a seven-digit code, and used the daily Code Guide for further references, the dish began to move very slowly to the prescribed coordinates. Milan wanted the dish moved in preparation so when NASA was finished with Star Wars, he could reposition the satellite.

After waiting another impatient ten minutes, Milan decided to take control of Star Wars. He locked in NSA's special override code: Tango-six-Mike/Alpha//.over-ride//Tango-NASA-Whiskey.Alpha Zulu 0405.

Sky watcher, the on-duty officer assigned to the War Room in the comcenter in the basement of NSA, informed Milan that Star Wars was moving. The NASA Bat. Line rang. "Captain Tobias, this a secure line."

Tobias listened to the bitching for three seconds, then hung up the receiver. "Seems they're upset at NASA," he said to MSG Milan, "guess they will have to get over it."

Members of the Ten Squadron laughed.

Once Milan had Star Wars in a beam contact with CATMANDO, he repositioned I-Spy, another image to voice system, which was used to listen in on worldwide telephone conversations.

When I-Spy recognizes specific key words, it locks in on a conversation. Then the system identifies the location of the speakers using a geographic world map, which is located in the War Room at NSA.

Once the locations are pinpointed, the voice or voices, numbers, locations, and pictures of the people speaking are directed through a mainframe at the nearest US Intelligence Field Station or a repeater substation. The information is then redirected through a complex system of multiplexes and computers to a Linguist who interprets, decodes, or classifies the conversation, even if the people speaking are on opposite sides of the world.

The system stores the information on hard disc in a huge computer system and creates a magnetic backup copy. The system has the capabilities of locking in on six million conversations at one time. However, when a key word is detected by the system, a buzzer and red light appear on the map alerting the on-duty officer. When this happens, agents and MI troops are dispensed to the location.

I-Spy can transmit thousands of conversations to the War Room at NSA in the blink of an eye. The dish can sweep the North and South American continent from east to west and pan back every ten minutes. One hundred Military Intelligence linguists at NSA, Hawaii, and Iceland listen in 24/7.

It took Milan twenty-five minutes to have all systems in synch. Images began to appear, and the computer began to printout those pictures while creating a CD of imagery and voice and time and date of the conversation. When the system went into the ready mode, Milan took out the CD, collected the pictures from the base of the printer, and headed for the conference room on the third floor.

Saturday - 2100 hours

Three events were taking place simultaneously:
Skip and Kristine were crossing under the Potomac River just northeast of the Beltway Bridge, and turning southeast towards Washington.

A Corps of Engineer Officer just arrived at Bloom's cabin with the maps Agent Rickard had requested.

And MSG Milan was handing General Hanalin the photos he had just acquired from the SIV's system, and was placing the CD into a laptop computer, which was connected to a sixty-inch screen in the conference room.

"Well, we only have about 25 more miles to go, Kristine," Skip declared when they reached the first iron grate, "let's step out lively, hey?"

Kristine glared at him. "What do you think I have been doing for the last five miles, dragging my feet?"

Skip turned around to look at her. She had cobwebs glued to her hair giving her ash blonde color a more granny look. "Quite distinguishing!" Skip declared as he began wiping the spider netting from her head and shoulders.

"What?"

"I do believe you are going to be quite stunning as an old lady."

Kristine could make out his sensuous color on his cheeks and his Irish twinkle in his eyes from the small amount of light coming from the grate opening.

"Oh! You've got to be kidding. *Not here? Not now?*"

Skip reached up and wiped the remaining webbing from her hair. "Thank you! But not here or now. We have far to go before we can rest."

Skip turned about to face the front and the way they were going and led off. It had taken them fifty-five minutes to cover the first five-mile stretch of the tunnel.

Agent Rickard reviewed the maps. "Agent Hicks, you take six men and enter the tunnel. Look here on the map and see how the tunnel goes? It ends at Constitution Avenue. The rest of the agents and I will post ourselves at the exit manhole cover." Rickard pointed to a mark on the map indicating a grate.

"I want you to drive Daggard hard. I don't want him to think, just react. I want that weasel to pop his head up out of the hole so I can shoot him."

Hicks looked at Rickard. He wanted to object but knew the futility of it. He and the six men going into the hole with him put on coveralls and calf high rubber boots the chief of the Corps of Engineers had brought for them.

"Here, Agents. You'll need these down in that tunnel." Rickard handed them each a flashlight.

While they were finishing sliding into their boots, the engineer took the dummy over to the grate. He took a pair of bolt cutters to the lock and cut it. Next he eased the grate up and dropped the dummy down the hole according to Rickard's instructions.

"No explosions, Hicks! Now get going," Rickard ordered.

Agent Hicks was amazed when they entered the hole without incident even though a dummy went first. "It's a long way to Washington," Hicks said to his team, "and if Rickard thinks we're going to pell-mell through this tunnel system, he's full of shit."

Rickard left the area with the rest of his team racing back to Washington to a deadly encounter. And by the time Hicks and company were starting their drive, Skip and Kristine were just stepping out beginning their sixth mile towards Washington and destiny.

MSG Milan slipped the CD into the computer and turned on the huge screen monitor. Captain Tobias handed a folder to General Hanalin.

General Hanalin reviewed the photos that were in the folder and began passing them around to the other officers as they watched events unfolding on the screen.

"Are you sure this is correct, Master Sergeant Milan?" General Hanalin asked.

"Yes, Sir."

"There is no question to the validity of this information, Milan?" General Toomey piped in.

"No, Sir."

General Stone spoke up, "This puts us in a difficult position, people."

"Yes! But it places the President in an even more crucial position," General Toomey said, "and if this info *is* correct, and Milan states it is, then either the President is part of the plot, or he is acting on advice from Secretary Kelly."

Captain Tobias went to the coffee table. He picked up the carafe, and went around the table refilled the officer's cups. They all leaned back in their chairs reviewing the new evidence while sipping their coffee.

"If the President is involved," General Hanalin broke in, "then that makes him...what?"

Every one looked at him. "Yes Mac, that makes him... a traitor," stated General Toomey.

The officers stared at General Toomey.

Agent Halbrooke and his team sat in chairs away from the main conference table close to a corner near the serving table. General Hanalin had ordered Halbrooke and his team back into the room, shortly before Tobias and Milan had returned with this new information. They observed the actions of their leaders and the information as that information was presented.

Halbrooke studied General Hanalin as the general stood, looking over at him.

"Stop the CD," Hanalin said to Milan. "Hal…"

"Sir?"

"We have overlooked a vitally important situation."

All eyes were now focused on General Hanalin.

"I do not know how important she is…"

Halbrooke broke in on the general, "Skip's mom?"

"Yes!"

The realization of the importance of General Hanalin's words was not quite clear to all of the occupants of the conference room.

"Sir, I don't think anyone in our organization would be that stupid!" Halbrooke declared.

It seemed as if the whole world had stopped and was holding its breath within the four walls of the conference room. No one in the room moved. The implications of Hanalin's words became inroads filtering through everyone's mental-processing facility as understanding began to take root.

General Hanalin began to pace the twelve-foot length of the conference table. He ignored everyone. Sometimes he cupped his hands behind his back. Other times, he rubbed his hands together in front of him as if he were washing them.

He did this for two minutes, then he looked over at Halbrooke. "How long will it take you to get to her house?"

Halbrooke rubbed his right hand over his chin, then looked at General Hanalin, "About two and a half hours, Sir. But I don't think me and my team should go."

"Understood! But you are going. Her home will be your post for the duration of this mess, unless I feel it necessary for you to be in Washington. Understood?"

"Yes, Sir. Understood! Any special orders, Sir?"

Hanalin weighed the question carefully before answering. "I do not believe you need any. *Do* you, Agent Halbrooke?"

The general's remark was perfectly clear. "No, Sir!"

Agents' Halbrooke, Furgeson, and Tenny rose in unison and left the conference room gently closing the hardwood door behind them.

General Hanalin turned to the fifteen officers of the various Military Intel units on Fort Meade assigned to NSA. "Ladies and gentlemen, it has been a *long* day. Tim, Ralph, I have assigned you a vehicle and driver. You are in adjoining rooms in the Marriott fifteen minutes from here. I have taken the liberty of assigning four agents for your protection. I really don't see CIA or anyone else coming after you, but an ounce of prevention is better than a pound of cure.

"Master Sergeant Milan, you have been provided a room at the Air Force Squadron barracks. We shall now retire and meet at the Four Winds dining facility at 0700. Good night!"

By 2205 hours, twenty-one hours and fifteen minutes after Chief Warrant Officer Skip Daggard intercepted Kelly's message to Schmirnoff and making the first move, the chessboard was set. The pawns were aligned, the knights were now on the offensive, and a king protected a lone rook. And all roads and tunnels were leading to a final match in Washington, D.C.

Eilis Daggard's house
Bud Lake, New Jersey
Saturday—2400 hours

Much had transpired at Eilis Daggard's gray-blue duplex situated on an acre lot on the east bank of Bud Lake in New Jersey since the afternoon broadcasts.

Bud Lake is a small community with a huge lake that lies gentle and peaceful between Netcong to its east and Stan Hope to its west.

Family and friends began converging on the Daggard home about 1:45 p.m. shortly after the first news story of the killing of the Secret Service Agents in Pennsylvania by MI Chief Warrant Officer Daggard head of the White House Communications Center.

To say this news had been earth shattering would be an understatement considering these convergents had been making a pilgrimage once a year to Arlington Cemetery and Skip Daggard's grave for about thirty-four years.

Eilis Daggard had accepted the fact that she would have much explaining to do when she watched the news broadcast and her phone began ringing immediately.

The first one to call was her daughter, Mary. "Are you watching TV?" Mary shouted into the receiver. "Just what in the hell is going on, Mom? They're saying Skip isn't dead."

It took several seconds before Eilis could get a word in. "Mary, you and John must come over. I have something I must tell you. Come over now, honey."

It had been that way throughout the day and into the evening hours. Eilis explained as briefly as possible without going into too much detail. She didn't know exactly what she was allowed to share without putting Skip in danger. Now; however, all of that was really mute because her Skippy was *in* about as serious a trouble as a body could be, being hunted the way he was. She had hoped and planned to make her son's homecoming a huge surprise. Her surprise had been shot to hell.

Eilis was surprised at how fast the time had passed. It was already five minutes into Sunday morning. Her daughter, Mary sat close to her at Eilis's antique oak, eagle-clawed pedestal dining room table. "I can't believe you never shared with me, Mom," Mary barked at her mother with iron in her voice. "All those years of going to Arlington...all those years, Mom, and my brother is alive! How could you do it? How could you be so cruel?"

Eilis Daggard, gray-haired and eighty-five, with freckles across the bridge of her nose and aging spots dotting the tops of both her hands, gently took Mary's right hand in her hands and smiled a motherly smile. "This may sound like an excuse, Mary, but it wasn't my idea. It was your brother's and our government. It was done to protect us."

By now, most people had gone home or to bed. Eilis Daggard and her daughter were the only two up. John, Mary's husband was curled up on the sofa in the living room.

"I still have visions of your brother standing in our doorway on that January 4th in 1970, all handsome in his army dress uniform..." Eilis became somber as she tried to continue. "He hugged me. And then he kissed me on my right cheek..." Eilis was now staring off into space as if she were reliving the events she was telling to Mary. "And then..." she said choking on her tears, "he broke my heart!"

Then Eilis began to explain to her daughter the whole sordid mess. How Skip was supposed to have returned from Vietnam by December 4, 1969. And that all of a sudden his weekly letters stopped by October '69.' She didn't think much of it for about three weeks because sometimes his letters arrived in a bunch. But by

November first, she new something was wrong, so she went to her friend, who was a Senator at the time.

"It was frightening, Mary. My friend had told me he had been ordered by NSA never to interfere with intelligence business again. I had no idea what he was talking about.

"Then, in January, your brother shows up on our doorstep and tells me…" Eilis broke off speaking because she couldn't hold back her tears any longer. Tears she had held in check for thirty-five years. Mary leaned over to her mother and gently pulled her into her.

Eilis wiped her face. He said, 'I came just to tell you the truth, Mom. I'm a covert operative for Military Intelligence. I kill people, Mom.'

"So matter of fact were his statements, Mary. And then…I looked into his baby-blue eyes…" Eilis choked down her tears again. "My Skippy was gone, Mary! The Irish merriment that once danced in his eyes was gone. His eyes were dead."

Both mother and daughter squeezed each other and cried. "Needless to say, your brother never contacted me again. His funeral was Intelligence's way of giving your brother free reign to operate without fear for us."

When Eilis finished her story, she rose on shaky legs and went into the kitchen to fix a pot of coffee. She knew that she and Mary wouldn't get any sleep.

Mary lumbered into the kitchen and wrapped her arms around her mother hugging her placing her left cheek against her mother's back. It was now twelve-thirty a.m. and a light knocking sounded at the front door.

Both women froze. The percolating sound of the coffee filled the silence as its aroma filtered through their nostrils.

"Who could that be, Mom?" Mary whispered in her mother's ear.

"I haven't a clue, Mary. I'll move near the door. You wake John."

The two women began to creep-step out of the kitchen. Mary went to the sofa in the living room while Eilis went close to the door.

"John!" Mary spoke softly as she gently nudged her husband. "John, wake up!"

A second light rap at the front door thundered throughout the living room. Mary shook John again harder this time. "John, wake up! Someone is at the front door."

John rubbed his eyes as he sat up. "Who is it?"

"We don't know…"

"What time is it?"

"It's thirty-five minutes after midnight, John."

John was about to ask more questions, when a third knock sounded on the door. It was louder then the first two raps. Mrs. Daggard saw that John was sitting up and attentive so she moved close to the metal door. "Who is it," she quietly called out.

"Mrs. Daggard? Snoopy sent us." A husky voice said softly.

John and Mary were now standing near Eilis. "Who's Snoopy, Mom?"

"That was your brother's code-name in Vietnam."

The voice from the outside spoke again in a more hushed volume. "Mrs. Daggard, I am Agent Halbrooke. I have agents Furgeson and Tenny with me. General Hanalin from NSA sent us."

Thirty seconds ticked off the dome clock while Eilis was trying to decide what to do. She barely breathed. Then she turned to her daughter, "This is precisely why your brother had to be buried, Mary. His death protected us all these years."

Eilis had formed a plan. "Mary, open the door slowly. John stand behind me."

As Mary began to swing the door inward, Eilis produce a .32 semi-auto handgun from the right pocket of her plaid skirt. She pointed the gun head high as the shadowy figure of Halbrooke showed in the doorframe.

Shock permeated from Mary's face, but Agent Halbrooke stayed stationary and smiled. "Come in, gentlemen," Eilis said in a calm and soothing voice.

Eilis was satisfied once she had checked their credentials. Agent Halbrooke put his wallet away then took out his cell phone to contact General Hanalin. "I have to inform the general that we have arrived, Mrs. Daggard." She nodded her head.

"Yes, Sir, we're here. Skip's mom is a game lady. I don't think CIA would have gained entrance if they had showed up."

"No Sir, no sign of them when we arrived."

"Stay alert, Hal! I'm sure they will not be to far behind you."

"Yes, Sir." Halbrooke put his cell phone back in his right outside jacket pocket.

Eilis filled her best china cups with fresh coffee as the somber group sat down at her kitchen table. Halbrooke sat at one end of the table while Mrs. Daggard sat at the other end, or the head of the table. Mary sat to the left of her mother and John sat next to Mary. Tenny was to Eilis's right with Furgeson next to him.

No one said anything for a while. They simply sipped coffee and stared at one another. Eilis broke the silence. "How is my son?" Her question was directed at Halbrooke.

Hal sipped two more sips of coffee before he answered. He was trying to figure out how to explain the situation or if he should. After all, she only wants to know how her son is. He inhaled deeply then exhales softly. "Well, that's a good question, Mrs. Daggard. You see, Ma'am, we haven't seen Skip. He and his fiancé…"

Eilis Daggard sat up, "His what?"

A quiet hush settled over the people sitting at her table. *"His fiancé!"* Halbroooke exclaimed softly.

"My son is engaged?"

"Yes, ma'am!"

"What is she like?"

Halbrooke looked at his fellow agents. "Well, she's tall and blonde and she is MI- army."

Eilis smiled. So her son finally found someone. "Where are they?"

Halbrooke wasn't sure what to say. He started to remember the handgun Mrs. Daggard has in her skirt pocket. "Mrs. Daggard…"

"Where are they, Agent Halbrooke," she demanded.

"Somewhere under the streets of Washington."

Silence prevailed for awhile except for the ticking of the second hand as three gold balls turned clockwise and counterclockwise mounted on a pedestal on a six-inch gold and silver domed mantle clock on the top shelf of a bookcase filled with cookbooks six feet from the kitchen table.

Eilis rose and refilled everyone's cups. Skip, had given the china to his mother on Mother's Day just before he went into the army. The white porcelain had been hand-painted with bluebells.

"He was coming home today." She stated in a trembling voice as she sat down again. "He was finally coming home!"

Eilis took a long sip of her hot black coffee. Before anyone could respond to her statements, she looked over her left shoulder at her mantle clock and corrected herself, "I mean he was coming home yesterday," and she broke down. She let herself have a few minutes of tears then collected her composure. Mary had reached over with her right hand and gently laid it on her mother's shoulder. "He'll be all right, Mom! You'll see. Skipper will be all right."

Eilis Daggard was staring over the rim of her coffee cup at Halbrooke as she sipped on her coffee. They had all heard the motor of a car as a vehicle pulled up to the curb in front of her house. All of their attention was focused on the outside noises. Early birds were chirping and singing announcing the dawn of a new day. They could hear the low purring of a car engine not far from the house. Then the engine went silent, as did all the morning sounds.

Eilis Daggard breathed a sigh of relief as she felt the reassuring metal of her weapon.

Chapter Ten
Eilis Daggard Takes Charge

Constitution Avenue
Washington, D.C.
Sunday—0205 hours

Director Rickard sat slumped down in a green-webbed lawn chair five feet from the grate at Constitution Avenue. He wore his full-length black raincoat and had an umbrella resting on his lap. Three agents stood in proximity of him and fifteen sat in five vehicles facing the grate with their feet flat on the dark, wet, green grass.

Rickard had his left hand wrapped around the brown handgrips of his weapon, which was in the left pocket of his raincoat. He sat there with the knowledge that Skip Daggard's and Kristine Anderon's time had just about run out. As he shifted in his chair, Rickard wondered what the repercussions were going to be once he had killed the two rogue NSA agents. But Daggard and Anderson were more than just NSA folks—they were Military Intel people-US Army. How was the Pentagon going to take to a killing of two of its own?

Director Rickard looked out over the bright, well-lighted scenery of all the monuments and the reflection pool. He stared off in the direction of the White House, which stood two miles south of his position, and wondered if the President's sleep was filled with nightmares of a man with a gun chasing him and Kelly. He studied the approach of Special Agent Kneedle the BATF agent who had been assigned as BATF's Task Force Leader directly under Rickard. Kneedle had one hundred agents with him, which were now deployed in and around the White House and the tunnel openings within the White House complex.

Just as Kneedle stepped up to Rickard's position, Rickard's cell phone rang. As he withdrew his phone from his vest pocket with his right hand, Rickard held his arm out lengthwise with the palm of his left hand facing out indicating to Kneedle to halt his advance. "Director Rickard!"

"Sir, this is Agent Altman. We have taken up our position in front of Mrs. Daggard's house. What do you want us to do?"

"Just maintain a vigil. No one in—no one out."

Rickard hung up and put his phone away. Kneedle stepped up to him, "Director Rickard, my men are in place."

Rickard studied the short, stocky ex-Marine for a few seconds. Kneedle was a thirty year-old Anglo-Saxon from Boston, with smooth skin, short-cropped brown hair and he wore SWAT style attire. "That's fine, Kneedle. I want you to stay here with me. In about ten minutes, Agent Daggard and SFC Anderson should be popping up out of that hole," Rickard pointed to the grate. "I want you to witness the fact that they came out shooting. I had no alternative but to return fire. *Understood?*"

Agent Kneedle turned his head right oblique and looked at the grate, then he turned his head back to stare at Rickard. In those few brief seconds, he understood all right. He understood two murders were about to take place, and Director Rickard had just ordered him to lie about the circumstances. He knew he had no way out. "Understood, Sir!" Why the hell did he come up here in the first place?

200 yards from Constitution Avenue
In the GW tunnel System
Washington, D.C.
Sunday—0215 hours

It took Skip and Kristine a little over five hours to cover the thirty miles to Constitution Avenue. At the right angle of the tunnel where the right fork branches off towards the grate 200 yards from Constitution Avenue, the left fork stops because of a wall. Skip felt along invisible seams. Kristine heard him chuckle as a stone moved and a section of wall opened. He smiled at Kristine. "This part of the old Washington tunnel we are entering is really deteriorated, but we have to go through it in order to access the one section of the Lincoln tunnel."

"Do you think they'll find the door once they realize we've eluded them?"

"Perhaps! But it won't matter. They'll never locate my hole."

"That's pretty conceited, Skip!" She shot back at him.

"Not really, Kristine. I know something they don't. Since I wasn't able to find the place we are going to hold up in on any maps, I feel confident Rickard and Company will not find my hiding place either. But I have taken precautions. I never take anything at face value"

Kristine glared at him. "You think this is a game don't you? But it's not. They're out to kill us, Skip!"

Skip stopped. He lowered his head accepting the admonishment. Then he turned around to face Kristine. He leaned forward and pushed on another rock—the wall closed. Skip pulled her into his arms, "Sometimes, Kristine," he inhaled and exhaled, "sometimes I treat it like a game. He held her tight in the dimly lit tunnel. "Sometimes…sometimes I think back to those days in the fifties when I was a kid playing war…just before I squeeze the trigger. To those days, Kristine, when we used peashooters, cap guns, and snowballs. When everyone who had been killed or wounded could get up and go home for supper." Skip dropped his arms to his side and became somber. "Yeah, honey, sometimes treating these types of situations as a game helps me…to kill and survive."

Kristine realized that Skip had just opened up to her, and she didn't know what to do or how to respond. So she leaned in and kissed him.

Sunday—0225 hours

Behind them, Hicks and his team were fast closing in on them. "We'll be confronting Daggard soon unless he's gone to the surface and has met Director Rickard," Hicks said to his men.

As they made the turn at the right angle, Hicks expected to meet Daggard and Anderson. He stopped. He and his men positioned themselves for a shootout. Only there was no one there. They began to move forward very slowly. Hicks knew this section was about 200 yards long. He expected Daggard to materialize out of the shadows at any second. Their progress was slow—guns at the ready. When he and his team reached the ladder, Hicks figured it was all over for Daggard and Anderson. He moved up the ladder, pushed up the grate, and found he was staring into the 'eyes' of seventeen semi-automatic handguns.

"*What the hell*! Hicks?"

"Sir," exclaimed Hicks, "they didn't come up?"

"No, Agent Hicks. They did not come up."

"That's impossible. Unless they went out one of the other grates along the way."

"What grates?"

Agent Hicks and his team climbed out of the tunnel through the opening at Constitution Avenue. They dusted themselves off. "We passed several along our line of march, Sir. They should have come up here."

"Well, they didn't." Director Rickard shot back at Hicks.

Agent Rickard queried Agent Hicks as to what he had seen down in the tunnel. "We noticed the grates. But after close investigation, we determined that Daggard and Anderson didn't use any of those exits. Nothing had been disturbed in a long while. There's a turn at a wall approximately 200 yards from here. The tunnel ends here."

"A wall?"

Agent Hicks stood up tall after he had removed his rubber boots and slid his feet into his black Cockrens. "Yes, Sir."

"Damn!"

The agents stared at him regarding Rickard's comment. They watched him pace around the grate in circles for about six minutes.

FBI Agents Boulder and Kitchen had their six-man teams move off towards their vehicles.

Rickard stopped pacing, "So, the bastard wants to play games, huh? All right, fine! I'll play one of my own." He turned to Agent Kneedle, "I want you to get about twenty loud speakers and an amplifier. Alert your men. Some how that bastard got past us."

Rickard took out his cell phone. Agent Boulder moved up to Rickard, while Agent Kitchen stood close by. "What do you plan to do with the speakers, Sir?"

"You'll see, Agent Boulder."

Rickard dialed his cell phone. When a voice answered, Rickard gave Agent Altman his instructions. "Agent Altman, I want you to kick in the front door, grab Mrs. Daggard and bring her to me. I will be in the subbasement of the White House near the entrance to the Lincoln tunnel. Do you understand?"

Agent Jeff Altman understood all right. He understood the orders he had just been give were insane. He saw his six-year career, and his life, being destroyed. He trembled at the thought of losing his life at the hands of Agent Daggard for accosting his mother.

Jeff Altman was wiry with thinning black hair. He was thirty-one and stood six feet-one inch tall. He had spent four years in Military Intelligence in the Navy, then went right into the CIA after his honorable discharge. Now, he had just been ordered to assault the mother of the meanest son of a bitch in the whole world.

Atlman sat behind the steering wheel of the dark blue sedan rubbing his hands. Jackson and Watt, Altman's team members, stared at him for a few minutes.

Agent Watt, a short five foot six-inch Italian powerhouse from the Bronx spoke up, "What did he say?"

Agent Jackson, a five foot ten inch black muscle builder from Alabama asked the same question.

"Director Rickard wants us to kick down Mrs. Daggard's door and bring her back to the White House."

They sat in their vehicle for another five minutes before exiting because all three agents knew and understood that Director Rickard had just ordered their execution should Agent Daggard live to fight another day.

Constitution Avenue
Washington, D.C.
Sunday—0240

Agent Ken Kitchen stepped up to Director Rickard. "I'm taking my team. We're going home." Kitchen was standing so close to Rickard, it appeared as if he was standing on Rickard's toes.

"You're *what?*"

Kitchen tried to control himself by clenching his fists. "Up until now, Rickard none of our agents have been hurt. Have you noticed? Or maybe you haven't been paying attention. How did you or any of your men survive that explosion in Dranesville Park? After all of the pressure we have put on Daggard, and all of the opportunities he's had to take us out, not one of our people have been wounded or killed, why?"

No one moved, but all the agents present began to analyze Kitchen's questions.

"I will tell you why, Director, because we're part of his team and he can elude us six ways from Sunday and every other day during the week. Therefore, we do not present a hazard to him. But now you have single handedly declared war on the baddest son in the whole corps. When he discovers you have bothered his mom, you won't have to worry about hunting him down any more..."

"That's my point, Kitchen. And that's my purpose for the loud speakers. Once I have Daggard's mother here, I will let her speak to him. Then when he comes out after me, we'll nail him and put an end to this."

Agent Ken Kitchen began to laugh hysterically. "You're a dumb-shit, Director Rickard. You have no idea...no concept of your quarry. I've seen Daggard's work in Nam. You don't know it, but you just signed the death warrant of every agent involved in this operation. Even if you torture Mrs. Daggard making her scream through those speakers, Skip will not come out. He won't come out until he can kill Kelly. Once that mission, his first mission is accomplished, he will begin his second mission..." Agent Kitchen paused to allow his words to seep into the brains of the listening agents. "His second mission, Director Rickard, will be to free his mom and terminate every agent involved. No, Sir, my team and I aren't going to be party to it. He'll come for us. But hopefully he will accept the fact that we weren't involved in the taking of his mother."

Once Kitchen finished with what he had to say, he collected his six men and left for the Federal Building.

A somber mood swept over the remaining agents. No one said a word for several seconds. Rickard's cell phone rang loud in the damp early morning air. Every agent jumped.

Eilis Daggard's home
Bud Lake, New Jersey
Sunday—0248 hours

The conversation around the table had been mostly about Skip. Halbrooke filled Eilis and Mary in on some of Skip's exploits since Daggard had arrived at the National Security Agency in May of 1982, and how it had taken Skip twenty-five years to break a spy ring within the organization. During a lull in the conversation, they all heard car doors close.

Halbrooke, Furgeson, and Tenny arrived at the front door just as the door was kicked in. Six agents faced each other over the threshold, pointing guns at each other. Eilis stood behind and to the right of Agent Halbrooke. She stood motionless for six seconds realizing that her son had spent thirty something years of his life protecting her from situations such as this one that was unfolding in her living room.

Eilis dipped her right hand into the pocket of her plaid skirt. The ratchet sound of the hammer cocking on her handgun arrested everyone's attention. "Gentlemen! Drop your guns please! My son taught me how to use this."

Slowly, the six agents complied. "Agent Halbrooke, please scoot them across the floor towards me with your right foot." Halbrooke did as he was ordered. "Mary, pick up the guns and give them to John." Eilis never took her eyes off of the six agents. "The coffee's fresh. I suggest we retire to my kitchen and have some."

Once they were all seated at the table, Agent Altman asked if he could report. Mrs. Daggard nodded her head.

"Sir," Altman said clear and plain, "we are prisoners in Mrs. Daggard's kitchen…"

Director Rickard responded to the news by throwing his cell phone on the ground and stomping on it, shattering it into tiny pieces. "Kneedle, I want those speakers in place by 0800 hours." Agents' Kneedle and Boulder and his six agents and Rickard's agents stared at him. "Altman explained to me that Halbrooke is there, but it is Mrs. Daggard who is holding all of them under her gun. We can't do anything else here so we will get some sleep. I want everyone at the White House at 0800 hours, understood?"

All of the agents acknowledged their understanding by nodding their heads. They all departed the area.

A secret room off a section of the Lincoln Tunnel between the Ford Theater and the White House
Sunday - 0325 hours

Skip and Kristine had moved quietly through a long section of the Lincoln tunnel. Skip stopped. Kristine stepped up and stood to Skip's left side because Skip had turned when he had stopped. He was now facing a wall. "Where are we, Skip? Why have we stopped?"

"We're situated between the White House and the Ford Theater. However, we are closer to the theater by three hundred yards."

Skip leaned forward and pushed on a stone with his left hand. A section of the wall began to open inward slowly making a scraping sound like metal on a grinding wheel.

"What is this place, Skip?" Kristine gasped.

"I have my theories, Kristine," Skip said as they stepped into a dark room. "But nothing concrete. When I first found this place, I discovered the names carved into the tabletop and dates, I would say this is where Lincoln's guards were kept on April 14, 1865. When I found the ten skeleton's and the Sergeant-of-the-Guard's diary, I learned some frightening truths."

"What do you mean by that?"

Skip turned around and pushed on a cut stone. The stone wall closed. Skip took out a penlight from his inside vest pocket of his jacket and turned it on. Then he walked over to a table in the center of the room and lit a hurricane lamp.

"Kristine, I have learned early in my career," Skip began to answer her question, "about collecting pieces of information and creating a puzzle using those bits of information."

She watched him rub his hand across the carvings. Then Kristine began to look around the room. It was a twelve by eight room off the tunnel. Skip told her the room had been constructed during the War of 1812, and was connected to one of the original tunnels which were constructed when Washington was first built in the latter part of the seventeen hundreds. The room was lighted from two hurricane lamps, which created shadows that danced along the walls once Skip had lit them.

"Skip!"

"Yeah?"

"What do you mean Lincoln's guards?"

Silence.

She could hear his breathing as he powered up a small Honda generator. Skip stood up and turned to her once he had the generator running. "Our government and Washington have a sordid history, Kristine, but most people don't know it, or choose to overlook it. Those who do know its history don't care to discuss it."

Skip sat at the antique table writing on several pieces of paper. On one small piece of paper, he wrote President Mantle. Then Skip created more puzzle pieces as he added CIA, FBI, BATF, Kelly, Schmirnoff, NSA, Secret Service killings, decode message, informed Pres about Kelly's plot.

"I don't recall how I acquired certain books, honey," Skip said looking up at her after she sat across from him, "but when I was a member of a Civil War company from Baltimore, A Company, First Volunteer Infantry, I ended up with two informative books. One was written by two ex-Pinkerton Secret Service Agents. They were in service when Mr. Lincoln was murdered."

Daggard began to move the pieces of paper around the tabletop trying to put them in order to create a puzzle.

"They had questions regarding Lincoln's assassination. Those two men conducted an investigation, which cost them their jobs and took six years to complete. They finally wrote down their findings and published their book in 1872."

Skip leaned back in his chair with a heavy sigh and slammed his fist on the table. Kristine jumped.

"Something's not right," he hissed. "These pieces should fit together neatly but they won't."

Kristine sat board stiff waiting and watching Skip slide the papers around and try putting them together in different configurations. "As a Civil War reenactor on the Union side, I began to study the Civil War and write down questions. For instance: Why did Booth kill Lincoln after Lee's surrender? And how was he able to get to the

President in the first place? Remember what I said about pieces of puzzles?"

Kristine nodded as she watched Skip begin to move the pieces of paper around the tabletop again.

"Well, the second book, <u>Mr. Lincoln's Lady</u>, I believe it was called, was about Ann Carroll of Kent County, Maryland. The book was published in 1953 or '54. Lincoln needed to make some changes—a restructuring of powers. Until March or April 1861 the President didn't have any war powers. Mr. Lincoln was tired of the crap from the officers and Congress so he had Ann Carroll write the Presidential War Powers, which are still in effect today. When she presented the document to Lincoln, he asked her if she could devise a plan so the Federal forces could invade the south.

"The problem with an invasion was that all rivers flowed towards the south. This presented a major problem for any flotilla taking troops down river because if any boat became disabled, then it would float the union troops into enemy hands.

"With the aid of an attaché, Ann Carroll was able to draw up what became known as the Tennessee Plan because the Tennessee River is the only river that flows south to northeast. So if any boats broke-down, they would float north back towards the union lines."

Skip stood up so suddenly, Kristine leaned back and almost sent her chair to the floor. He glared at the pieces of paper on the table.

"Ann explained her plan to the President in November 1861. The attack was to begin in February 1862, which it did, and would take about seven months to achieve the surrender of the southern forces. Grant was to proceed down the Tennessee River with a Union Armada. Rosecrans was to take his forces through the Shenandoah Valley, while chicken-shit McClellan was to take the Army of the Potomac along the eastern seaboard. It was a three-prong invasion bringing all three union armies together at the Confederate Capitol."

Skip paced back and forth near the table. He was trying to figure out the puzzle in his head to no avail.

"However, the present Secretary of War would not accept such a plan because a civilian had written it—a civilian female. The only way to get the proposal before Congress was to fire the secretary and hire Stanton. The only flaw was Stanton and Lincoln hated each other. But both men agreed to put aside their differences for the country."

Daggard swept up the pieces of paper in his right hand crushing them. Then he threw the crumpled forms onto the tabletop with a viscous curse, and sat down again facing Kristine.

"History has shown us, Kristine that hatred doesn't diminish—it only grows, especially if you have daily contact with that which is hated."

"Let me see if I get this. Because of what you have read, you're saying that Stanton plotted as far back as 1861 to assassinate Lincoln?"

"No. But he was offered an opportunity to be placed in a position where he could insure that Lincoln would not be reelected..."

"But Lincoln was reelected!"

"Yes, only because Congress believed they had control over him. They didn't want someone else as President at the time when the war was coming to a close. Certain members of both parties were ready to reap the fruits of the war they had started. So they conspired to set up what would be the first of many electoral scams on the American people."

"How did they do that?"

"Manipulation. They hyped up Lincoln, and the Democrats chose a weak candidate."

"Wait a minute! You said that Congress started the war?"

"According to the pieces of the puzzle, it's the only thing that makes sense. It wasn't the whole Congress, Kristine just a handful. And because of that conspiracy, Lincoln had to die. Congress knew about his plan to bring the South back into the Union with a "forgive and forget" policy, and let things go back to the way they had been. Also, he was going to tell the people about Ann Carroll's role, which would make the Congressmen, look silly, especially after giving medals to Grant, Rosecrans, and McClellan for the Tennessee Plan back in 1862. Actually, he was going to Congress on Monday April 17, 1865."

Daggard rose again and began to circle the table with his hands clasped behind his back. He looked down at the pieces of crumbled papers several times. He had written names and places and events on each piece and had tried to create a puzzle of sensibility, but the pieces would not fit.

"There had been compromises in the late 1850's because the North wanted the South to get on the industrial revolution band wagon. Machines were doing the work of a hundred men. The South had all those cotton, tobacco, and sugar fields ripe for picking. A select few in the Northern Congress envisioned wealth. Their idea was to get the human factor out of the fields, put in the machines, and the financial rewards would be unlimited—for them not the South."

"Are you trying to tell me..."

"That certain members of the US Congress started our Civil War for financial gain. It's the only sensible answer when you put all the pieces together, Kristine. Of course, many could and would argue my hypothesis even though I have substantial proof. And, Kristine I've been part of the government that creates havoc around the world to start wars for one gain or another, so my theory is not far-fetched."

Kristine became subdued thinking to herself about lessons she learned by studying history. Not what was printed for public knowledge, but those documents such as Skip had just mentioned. Books kept hidden by governments away from public view.

"Why was Lincoln's personal guard here?"

"Ah! The mystery question."

Skip sat down at the table and began to unfold the crumbled pieces of paper and lay them out in a single line. Daggard started from left to right; Mr. President, SOS, Secret Service at PA, CIA at D.C., SOS spoke to Schmirnoff, decoding message, spoke to Pres at Camp David, SOS spoke to SS, CIA after Skip, NSA response. He began to move one piece at a time forming four corners of a small frame, then placed the remaining pieces in the center.

"According to the investigative findings of the two Secret Service Agents, Stanton was part of the assassination plot, but because he covered his tracks well, they could not prove it beyond a reasonable doubt. Their investigation revealed three important facts, which were kept from the public.

"The officer in the box with the President was unarmed and sat well back in the shadows of the Presidential Box. Lincoln's military guard was dispatched to parts unknown, and an alcoholic off-duty detective was posted at the door to the President's Box with strict orders not to leave his post for the bar across the street."

Skip moved some pieces of paper on the table. He looked at Kristine with flaming eyes. "Pieces of the puzzle, Kristine. But I'll be go to hell if I can figure this one out. So please be still for awhile."

"What are you trying to figure out," she asked as she got up from the table and walked around him and began to massage his shoulders.

"Why the President is so hell-bent on protecting that traitor, Kelly."

She was standing behind him working the muscles of his shoulders so Skip could not see her face. Kristine argued with herself for ten seconds determining whether this was the time to tell him.

While Skip shuffled the papers around, Kristine moved over to the army cot, which was positioned against the right wall six feet from the table, and sat down. The green canvas moaned as it took the tension of her weight. She watched his face turn red as he swiped his left arm across the table sending the pieces of paper to the floor. Kristine watched as he stood up and stretched. "Oh well," he said taking a deep breath, "No sense on loosing control."

She felt her heart pound against her chest. "What have those incidences got to do with Congress starting the war, Skip?"

"They're important pieces to the puzzle, Kristine. Just like the damn puzzle I'm working on now, but I believe specific pieces to this puzzle elude me."

Kristine heard the echo of her silent prayer as she said, "Maybe your target is not the Secretary of State but the President."

She knew by the cold expression on his face and the blank stare in his eyes, that she had his attention.

"*Excuse* me!"

Kristine couldn't stand. Her trembling legs would not support her meager weight of one hundred twenty pounds. The moment she had feared for two years had finally arrived. Kristine knew she had to go all the way now. Perhaps he wouldn't shoot. Perhaps he would not kill her! She hoped he loved her that much. Yet she had to proceed. The words had to be said.

She swallowed hard and forced herself to rise. "Your target is the President of the United States, Skip."

Silence filled the room like water filling up a glass.

The thunder in her ears came from the palpitating of her heart beating in her chest. She heard her mind shout, "Say something, Skip." But he only stood there glaring at her.

In an instant, his glare was replaced with an icy stare of hatred. "KGB or Russian Secret Service," he asked in a chilling tone as he drew his 9mm and pointed it at her.

Here it was. The time when the man she loved would kill her. All she ever wanted ever since she had turned twelve was to marry this marvel of an agent. Now he stood before her with his weapon drawn ready to shoot her. "KGB," she blurted out, "but before you squeeze the trigger, you *must* hear me out."

Kristine saw his finger relax on the trigger. The whiteness of his knuckle returned to a pink tint. She had his full attention and seized the moment. "I love you, Skip. I have since I was twelve. But the traitor isn't the Secretary. He's following orders from the President."

Kristine gulped down air. "We've known for a year about the President's condition…"

"The President's condition?" Skip snapped.

Kristine inhaled, then exhaled as she said, "He has terminal cancer."

His eyes widened as he lowered his weapon. Skip lowered his eyes straining them as his forehead wrinkled. "Go on!" he said as he looked back at her.

Daggard was staring at her. Lumps filled her throat. She coughed. "He wants to be a martyr, Skip. With the entire world in such a state of depression, and the war on terrorism coming to its completion, President Mantle wants to die a hero. He figures he can do this by starting World War Three to end the world's depression and restore economic stability once again."

She waited a few seconds for Skip to respond. He stood with his weapon at his side glaring at her. Somewhere far off, she heard water dripping. Was it her imagination, or was it her own perspiration dripping off of her fingertips splattering on the stone floor at her feet?

"He has approximately eleven months left to live. He conspired with the Soviet Socialists who want to regain power in Russia, and to once again enslave those countries they had lost when the Berlin Wall came down, and they had been run out of office.

"The plan is quite simple. A Socialist assassin will kill the President in Munich. The Germans will be blamed. The Soviets have already planted the evidence. Unfortunately, our people." Skip scowled at her. "My people have no clue on where to look for it." Kristine corrected herself.

"We do know that the Soviet Socialists have a significant military force well hidden ready to ally itself with the US. Attempts to locate them have failed as well."

She shifted her weight, but Skip raised his gun arm as she moved a few steps towards him.

Skip was completely at ease. He hardly breathed. He was poised like a snake ready to strike. He waited pointing his weapon at her.

"Schmirnoff is a Socialist. He is the President's main contact. The President is using Kelly as a go-between to set up the assassination. That way it will never appear the President had anything to do with the plot. You were supposed to have started your leave, Skip. They didn't expect you to be on duty or in the comcenter. I think that's what makes you so dangerous! You seem to be where you are not expected to be!"

She saw the crack of a smile on his face. Kristine watched him holster his sidearm. She rushed into his arms. "Skip, I love you," Kristine declared and kissed him deeply.

He reached out and grabbed her, holding her at arms length after a long embrace. "Go figure," he said, "I wait thirty-odd years to fall in love and she's a KGB Agent! Somehow, Kristine that seems quite appropriate."

"Are you angry," she asked as Skip drew her to him.

Kristine felt his chest rise and fall in even cadence against her breasts. They held each other in the dim light. The only sound in the small confined room was their pulsating hearts.

"No, I have learned long ago never to be surprised or disappointed," Skip whispered in her left ear, "What's disheartening is, I should be working with my colleagues to protect the American people. Instead, here I am with an enemy agent, my nemesis from the Cold War. It's true, Kristine…life is stranger than fiction."

Skip bent his head and kissed her. He felt his heart pound and his blood rush through his veins. "How he loved this woman," he thought.

"Now let me see if I have this straight. Mantle has cancer, and he has only eleven months to live?"

Kristine nodded her head.

"So the President devised a plan in which he could die a martyr, and the Soviets regain Russia and all of its lost territories?"

Again, Kristine nodded her head.

"And Mantle believes the only way to Heroville is to send our troops off to a phony war?"

Kristine felt her heart jump as a lump lodged in her throat at Skip's implication. She stared at him finally understanding where his questions were leading.

Skip stood there not two feet from her turning several shades of red as the demon's rage took control of him.

She could feel the stale air go frigid around them. She could feel, on her face, the venom in Skip's words.

"Not on my watch!"

Skip turned so suddenly his movements threw Kristine off balance. She watched him as he began to move the pieces of the puzzle around. They both stared at the completed puzzle.

"Son of a bitch!"

Kristine watched as her strong man fell into his chair. His shoulders sagged.

"I'm getting too old for this shit, Kristine. I hope you're not lying to me." He said staring into her eyes. "Because, if you are…"

"I'm not, sweetheart." She responded, and went to him.

"Let's get some sleep," he grumbled, "I'm exhausted." Skip looked down at the completed puzzle once again. He let the rage drain from his body, and then he spoke, each word crystallizing in the cool air, "So, it's the President who is the traitor!"

Skip looked at Kristine. She was standing next to the cot taking off her clothes. He could feel the heat of his excitement rushing through his body. "I will reexamine everything when we wake up," he declared as he sauntered towards her unbuttoning his shirt.

NSA Conference Room
Fort Meade, Maryland
Sunday—0730 hours

Most of the activities at Fort Meade and NSA for the past ten and one half hours, dealt with MI recalls, MI soldiers relieving FP Security Personnel at NSA, and locking down NSA and the MI barracks and operations complexes.

Barricades had been placed with checkpoints established at Canine Road and Route 32 and every road junction leading to the NSA-MI complexes on Fort Meade.

The Generals and officers had just returned to the conference room from breakfast when MSG Milan arrived at 0745. He placed a CD into the multifunction CD, VHS player, and handed the officers printouts and photos. Rickard's voice and image was clear. The officers listened for ten minutes. "Sir," Milan spoke directly to General Hanalin, "I used I-Spy to try and discover what was happening in Washington before I went to bed. I thought that you all would want this info, so I made a CD and photos."

General Toomey took out a cigar from his tin. He studied the long, cylindrical, tobacco-leafed BlackStone for a few seconds. He put his cigar to his lips and moistened the tobacco leafs before he lit it. "Where did Skip and Anderson disappear to?" he asked with his cigar dangling from the right side of his mouth.

"Skip had three years to explore those tunnels," General Hanalin piped in, "so it's any bodies guess where they are. But my concern is Altman and our team."

As General Hanalin picked up a phone receiver to call Agent Halbrooke, he looked at General Toomey and said, "Agent Kitchen is correct. Daggard will make all of them pay for molesting his mother."

Hanalin breathed deep of the air filled with the aroma of fresh brewed coffee. "I think it's over, people. When Rickard makes his announcement referencing having Mrs. Daggard as a hostage, Skip will come out of his hole fighting-mad."

Milan went around the room filling the officers cups with the fresh-made coffee. Everyone was lost in his or her own thoughts.

General Toomey broke the silence. "If that happens, Mac we're all screwed, blued, and tattooed."

"Well, it will all be over shortly, or it's going to be a long day," said General Hanalin. He dialed Halbrooke's cell number. "I'm going to bring Halbrooke back here. I am thinking about sending him to Washington with a copy of the decoded printout to Rickard."

As General Hanalin was explaining about Agent Halbrooke's returning to NSA with the three CIA Agents, Director Rickard was beginning his explanation to President Mantle on his ploy to extract Daggard and Anderson from their hiding place.

Chapter Eleven
Director Rickard's Follies

Eilis Daggard's house
Bud Lake, New Jersey
Sunday—0800 hours

Eilis Daggard had fixed breakfast for Mary, John, herself, and the six agents. She fixed scrambled eggs, ham, and fried potatoes.

As everyone sat at her dining room table eating, Eilis turned to John, "John, give Agent Halbrooke the CIA agents guns." Then she looked at Agent Halbrooke. "I want you to take all of your people and leave my house after breakfast. You can tell your General Hanalin that I do not want any more of his agents sent to my house. Next time, Agent Halbrooke, I will not be so hospitable."

At 0815 hours, Halbrooke handcuffed Altman, Watt, and Jackson with their hands behind their backs. Then he turned to Mrs. Daggard, "I will relay your message to General Hanalin, Ma'am, but I can tell you that if he feels your health and welfare are in jeopardy, he will send us back. Furg, you ride with me in our vehicle. We'll put Altman and his crew in the backseat. Tenny, you follow us in their vehicle. Good-bye Mrs. Daggard!"

"Good-bye, gentlemen. Don't hurry back!"

As the agents drove away, the sun was making its appearance on the eastern horizon. Eilis turned to Mary and John, "Now do you understand why Skip had to be dead, Mary?"

Mary nodded her head. "Yes, mom! But what's going to happen now?"

Mrs. Daggard could feel the cancer at work. She turned back around and opened the front door to let the new sunshine filter in. Dust mites danced in the sun's white rays inside the doorway of her house as if they were human performers. Eilis said a silent prayer. "You've watched over him this long, God. Don't stop now!

"I'm going to lie down for awhile, honey," she said going slowly upstairs.

Oval Office
White House
Sunday - 0810 hours

The early June day exploded on the eastern horizon warm and golden with tentacles flaming forth with colors of scarlet and pumpkin.

President Mantle stared out the Oval Office window admiring the clash of colors in the sky.

Director Rickard sat quietly sipping fresh coffee. He was thinking. *Where the hell did that son of a bitch go?*

Director Higgins said, "Mr. President, Rickard's plan is a good one. Now we know where they are, we can flush them out."

President Mantle spun around catching his balance. His eyes shone like cold steel, and his face flushed with rage.

Rickard had just finished explaining his idea about using loud speakers in the tunnel systems demanding that Daggard and Anderson surrender or his mother would suffer the consequences. "*Do we?*" He asked, falling into his seat behind his desk.

"We have an approximate location on them, Sir," Rickard said, "I have people positioned at all the manhole covers and in key locations throughout the tunnels. At 0830 hours, I will begin my announcement while two teams of fifteen agents in each group will begin to sweep through the Washington and Lincoln tunnels. They will depart from the White House entrances. Each team will begin to advance through their respective systems."

The President sat at his desk. He picked up some papers he was supposed to have signed, but he hadn't read them yet. He couldn't read them now. "You all know this operation has gone to shit don't you? And for the life of me, I can not fathom how Daggard and Anderson have managed to elude 300 top trained US Agents!

"In twenty-four hours, you have failed to capture them. FAILED," the President exploded, "to locate them! And bungled what I perceive to be a simple operation. It boggles my mind, gentlemen how we ever managed to win any wars, and how we are holding our own on the war against terrorism."

Rickard was about to answer, and then thought better of it because of the way the President's piercing scowl penetrated him. But

Rickard knew the answers to the President's sarcasm. He knew it was the US military might that was making the difference, and made the difference between victory and defeat. He also understood that at times too much intelligence got in the way, or things went badly for military ventures when Congress hand-tied military operations.

President Mantle rose. As he turned to peer out the window again, he stopped and stared at the American flag behind his desk. *One damn patriot is all that stands between me and my quest for glory. One goddamn patriot. Yet, he's not just any patriot. Oh no, he has to be the best we have.*

"I want them dead by noon. *Do* you understand?" President Mantle spit out venomously.

A cold silence hung frozen in the air.

President Mantle came back to stand behind his desk.

Directors' Rickard and Higgins rose from their seats and stood in front of the President.

The President's face was a sculpture in rage. "I want to see their bodies before I have lunch," he hissed while grinding his teeth. "Now get out."

As Rickard and Higgins started to turn, Mantle interjected, "Oh, one more thing. I have moved-up Tuesday's dinner ball to tonight." Mantle leaned on his desk. "By six o'clock tonight, these past thirty hours *will* be a memory. Take care of it."

"Yes, Sir, Mr. President!" Rickard and Higgins echoed.

"Gentlemen," the President said serenely, "this meeting is adjourned."

NSA Conference Room
Fort Meade, Maryland
Sunday - 0845 hours

The sun was bright in the eastern sky, and the rainbow created a perfect hue across the serene horizon.

Generals' Toomey, Hanalin, and Stone were sitting at the conference table with the MI officers in charge of the units at Fort Meade. Everyone sat rigid and silent. Master Sergeant Milan had just arrived with four boxes of assorted Dunkin' Donuts. He opened the cartons, then placed them on the table before the officers.

As General Stone began to speak, Milan took a seat against the north wall close to the coffee bar. "All right Sergeant Milan, give us a report."

The general's demand momentarily caught him off-guard. Milan stood and moved to the head of the table. "According to our satellite surveillance of Rickard's operation, we know that Agent Daggard and SFC Anderson are in the tunnels under Washington, D.C. We also know that they have eluded capture."

"Is there any way we can aid them, Sergeant," asked General Hanalin.

MSG Sergeant Milan lowered his head his face a mask of sorrow. He looked up at the officers and shook his head. "No, Sir. I believe if we send in a team, they might get caught in a cross-fire if shooting starts."

Eighteen officers dipped their hands into the containers of donuts. The atmosphere was filled with the aroma of fresh-brewed coffee and fresh baked donuts. The mood was subdued.

"So what do we do," asked General Toomey.

All eyes were fixed on General Hanalin, waiting for his reply as he finished his first donut.

"We put four platoons at Tipton Airfield. That will be our demarcation point. They will be ready to lift-off at a moment's notice," Colonel Hempden said. "If Agent Daggard and Anderson are captured, we'll go in and get them?"

It was a general consensus of all the occupants in the conference room that Col. Hempden's plan was doable, and General Hanalin assigned her as commander of the operation. "Do we give this operation a name, Sir?" asked Colonel Hempden.

General Hanalin looked to General Toomey. Both men shrugged their shoulders.

Slurping sounds filled the room as everyone sipped their coffee. Seconds ticked off the wall clock as Toomey dipped a sugar doughnut into his cup. General Stone took two long drags from his cigar. All eyes were on General Hanalin. "No," Hanalin finally blurted out, "if the time comes, you will receive a "go" signal."

Colonel Hempden rose. "We have to end this soon because our resources have been diverted from the Middle East. I'm sure it's on your minds as well, but we have three hundred thousand special ops soldiers over there depending on us to provide them with up-to-date info and strike positions. Not to mention the 9th and 25th Infantry Divisions, and half our Naval forces."

Colonel Hempden stopped at the door and slowly turned to look at her superiors. "Sir," she focused in on General Hanalin, "I have never felt so distraught as I do now." Then she disappeared behind the closed door.

General Toomey jumped up and threw his coffee cup against the far wall. His face aflame as he turned to his constituents. "We should arrest them all. Declare Marshall Law and put the Speaker of the House in as acting President until we can sort this damn thing out!"

"I agree, Tim," said General Hanalin, "But…"

"In the name of "National Security", Mac! That's our authority."

"Oh yeah," Hanalin muttered, "In the name of *National Security*. That should cover it, and protect us from our actions. After all, how many times had that phrase been used to justify questionable actions?"

However, it was a loophole that always worked, so far.

Washington, D.C.
Sunday - 0900hours

Like an accusing finger, the obelisk shaped Washington Monument pointed towards the marshmallow-dotted blue sky. The planning for the monument had begun while George Washington still lived. However, he did not want money wasted on such foolery. So the Washington National Monument Society had waited until 1833, thirty-four years after his death, before they began raising money for the monument.

The early morning misty rain had vanished. A warm gentle breeze had quickly dried up the grass as scores of visitors walked around the square, lounged on the lawns, and soaked their feet in the Reflection Pool.

Three men dressed in dark suits stood close to the door turning visitors away from the G.W. Monument, "The monument is closed for repairs."

Director Rickard stood just inside the Lincoln tunnel, fuming because the President had already reamed him out four times in the past half-hour. Rickard felt as if the President had become the Rotor Rooter Man. "What the hell is your problem, Agent Brown?" Rickard demanded. "You are supposed to be an audio specialist, so why am I not broadcasting over those loud speakers yet? Do you realize it is now nine o'clock? I was supposed to have broadcast my demand to Daggard thirty minutes ago!" He exploded in profanity.

Agent Brown sat in front of his amplifier system just inside of the Lincoln Tunnel entrance in the subbasement of the White House. He was hand tightening the tenth and last speaker wire terminal bolt while Rickard was having his temper tantrum.

Unable to control his temper as his face turned purple with rage, Director Rickard grabbed Agent Brown with both hands jerking Brown off of his seat. The two men stood nose to nose. "Five minutes," Rickard snarled, "if I am not speaking through that microphone in five minutes, I'm going to shoot you."

Agent Brown was fifty-eight years old. His pitch-black skin was a roadmap of acne scars, but the old agent maintained a sense of humor. "Director," Brown taunted as he reached up using a defensive maneuver with both hands, bending Rickard's thumbs back causing Rickard to wince in pain and release his hold on Brown, "You should be thanking me, Sir. I just gave you another half-hour of life," he said and began laughing, "but for your stupidity to be effective, the loud speakers had to be positioned further than you had anticipated. Now, get the hell out of my way and let me do my job."

Rickard didn't know whether he should shit or go blind; his rage was that intense. He decided to conduct a radio-check with his agents in order to keep himself from shooting Agent Brown. He first checked-in with Beal, Tittle, and Butts at the Washington Monument. Next, he checked with the two teams waiting to move through the tunnels. It took him ten minutes to complete his radio-check with all 300 agents stationed at all the manhole positions in Washington and along the Potomac to Dranseville Park.

At 0915 hours, Agent Brown said, "Now Sir, you may announce your death-call. The speakers are connected to the amplifier. However, if I were you, and knowing what I know about Chief Warrant Officer Daggard, I'd take that mic in your hand and throw it in the Reflection Pool. Or, you could shove it up your ass," Brown taunted again as he started to walk away.

"Where the hell do you think you're going?"

Agent Brown slowly turned around to glare at Director Rickard. "As far away from Washington as I can get within the hour," he enunciated, "because once you announce to Chief Daggard that you have his mother that's about all the time all of you have left to live."

As Agent Brown's footfalls echoed down the corridor, the six agents with Rickard involuntarily began to shift in place.

Director Rickard made his announcement exactly once, recording it as he did so. "Chief Daggard, this is Director Rickard. You and Sergeant Anderson have until 1300 hours to surrender to any of my agents or I will begin interrogating your mother. Oh! Did I not tell you I have her here? Yes, Chief Daggard, I have had my agents go to her house in Bud Lake, She is currently drinking coffee at CIA Headquarters. In my office to be precise."

Rickard turned off the recording device. "Now," he instructed two agents, "I want you to play that tape every fifteen minutes until you receive orders from me to stop. Any questions?"

Agents' Books and Reams stared at each other for thirty seconds. "Sir," Books questioned, "What if Chief Daggard attacks us?"

"Shoot the son of a bitch! What else do you think you should do? I am going to leave four other agents here with you. That should be sufficient."

"Where will you be, Sir?"

Director Rickard stared down the sixty yards of tunnel before it made a twenty-degree bend to the right. He knew his men were frightened, and he had Brown to thank for it. He looked back as his agents, especially Sarah Martin and Blasé McKenzie. His two female agents appeared to be the only ones not shaking in their shoes. "I am physically going to inspect our positions," Rickard announced as he left his agents staring after him as he walked the White House corridor towards an unknown future.

Washington, D.C.
Sunday—1200 hours

Director Rickard spent two and one half-hours reviewing the posts. He was satisfied that he had covered every avenue Daggard could use to get at the Secretary. His only concern was the time. It was now 1200 hours and Daggard and Anderson were still alive and their whereabouts were unknown. Now he was late with his report to the President.

He had just crossed over the bridge from Arlington Cemetery into Washington when his cell phone rang. "Rickard here!"

"Sir," it was Agent Hicks, "we found the route Daggard used to elude us. The wall at the angle is hinged. We are now entering another tunnel."

"What angle?"

"The angle in the tunnel my team and I followed last night when we lost Daggard and popped up at your location at Constitution Avenue.

"This tunnel is not on any map I have. We're going to follow it. I'll be in touch."

"Hicks, if and when you find them…kill them, then report to me immediately. I will be with the President in the Oval Office."

Agent Hicks started off down the dark, raunchy-smelling tunnel. "Yeah, right!" He thought, as if finding, then killing Daggard was as easy as making a peanut butter and jelly sandwich.

"Yes, Sir."

Now Rickard had something to tell the President.

NSA Conference Room
Fort Meade, Maryland
Sunday—1210 hours

General Hanalin dropped the telephone receiver in its cradle. He turned to the other officers, "Colonel Hempden is at Tipton Airfield with 300 troops ready to deploy."

Captain Tobias entered the room. "Sir," he addressed General Hanalin, "Echo Group just intercepted a conversation between Agent Hicks and Director Rickard. Hicks found a secret passage, which leads into another unknown tunnel. Hicks believes it is the route Daggard and Anderson used to escape. He is following according to Rickard's direction..."

"Is there something else, Captain?"

"Yes, Sir. Director Rickard ordered Hicks to terminate Chief Daggard and SFC Anderson when he locates them."

General Hanalin sipped his coffee. His thoughts brought a smile to his face. He has known Daggard a long time—Christ, since Vietnam, 1968. "Ladies and Gentlemen, we're going to sit back and wait. Hicks has just intruded into Skip's domain, providing Skip and Anderson are still in the tunnels. No one is better at cat and mouse than Skip Daggard.

"Captain Tobias, would you please pass my order on to Colonel Hempden to have her troops stand-down, but remain in place."

Once the captain left, General Toomey looked over the huge table at General Hanalin. "You're not concerned, Mac?'

"No, Tim. They're in Skip's playing field now. We have troops standing by to aid Skip and Anderson if things go to shit."

The consensus was universal. Hanalin felt he had done everything possible. He had just sent Halbrooke, Furgusen, and Tenny to Washington a little over an hour ago to return the CIA Agents to Director Rickard and meet with the President. Now they would sit back and let developments play themselves out.

White House Oval Office
Sunday - 1230 hours

The Oval Office is in the West Wing of the White House. Its doors open to the Rose Garden and the Cabinet room. The room was added in 1902 under the direction and order of President Theodore Roosevelt. Its purpose was to provide ample workspace for the President and his staff. Prior to the addition, the President conducted business on the second floor close to the First Family's living quarters.

President Mantle sat behind the large oak desk glaring at Director Rickard.

Director Rickard did not like being reprimanded, especially in the manner in which the President had just done it, and in front of the FBI director and three NSA agents.

"My orders were specific, you worthless bastard. I wanted them dead by noon; no fucking, goddamn excuses. Now you have the unmitigated gall to sit there and tell me you have no idea when you will pluck these thorns from my hide. Get out! Get the fuck out of my office and my sight!" President Mantle was now on his feet shouting at Rickard, and pounding his left fist on his desk.

No one moved, especially Director Rickard, but at that moment he was tempted to harness his agents and call a halt to searching for Daggard and Anderson. He wished that Daggard would shoot this arrogant bastard instead of Kelly.

Rickard was about to rise and leave the room when Agent Halbrooke interceded.

Special Agent Halbrooke didn't appreciate the President's explicit adjectives he directed towards Rickard. "Mr. President," Halbrooke said, standing up wearing a stone-cased face as he glared at the President. "We NSA types do not take kindly to your assaults against one of our own; Director Rickard is doing the best he can. But all of your attempts are futile. You don't have enough resources or months in a year to bring down Chief Daggard."

President Mantle looked at Agent Halbrooke for the first time. "And just what in the hell are you doing here?"

Agent Halbrooke felt a burning desire to ignore the President and take Rickard out in the hallway and give him the copy of the message. However, he answered the President. "My generals have decided to take a wait and see policy regarding the actions you have set in motion.

"However, General Hanalin, you remember him don't you Mr. President, General Hanalin, the Director of NSA? Well, Sir, General Hanalin has decided that me, Furgeson, and Tenny will accompany three of Director Rickard's search parties.

"I am to marry-up with Hicks."

"We do not need your help, nor do I want it, Agent Halbrooke."

President Mantle's twitching jaw was a sure indication that Halbrooke's smirky grin was beginning to grate. "I think you misunderstand, Mr. President. General Hanalin isn't offering help. We're the forward observation team. We're joining your search-teams whether you like it or not."

President Mantle stood behind his desk shaking with rage. He tried to scream at Halbrooke, but all that came out of his mouth were showers of spittle and bursts of profanity.

Director Rickard looked over at Halbrooke and smiled. Halbrooke looked back and shrugged his shoulders. And in that instant of eye contact with Rickard, and with the President's verbal assault on Rickard, Halbrooke knew that he was going to share the information on the printout with Rickard no matter what the consequences would be. Besides, General Hanalin had given him free rein to act during this mission without having to report for permission.

Chapter Twelve
Secrets are Shared

Secret room off the Lincoln Tunnel
Washington, D.C.
Sunday - 1235 hours

Skip did not move. He lay with his eyes opened, listening, trying to identify the sound or sounds that had awakened him. He studied the sounds of the room with his ears while allowing his mind's eye to see the room and identify the sources of the noises within the room. Kristine was awake, but Skip made no attempt to move or acknowledge he knew she was there.

Daggard's mind's eye focused on the entire room taking in the position of every object and their locations, and the normal noises associated with them.

He and Kristine were against the center far right wall lying on the OD army cot with an OD wool blanket draped over them. Their breathing was normal, at least hers was. Skip was barely breathing as his mind searched the room for the disturbance.

He could see the old oak table in the center of the room. A small, clear-glass hurricane lamp was in the center of the table. It was the only source of light in the room. His mind selected the Honda generator, which sat on the floor near the back wall directly across the room from the door. The generator was used to pipe-in fresh air from the tunnel. It was connected to an air-filtration unit that had a three-inch black plastic flexible hose connected to it. The hose went up the wall near the generator secured by clear plastic tie-downs fastened to metal wall-brackets, which Skip had installed. The hose snaked along a seam where the wall and ceiling joined, and ran along that upper seam until the opened end disappeared into the stone wall to the left of the entrance. The soft, quiet, whisper of the humming from the two units was normal-no problems there.

Skip sat up and placed his feet on the cool, stone floor. Kristine sat up and leaned against him. "What's wrong," she asked.

Skip was surveying the room. Nothing was in shadow. The lamp provided amble light. "I don't know. But do you hear that sound?"

She wrapped her right arm around his waist and laid her right cheek on his left shoulder. "Something woke me," she answered, "and it wasn't your stirring."

"Do you hear it now?" He queried.

She strained her ears, "Yes! Faintly! Where is it coming from? And what is it?"

Skip could not answer her questions because he had no idea what the noise was, or what was making the strange, distant sound. He stood up and went to the section of wall that was the door, and placed his right ear to the stones. "It sounds like someone moaning and a high pitched dentist's drill," he said with a hint of anger in his voice.

Skip could hear the noise as he pressed his ear against the stone, yet it was not loud enough to be recognizable. "It's coming from the tunnel what ever it is." Skip said to Kristine as he walked towards the right corner of the room.

There were four black Homak Home Security, waterproof gun cabinets standing in the corner. Skip had labeled them cabinet 1, 2, 3, and 4. The security cabinets labeled 1 and 2 were lined up against the outer wall of the room with the second cabinet situated in the corner. They were bolted together. The other two security cabinets were lined up against the right inner wall but not side-by-side like cabinets 1 and 2. Instead, Skip had arranged cabinet 3 with its back against the wall; however, cabinet 4 was aligned with its back to the right side of cabinet 3 and bolted together. The head of Skip's cot had been positioned two feet from the door of cabinet 4.

Cabinet 1 contained electronics equipment such as listening devices. Cabinet 2 held an assortment of food-stores; whereas, an array of clothing and footwear was contained in cabinet 3, and cabinet 4 was used to secure a wide assortment of weapons and ammunition.

On his way to cabinet 1, Skip retrieved a small ring of keys from the right pocket of his wash-faded blue jeans that were draped over the back of a chair at the table.

Once he had unlocked the gun cabinet, he took a hand-held dish. "This is a special audio amplification device. I had a friend of mine at the Patuxent facility make it for me two years ago."

Kristine rose from the cot and followed Skip to the door section of the wall. He flipped a switch on the device, and placed the center-cone against the stone wall.

"Chief Daggard, this is Director Rickard! You have two hours for you and Sergeant Anderson to give yourselves up. I have your mother here all the way from Bud Lake, New Jersey. If you two haven't surrendered by 1300, I am going to begin torturing her."

Kristine watched his face for a reaction after the announcement ended. She witnessed his eyes become slits, his breathing slow to where she wasn't sure he was breathing any more.

They were both standing close to the cold stone, naked. She became infuriated with him when he turned to her. His eyes were open and he was smiling. The smile didn't go past his lips, but the fact that he was smiling after listening to that announcement brought-forth a rush of anger from deep within her stomach. "I *know* you heard what he said! Why are you smiling? Why hasn't your demon raged forward?"

She studied his body language. "Oh, *you have got to be kidding?*"

Skip had her pressing against him with his arms wrapped around her. She could feel the stinging cold of the device as Skip pressed the metal, round, listening dish against her exposed, warm flesh of her behind. She felt his urgency as his tongue darted into her mouth and down her throat, probing and caressing her pallet and teeth. His passion was exploding with each kiss igniting her. She responded as they helped each other move across the floor to the cot.

White House Conference Room
White House, West Wing
Washington, D.C.
Sunday - 1330 hours

Washington basked under a brilliant, warm sky. The calm ocean-like ceiling extended to the horizons void of the marshmallow clouds that had dotted the blue vastness earlier.

Imagine this bustling metropolis of about 700,000 people was rolling meadows and farm lands just two hundred and ten years ago.

L'Enfant, a French Architect, the first architect, was pressed into service by George Washington to design, layout, and construct the new capital city. L'Enfant would not complete the task. George

Washington would turn the project over to and Irish-American named James Hoban.

Hoban also designed the White House, a Georgian Mansion in a Palladian style. The original floor plan displayed three floors with 100 rooms. The cornerstone was laid on October 13, 1792.

Because of the pale gray sandstone used in the construction, the citizens had called it the White House, but it had been Teddy Roosevelt in 1902 who had made the name official.

Director Rickard stood at the podium, his face flushed with anger. He had left the entrance to the Lincoln Tunnel at 1305. Daggard and Anderson had been a no-show. He had checked with all sentries. No one had good news for him. At 1315 hours, he had radioed to the three teams to proceed to the conference room in the West Wing.

Rickard did not appreciate the fact that he had to inform the President that his plan was another failure. But he did, and President Mantle's abuse could be heard throughout the White House. Now, he watched his agents fill up the seats as they entered the conference room.

The conference room was laid out like a small theater. There were ten rows of twelve cushioned seats, a stage, and a podium. The American and Presidential flags were appropriately aligned seven feet behind the podium.

Director Rickard stood behind the podium reviewing his plan in his mind as the agents took their seats. His new plan was simple. There would be three teams of thirty-five agents. They would enter the tunnel systems through the White House manholes, proceed to intersecting junctions, and crisscross each other until the quarry was found-and terminated.

Agents were posted at every manhole, so there was no way that Daggard and Anderson could elude him this time. Rickard smiled. A subtle, uneasy shiver rippled up his back invading his nerve fibers. The invasive tremor wrapped itself around his skin, and penetrated his guts and stomach, pounding the walls of his brain, shaking his mind out like an old rug on cleaning day.

The ominous feeling shrouded his entire being dampened his spirits and unnerved him to his core. Even so, through the damnable feeling, Rickard was able to create a small smile on his taut face because he knew, no matter what the outcome; it all would be over in a few hours.

Director Rickard explained his plan to his agents. "Hicks, you will be team leader of Alpha Team. Altman, you will lead Bravo Team, and Boulder, you will take charge of Charlie Team. Each team will now be comprised of thirty-five agents. Find them. Terminate them. And bring back their bodies to me. Any questions?"

Agent Halbrooke, Furgeson, and Tenny had not gone unnoticed by Rickard, so when Halbrooke stood up from his seat in the middle of the agents, Rickard was not surprised.

"Sir," Halbrooke began deliberately, "I will be going with Agent Hicks' group. Agent Furgeson will go with Agent Altman's, and Agent Tenny will accompany Agent Boulder's team. But before we begin this *witch hunt*, I have something you need to read."

Agent Halbrooke proceeded to the podium.

"No one outside of NSA has seen this," Halbrooke informed Rickard in a low voice, "but my generals felt you should be privy to this info." He handed Rickard a copy of the printout.

Rickard's eyes widened as he read the message. "What the hell *is* this?"

The agents in the conference room watched and listened to Director Rickard wondering what he was reading.

Halbrooke answered taking the paper from Rickard. "It's what this whole bull-shit has been about, Sir. Daggard intercepted this communiqué yesterday morning. He had it decoded at NSA. No one has been able to determine or understand the President's involvement." He said quietly.

"My men and I are here for one purpose, Director Rickard," Halbrooke stated loud and clear, "to take Chief Daggard and Sergeant Anderson back to NSA. Alive!"

The two men glared at each other. Both men knew and understood that their individual orders and end results to this operation were totally out of sync.

"Sir," Halbrooke said, "I didn't say anything to the President, but NSA has three hundred troops at Tipton Air Field at Fort Meade ready to deploy on my order."

There it was. Spelled out with no misunderstanding. Now he knew to what extent NSA would commit to protect Daggard and

Anderson. The possible blood bath that had been avoided yesterday near the White House Communications Center might happen in one of the tunnels close to the President's home.

"I must tell you, Sir that this information I just shared with you is for your eyes only. You are not authorized to disclose the contents with anyone—including the President."

Director Rickard nodded his head that he understood. Then he gave the order for his teams to deploy.

When his agents had left, Rickard sat near the podium trying to comprehend the meaning of the message and the President's involvement and how was he going to carry out his assignment with the NSA agents on-hand.

Rickard rose to his feet feeling very old and weary. He knew of only one solution-Daggard, Anderson, Halbrooke, Furgeson, and Tenny—would all have to die.

Tipton Air Field
Fort Meade, Maryland
Sunday - 1400 hours

Tipton Air Field was somewhat secluded. No one could see the three hundred MI soldiers positioned on the far side of the asphalt runway.

The assault force was spread out over the length and width of a football field. Some soldiers leaned against their field packs taking catnaps with their hands resting on the barrels and stocks of the M16A4's. Twenty groups of four to five soldiers played Hearts, Spades, and Gin rummy. Two crews of automatic crew-served weapons teams were cleaning and checking their old-style M60 machine guns and ammunition.

Two teams of two soldiers-to-a-team were field stripping their new model M249's that were called Squad Automatic Weapons (SAW), wiping them down and reassembling them.

Sergeant First Class Keno sat cross-legged in the middle of the grassy field surveying the surrounding troops. He was a discriminating pipe smoker who did not purchase his tobacco over-the-counter, but chose his blends fresh at a pipe store called Fielder's in the Eastpoint Mall in Dundalk, Maryland.

He took out his brown leather, zipper-sealed tobacco pouch and began stuffing the bowl of his well-used corncob pipe. While filling his pipe, Sergeant Keno studied the faces of the soldiers closest to him—men and women in his own platoon. He could see the strain on their faces.

Keno thought how strange their outward appearance of calm was while waiting on the line of debarkation to deploy yet inside every nerve fiber taut-they were ready and could respond to the "saddle-up" call instantaneously.

SFC Keno had kept a vigil on the Colonel as well. He knew her capabilities because he had served with her during Desert Storm, the Iraqi War, and had seen her yesterday at the White House. He watched the approach of Staff Sergeant Bento, a squad leader in his, Keno's Bravo Platoon.

Staff Sergeant Bento, assigned to the 704th a year ago, dropped his pack then plopped down next to Keno. Bento pointed towards Colonel Hempden. "What do you think of her?"

Keno looked out at the runway and the squadron of Chinooks and the ten Huey gun-ships that would provide fire support for them. "I'll put it to you this way, Bento," Keno stated matter-of-fact, "Colonel Hempden is the only officer I would follow into Hell holding an empty bucket in one hand and my ass with the other."

The two sergeants heard the stirring of the troops around them and looked around. The nods of the soldiers who surrounded them emphasized Keno's sentiment regarding their Colonel.

SFC Keno decided to get up and check his troops. As he stretched, Keno looked at the faces of the MI soldiers. He saw the doubts and questions in his soldiers' eyes that he, too, had about this mission.

These were mere mortals. Military Intelligence people. They were cryptologists, linguists, and technicians. But they were all soldiers, foremost and above everything else, soldiers sworn to defend the Constitution and the American people against all foreign and domestic enemies. And here they were. Three hundred MI troops-one hundred forty-one females and one hundred and fifty-nine males poised and ready to strike at the heart of America-its capital. "How in

God's name" Keno said to himself, "can you ever explain such an assault like that to "Joe Public?"

All any of them knew was that Hydra, the many-headed serpent, has shown itself and was ready to strike at their President. Chief Warrant Officer Daggard was spearheading the attack, and NSA had taken complete control of all US Military forces.

They would go because they were soldiers. They would fight to the death for their nation and people because of the oath they made when they signed-up. And they would have no mercy for any enemy on American soil, no matter who that enemy was.

Secret room off the Lincoln Tunnel
Washington, D.C.
Sunday - 1430

Kristine Anderson lay on her back wiping sweat from her forehead and face with her left hand. She looked up into Skip's eyes, "My God, Skip! Where did *that* come from? *That was intense!*"

"Are you ok?"

She nodded her head. He always asked her if she was ok after they had made love. She loved him for that because it made her feel special. Once, she had come close to saying 'No' just to see what his response would be, but had decided against it.

Skip was propped up on his left elbow looking down at Kristine trying to catch his breath. He was caressing her face with feather-light touches, as his breathing became even and rhythmic.

She prodded him again with the same question destroying his mood.

He wondered why she couldn't lie still and enjoy the after-shocks of the most explosive lovemaking they had ever shared.

He sat up naked once again, placing his warm feet on the cold stone floor.

Kristine rolled onto her right elbow and began gently to rake his exposed back with her long fingernails. She felt Skip's body tense through her fingertips, and realized she had shattered the mood with her questions.

She sat up next to him, but did not touch him or say anything.

The quiet humming of the generator filled the silence.

After five minutes had passed, he turned towards her putting his left leg on the cot. "It was the danger..."

Kristine was puzzled, but then understood, by the expression on his face, that this was going to be one of those rare occasions when she should sit quiet and listen.

Skip took her hands in his. He began to gently caress the tops of her hands with his thumbs. If she had only known what was coming, she could have tried to prepare herself. But maybe...maybe there was no way she could have prepared herself.

When she tilted her head to look at him, Skip looked into her eyes. Her heart stopped.

Time stopped. All noises stopped, and Kristine felt a squeezing pain crushing her heart. She was frozen in time and place...she had become an immovable object.

She had never seen such unfathomable sadness before, and the drooping of his face caused her to skip breaths. She was unable to stop the tears swelling up in her eyes.

Skip continued to gently hold her hands as he allowed his tears to fall unchecked. His sobbing was out of control and gut retching.

Kristine felt the burning of an overpowering need to reach out and pull him into her, to protect him and smother him in her love, but instinctively she knew she should not move. Her tears flowed down her cheeks as well.

She had been witness to Skip's outbursts before; however, he had only allowed himself 3 to 4 seconds of grief, and then he sucked down what ever was the source of his pain. He had never shared any of it with her before-not with anyone.

She knew that from this moment on and until her death, that depth of the sadness in his eyes was going to haunt her, and that he was about to violate one of his self-sacred codes. Skip was going to share something horrible with her.

Kristine witnessed how the intensity of his sadness had changed the color of his eyes from sky-blue to pale-blue. She had no understanding of what had triggered his intense sadness. If she had known, she would have fled from the room.

She felt that a lifetime had elapsed, but it had only been several seconds since Skip had last spoken.

"I can't expect you to understand," he began slowly, "because you've never been there, so you don't have any gauge of reference."

He paused to gulp down air and wipe his tears from his face. "I guess you thought I had lost my mind when I grabbed you for lovemaking after such an announcement that Rickard was going to torture my mother?"

"I didn't...yes. I was shocked that you wanted sex after hearing your mother was about to be tortured."

She could see color begin to return to his cheeks.

"I knew Rickard didn't have her, Kristine," he said almost purring his words.

Kristine raised her eyebrows.

"Because if he had, Rickard would have forced mom to make the announcement. But it was in that instant, Kristine...in that instant hearing him make the threat, that I knew I was going to destroy Director Rickard and the whole of CIA. It was the rage of combat and the memory of the smell of blood that fired up my loins."

He still held onto her hands, but he had stopped caressing them with his thumbs. The low hums of the equipment had seemed to escalate in volume.

They sat quietly looking deep into each other's eyes. She still felt the overpowering need to hold him but restrained herself.

"In combat, Kristine, a soldier has only one second...one second to live...one second to die...one second to kill. That's all there is. That's all he has, so a soldier crams all the living and killing he can into it because he may not be around for the next tic of the second hand."

Kristine felt her life drain from her body. She felt a demoralizing ache in her heart, and her breath catch in her throat. And she felt a burning need to pee.

Skip lowered his head staring at Kristine's smooth hands. He did not look up at her when he began again. "When a soldier closes with the enemy, death is poised on the sidelines waiting...watching. It has no conscience, nor is it prejudiced. It drifts over the battlefield taking with it the souls of whoever it can."

Skip shifted his position slightly, but never let go of Kristine's hands. He slowly lifted his head until their eyes met. "People fear death, Kristine, I don't. People say they believe in God because the

Bible and their religious leaders say so. I don't believe in God, Kristine-I know there's a God. I met him when he snatched me away from Death's skeletal fingers.

"It was 0045 hours on September tenth 1968 when Death came for me, Kristine," he said choking on his words. "I was still innocent-a happy-go-lucky kid, but that was all about to change."

Kristine couldn't breathe. She felt her body contract, her stomach convulse, and her heart shatter into pulsating pieces of pumping blood.

As they continued to stare at each other, Kristine could see he was leaving her, going to that place only he knew. Yet, this time it was different because his eyes were not completely vacant. He was still looking at her-not through her.

"The VC came, Kristine. They came on that half-mooned, warm, black night. We were unarmed and no place to run...in the middle of a rice-paddy."

She wanted to ask why they didn't have weapons, but was too frightened to speak.

"The atmosphere had an ominous feel to it as I crossed the compound heading for the Command building where the mess hall was located. I was going for mid-night chow."

Kristine felt Skip shiver and tremble as his eyes held hers.

"I could feel it, Kristine. Death! But it wasn't until after chow that I knew..."

All at once, Kristine witnessed his change. His sadness was being replaced with a burning hate and anger. She saw the hate in his eyes, and the rosy tone flame up on his cheeks.

"After chow, I left the mess hall, and entered an alcove to leave the building. I waited in the dark between the two outer doors and two inner, lobby doors with my eyes closed in order to acquire my night-vision."

She felt his hands grip hers, holding onto her as if to say, 'Don't let me go.'

"It was during those brief seconds that a realization flooded over me...that when I walked through those outer doors, I was going to die. I didn't know from what quarter, or from whom...whether it would be human or reptilian."

Kristine gently squeezed his hands trying to settle his trembling.

"With my right hand, I reached over taking hold of a door knob. My eyes were still closed. Titling my head back, I whispered, 'Goodbye, Mom.' Then I spoke out to my girlfriend, 'I'm so, so sorry Bryana.'"

She winced as Skip tightened his grip, but she didn't move or complain.

"Slowly, I turned the knob easing the door open. I said my good-byes once more, opened my eyes, and slipped out through the small opening. My eyes were riveted to the ground closest to my feet, but no creepy-crawlers. No."

She squealed as Skip's grip intensified, but he didn't loosen his pressure as his fathomable sadness returned to his eyes and face.

"As I stepped away from the building out into the compound, I stepped into the path of the enemy...we were surrounded. They had come in rice-boats and were now taking control of our perimeter. I stood in the middle of our compound, frozen with four AK-47's aimed at me."

She watched him, through his eyes, disappear into that world she had seen him loose himself in so many times before. And she did then what she had always done before, held him while she waited for him to come back.

"I tried calculating the distance, my speed, and their reaction time. Could I cross those seventy-five yards, leap into the air over our concertina wire, and kill one of those bastards before they killed me? No! I couldn't. So I took up an astute position of attention...I never heard the report of their AK-47's... I never saw the muzzle-flashes... nor did I feel the bullets, but at approximately 0047 hours on that early black morning in an unknown, insignificant rice-paddy called Bang Pla, Mrs. Daggard's son...died."

She leaned into him, squeezing him and kissing him. She cried. He was filled with rage.

Then came the horror.

Skip began to kiss the center of her head planting his kisses as he kissed his way down her face to her right ear. Ever so softly, like a gentle whisper of leaves being tickled by a breeze, he let his words flow into her ear. Words that froze her blood to the linings of her veins.

"Death, at first, was part of the shadows. Then the shadow moved, and Death stood before me, reaching with its fleshless fingers to grab me. The next thing I knew, I was plunged from my body, whisked across the gravel, and sucked up into a vast blackness."

Skip released his grip, but continued to gently hold her hands.

"I was incased in a sphere. Maybe the abyss was Purgatory, I don't know. But Death was there, probing my protective sheath with his bony fingers and pointy nails. Then I heard a distant voice to my left. I was facing north towards the jungle...the way the VC had come.

"Like an exploding flash, A sphere of light was close to me. From this light came a voice. 'Believe in me! Trust in me!' Over and over, 'Believe and trust in me.' I believed, Kristine. I believed so I stepped through my sphere and embraced the light.

"I felt a peace and contentment that was so total and complete. A love and joy that was so powerful it washed away any hate I had for anything...I was going home, Kristine. God was taking me home to Heaven.

"But when I opened my eyes, I was back in my body, and the enemy was still there pointing their rifles at me. Then they simply...left. The bastards got into their boats and paddled away disappearing back into the jungle.

"Then came the hate...the anger...the rage. It started subtle and deep down. A slight burning at first, then it swept over and through me...a raging inferno. It was a need, Kristine, a deep burning need to kill, pulverize, and destroy...and...to die!

"I had been cheated, Kristine. I had met the enemy, crossed over, and then cheated.

"Then came the realization, Kristine...I didn't belong here any more."

His words shut down her brain because they were incomprehensible. She lost all control of her body-functions and urinated uncontrollably.

Skip stroked her face with a gentle touch as if to say, 'I understand,' as her wetness spread out along the cot and the green canvas soaked it up.

Skip rose in one quick easy motion, and padded over to the washbasin and began to wash-up.

Kristine sat there…she couldn't cry…she couldn't breathe, but through shear willpower of her mind, she was finally able to rise. Once she gained her feet, Kristine rushed across the cold stone floor to Skip.

She wrapped her arms around his waist, pressing her warm breasts against his back squeezing him into her. She laid her right cheek against his back between his shoulder blades, and squeezed her eyes shut.

Skip gently placed his hands up against hers.

Try as she might to obliterate his words, Kristine could not. They echoed through her mind, reverberated throughout her brain, and invaded every fiber of her soul. She couldn't stand the assault any longer. She fell to her knees bursting into a raging torrent of tears with her arms wrapped around his legs.

Her question had become a branding iron searing her heart. That question she had asked while he had been kissing her as they had sat on the cot. "What had they done to you over there, Skip?"

His breath was hot and venomous in her ear. "They *killed* us…our government and our people…we *all* died."

She let him pick her up from the floor and hold her and support her dead weight. Kristine felt Skip washing her face with a washcloth. "You see, Kristine, it's the danger that triggers my emotion. Death is omnipresent. I have learned to live for each second…only that second I breathe…to cram a lifetime into it…into each one."

Skip gently laid his hands on her shoulders and guided her back away from him. "Lovemaking is the only gauge I have of knowing, Kristine…knowing… that I am still alive."

Kristine felt her heart sink again. She reached up and gently squeezed his forearms.

"War is Hell unchecked; man's inhumane insanity against himself, which is filled with explosive seconds of death. Orgasms are my explosive moments of life," he stated strongly, then pulled her into him for a long embrace.

Once again, Skip whispered into her right ear, "And that's why the traitor in the White House *must* die!"

The tunnel systems
Washington, D.C.
Sunday - 1515hours

While Skip and Kristine were sponge bathing, Rickard's three teams were moving through their respective tunnels slow and easy like, and trying to be quiet.

Rickard had given clear and decisive orders, "I want strict radio-silence integrity, so turn off your radios and cell phones."

Hicks took his team into the Lincoln Tunnel. Altman led his team down the hole at Constitution Avenue where some dramatic scenes had unfolded earlier, and Daggard and Anderson had eluded capture, again. Boulder took his group into the Washington Tunnel. As they proceeded, Boulder saw a small cutout in a wall, and led his team through it into a section of the subway system. There, he split up his team. Seventeen of his agents would search the subway system, while Boulder took the second seventeen agents back into the Washington Tunnel. NSA Agent Tenny decided to stick with FBI Agent Boulder.

When Boulder's group reentered the Washington Tunnel system, Tenny contacted Agent Halbrooke. "Agent Boulder split his group. I am staying with Boulder," Tenny informed Halbrooke.

The search continued for a few hours, then Hicks' group passed a section of the Lincoln Tunnel. A malodorous, decaying stench was filtering out from a stone wall.

"*P-U!* What is *that* smell?" asked Hicks as he pinched his nose closed.

"I don't know, replied, Halbrooke, "but let's move a little faster, so we can get passed it." He said as several agents began to choke and cough loudly in the quiet tunnel.

Hicks glared at his noisy squad as he led them quickly beyond the section with the odor. All of the agents were holding their breath and moving fast. All of a sudden, they found themselves standing on a platform facing a four-foot ditch, with shallow water flowing through it disappearing down another channel.

The section they had been following continued through a narrow passageway. "All right," Hicks said, "we will continue through that passageway for awhile. If we don't see anything, we will come back to this point and follow the watercourse."

Hicks took the lead with Halbrooke next in line.

As they dressed, Kristine kept glancing over in Skip's direction. She had spent many sleepless hours thinking about Skip, and what was it that had made him so special as an operative. Now, she was being spoon-fed certain events in Skip's life, by him, that were beginning to help her understand the man. She was beginning to realize that he was not a cold-blooded killer, but could kill in an instant if provoked, or in the defense of his people, or whenever the raging demon inside of him took control.

Skip looked over at her as he zipped up his cotton, waterproof jump suite. "You're thinking!"

"Yes! Now I know why our lovemaking has been so intense. And why my father was so fervent about my divulging the information to you about your President. Obviously, he knows you better than I."

Before he could respond, Skip was pressing his right ear up against the stone doorway. He held up his left hand signaling Kristine not to move. He stayed in that position for ten minutes...barely breathing...barely existing. "If I was with *that* group, I'd shoot 'em to shut them up!"

"What group? What are you talking about? Have we been found?"

"Questions! Always questions! That's the problem with you KGB-types, you're always asking questions instead of solving the equation. A search-party just passed by."

"Do you think they will find us, Skip?"

"No!"

Then it hit her what Skip had just said. She became infuriated; face flushed red and eyes aflame, she advanced on him uttering a string of dignified profanity.

"Temper, temper, sweetheart," he warned her off with a clenched fist.

"Like I said before, no they won't find us, but at 1600 hours we will leave here to ascend to the site I have chosen to terminate the traitor. By 1800 hours it should all be over."

As they hugged each other Skip thought, "Yeah, by 1800 hours it should all be over one way other the other...and somebody is going to be dead! Who?"

Chapter Thirteen
The Irony of Deceit

Secret room
Lincoln Tunnel
Washington, D.C.
Sunday - 1600 hours

Skip walked over to the massive grave he had dug three years ago when he had first located this room and buried the ten dead Civil War soldiers, buried them as they had died—together.

He held his black watch cap in his left hand as he bent down on his right knee. "Life holds many mysteries," he said in a prayer, "you died in this room, so you couldn't protect *your* President. I'm leaving this room so I can kill mine."

Kristine stood near the table watching and listening. She knew that the reason Skip had decided his target was the President had nothing to do with her. It was his puzzle. Once she had given him the information she had, he went over to the table and completed his puzzle. If the pieces hadn't gone together, he would have shot her.

Skip slowly rose, and then turned to face her. He surveyed the small room as he sighed. His mind was racing—processing events. *What had it been like for these men, Lincoln's guards, to be trapped here with no way out?*

"The Sergeant-of-the-Guard's last entry in his diary, Kristine, was heart wrenching. 'We were killed, but we do not know why.'"

Kristine watched him approach the table. She didn't understand the significance of that diary entry. She stood by him as he sat down and began to play with the pieces of paper until he had recreated his puzzle. She leaned against him placing her right hand on his right shoulder. "I don't understand, Skip!"

"They," Skip pointed to the grave, "didn't have a clue to why they had been entombed here, but *we* know why those who are about to die must die. We may be among them."

She felt a tremor rock him. "Skip…"

"I know, sweetheart, it is 1405, but I have a few things to do first. Would you please get me your purse?"

Kristine looked at him as she furrowed her brow. "I packed it away in the backpack you had given me. You know! The heavy pack I am supposed to carry when we leave here! The camouflaged bag you packed with three days rations and..."

"Yeah, Kristine I know the pack. You don't have to be sarcastic. One of the things I learned in the army was that you couldn't depend on anyone for support.

"You have to be self-sufficient. Since I don't know what we are going to encounter once we leave this sanctuary, I over packed for the both of us as usual. That way, we have enough essentials for three days.

"Now, if you've gotten your bitching done, would you please get your purse!"

Skip was cognitive of her movements as he watched Kristine retrieve her purse and drop it in front of him. "Well, the shit's going to hit the fan when she sees what I have done" he thought.

He pulled her purse across the table until it was in front of him. Next, he removed the specially designed Velcro strip that held the secret compartment to the bottom of her purse. Then he peeled back the black leather concealing the secret compartment and removed a copy of the printout and the canister containing the tape.

It took about thirty seconds for Kristine to realize she had been used. "You son of a bitch. That's the purse you had given me for our six-month anniversary. And all this time, you...you! Oh, you!" She said stamping, and grinning in spite of herself.

Skip looked up at her as she leaned on the table across from him. He wasn't sure if she was mad or not. "Kristine, you know some of my quirks by now. And one is, I don't completely trust anyone, so I felt the best way to alleviate any concern was to give you a purse with a compartment in it that only I knew existed. Life is filled with many unknown variables, and the situation we're in now is a prime example."

"You're a piece of work, Skip Daggard."

"Oh, don't pretend to be mad; after all, you dropped one hell of a bombshell on me! And the secret compartment in your bag doesn't even come close in comparison to the fact that you've duped me about your being KGB. Speaking of that, were you ever going to tell me?"

"Well, Mr. Smart Ass, I was going to tell you I was KGB at the moment I felt it was necessary." She said sarcastically.

Skip scowled at her.

"And I did. At the precise moment I felt *you had a need to know.* So there!" She stuck her tongue out at him as she placed her hands on her hips.

They both broke out in hysterical laughter that echoed around the room.

Skip studied the completed puzzle. He closed his hands as if in prayer, gently squeezing the center of his lower lip between both of his index fingers.

Kristine moved over to sit down on the cot, then she remembered, and raised herself.

She instinctively turned, and saw the wet stain, and moved over to a chair opposite Skip and sat down. She watched Skip stare at the puzzle for five minutes.

He finally looked up at her. He wasn't actually seeing her; it was more like he was still lost in thought, but felt her presence, so he spoke, not to her, but more around her speaking his thoughts out loud.

"Greed! How one person's greed can alter the course of history. Or, maybe more precise, how one person's greed follows the destiny of history. And who am I? Perhaps I'm just one of the select few; simply one instrument of the Fates." Then he focused on her, "You know, mythology, the three Fates?"

Skip slowly rose to his feet leaning his palms on the table over the puzzle. "Maybe the greedy ones are the Devil's minions, and people like me fill the rank and file of St. Michael's army-God's General of all Angels."

Kristine sat riveted to her chair listening and studying Skip's facial expressions, distorted in questions. She watched him shake off his thoughts and go over to the cabinet with electronic devices and get out a large brown envelope with two silver clips and a white-lined stationary pad.

"What are you doing?" she asked him as he sat back down at the table.

"I am going to write a letter to General Hanalin. I don't know how this is going to turn out, Kristine, but in any event, we have to be covered. Besides, I have to cover Hanalin. He has over-stepped protocol, so this letter should exonerate him of all wrong-doing."

Ten minutes later, Skip placed the letter in the envelope along with the canister containing the original taped conversation between Kelly and Schmirnoff. He addressed it to Hanalin at NSA, and he wrote the President's address in the "from" line. After he placed four stamps on the envelope, he said, "I'll mail it when we get top-side, but it sure would be nice if I could just see one of our agents. Hey, Lord!"

It was now 1630 hours.

"One more thing, Kristine, then we'll take a hold of the Fates' hands and go wherever it is we are supposed to go."

Skip went to the gun cabinet and took out a mailbag-sized olive drab satchel. He opened the flap and counted fifteen incinerator grenades. He returned to the table and set the bag down. "Incinerator grenades, Kristine," he said as he looked around the room, "they melt away metal, destroying equipment and paper."

Kristine watched Skip as he moved around the room, attaching incinerator grenades to all of the equipment he had brought into the secret tomb. It took him fifteen minutes to complete his task. Skip knew time was running out, but he knew, too, that the letter and what he had to do in destroying his equipment were necessary and vital. He didn't exactly know vital to what, however, it was another lesson he had learned: *never leave any evidence behind of your presence or passing.*

Once he was finished placing the grenades, Skip went to the table, and surveyed his work with satisfaction.

Skip put the pieces of his puzzle in the envelope with his letter and the canister. Then he sealed it with scotch tape. As he put the envelope in his backpack, he looked over at Kristine, pointing to his right vest pocket. "I have a remote control detonation device. I won't set them off if I don't have to. I don't know if I'll ever have need of this place again."

Next, he went to the gun cabinet and selected his Ruger bolt action, Model 77 in caliber 7mm. He spoke to Kristine with his back to her as he checked to see if the 40X100mm scope was secure and the mounting rings were tight, "This is one of the best flat-shooting weapons I have ever owned. Not much of an arc-path of the bullet as it goes down range."

Skip also took two Springfield .45's and six ten-round clips, loaded, and one black holster for himself. Then he locked the cabinet and put the cabinet keys is his pocket. He returned to the table, and tested the infrared night-vision mechanism attached to the scope. He took a cleaning rod, patch, and a dry cloth from a small green-pouch cleaning kit, and swabbed the bore, and wiped down his rifle and cleaned both handguns. Next, he loaded a clip into each handgun, and placed one in his shoulder holster he had put on, and the other gun he placed in Kristine's backpack.

Skip slipped the rifle sling over his shoulder. "Ok, honey saddle-up," he ordered.

They settled their packs on their backs and moved to the door.

Skip and Kristine stood in the threshold of the open wall. "Skip, I have a question…"

"Of course you do, you're KGB! What's the question."

"How is it that *we* can get out, but Lincoln's guards couldn't?"

"Because there wasn't an exit lever, honey. I put it in. When I found the stone lever that opens the door and discovered the bodies, I exited quickly.

"During several trips to this place and investigating the area where an exit lever should have been, I couldn't find one, so I installed one. It's obvious an exit lever had been left out intentionally."

With one more look around, Skip turned towards the grave and saluted. He pulled his watch cap down over his head and stepped out into the tunnel next to Kristine and pushed on the stone. As they watched the wall close, emptiness filled both of their stomachs. Then the gladiators turned from their sanctuary and walked away towards whatever destiny the Fates had waiting for them.

The Lincoln Tunnel
Near Fords Theater
Sunday - 1700 hours

Skip and Kristine proceeded down the tunnel moving slowly. Kristine was one step behind him. The old lighting system used 15-

Watt bulbs spaced at intervals twenty-five yards apart, which left many sections of the tunnel cast in amber, eerie shadows.

They had traveled about one hundred yards when Skip suddenly stopped and stepped into an area deep with shadows.

Kristine stepped in on his left side watching him shift his gaze up and down the tunnel. "What is it?" She whispered in his ear.

"We're not alone."

Skip was attuned to the tunnel's atmosphere-it had been disturbed. He strained his eyes and ears, looking and listening, while his senses warned him of danger. He leaned into Kristine whispering into her right ear, "No more talking. When I say drop, you fall to the ground immediately. Don't hesitate. Just do it!"

Five minutes passed, then Skip led them back into the center of the tunnel, and they began to proceed along the same path that Hicks and company had followed just a few hours ago.

Skip led the way at a slow pace. He had not drawn his .45 yet because he didn't feel there was a need. They reached the same platform that the search party had stood on earlier. Skip froze with his right hand on the butt of his side arm.

Slowly, Skip began a systematic search of the area from left to right. He had learned this process of investigating a crime scene during his Criminal Investigations studies. The process had saved his life many times.

Skip Daggard stood at the edge of the stone-floored platform with his back towards the tunnel he and Kristine had just stepped from. The tunnel continued on the other side of the platform. Another system ran parallel to the Lincoln system, but was about four or five feet lower and had a stream of shallow water trickling towards to Potomac River, which meant the tunnel ran north to south.

As he continued his survey, Skip checked the ladder fastened to the opposite wall from the platform, studying all twelve rungs suspiciously. He had been through these tunnels many times and knew where the ladder led; what he was looking for was those things that were out of place. His hand clasped the butt of his .45 lightly. Its feel was reassuring. He was staring down at the stone flooring near the edge of the platform.

Slowly, he squatted.

Kristine was straining her eyes to see what he was seeing, looking over his shoulder.

"They were here!" He said pointing to two tiny pebbles, which had been over-turned.

She stared in awe, and wondered how in the hell he had noticed those tiny stones were out of place.

Skip swiveled around to his left and right as he continued his investigation still squatting.

During the past two hundred years the tunnel had been in existence, stone fragments had broken-off from the larger stones that made up the floor, walls, and ceiling of the tunnel. A quarter inch blanket of sediment had accumulated along the floor of the tunnel, which had been left by bygone water run-offs.

"Twenty-five, maybe thirty of them!"

"Oh! So now you're an Indian Scout?"

Skip shook his head in disgust as he stood up. "You know, sweetheart, at times you sure can tax me."

"Well, lover! Here is another taxing moment for you, I have to pee."

Skip looked over at her and scowled.

"Hey, don't blame me! I think I'm pregnant."

Skip's eyes widened. "Now how the *hell* did that happen?"

Kristine glared at him as she widened her eyes and furrowed her brow. "Geee, I wonder? It wouldn't have anything to do with the fact that you need it every day and three times on Sunday. Oh, no! *Not you.* I mean, *honnney* for the past two years you have pressed me into our mattress, slammed me up against the wall, on the floor, on a table, and just about any other place you could find when the mood struck you. And now you have the audacity to ask me how in the hell I got pregnant." Her voice was rising hirer now.

"Shhh! Didn't I tell you no talking?"

Kristine's eyes flashed wide-open, her nostrils flared, and her cheeks turned rosy with fire as she took one step towards Skip, raising her right arm, and clenching her right fist in his face."

Skip stepped towards her and wrapped his arms around her waist. "Do you really think you're pregnant?"

Kristine leaned up and kissed him, "Yes!"

"Wow! A little Nikita," Skip's sarcasm did not go unnoticed.

Kristine became infuriated, "Oh, yooou are incorrigible," and broke away from his grip." And besides, Mr. Smart-ass, Nikita is a male name. It is the Russian form of Nicholas, meaning victory of the people," she corrected him, then stuck out her tongue.

They both laughed silently.

"You really have to pee?"

She softened her facial expression, "Yes, darling!"

Skip used the edge of the platform to support his weight as he eased himself down into the lower drainage ditch, and into the ankle-deep water. "All right, sit on the edge and I'll lower you down." He whispered while looking towards the tunnels to his right.

Kristine moved over to the edge of the platform and sat down, "Why?"

Skip shook his head. "Those damn questions again," he said sarcastically. "Two reasons: One, so you can squat in the shadows to our left, and the water will carry your urine away, and two," Skip pointed to the opposite wall, "that's the ladder we're taking up to another level."

While Kristine lowered her jump suite and panties, Skip was leaning against the slime-covered wall where the platform and wall joined. He quietly drew his .45 as he watched the infrared dots and red beams of light dance along the walls and across the platform floor. He turned his head looking at Kristine. He placed his index finger to his lips. He looked back towards the platform. "That's far enough, ladies and gentlemen. Raise your hands and turn around."

It took Hicks and his team-members about five seconds to realize that they had just walked into a trap.

Hicks swore as they did as ordered. "Goddamnit, I don't believe we just turned our backs on him! And where the hell did you come from, Daggard?"

"You passed me once, but I was concealed," Skip declared, "now, we're going to do this by the numbers, folks, so listen-up."

Skip looked back at Kristine. "Are you finished, honey?"

"No! It stopped because I am frightened. I'm sorry, Skip. It's my fault we got caught."

"Caught? We're not caught, sweetheart. I'm the one holding the gun on them, while theirs are pointing towards the ceiling."

His words were reassuring, and as her tension drained from her body so did her water. "Always the soldier, aren't you, Skip. My hero," she praised him as she stood.

Skip went warm inside as he turned to look at her and smiled. But when he turned his attention back to Hicks and Company, his eyes became vacant, his heart a chunk of ice.

As Kristine fixed her clothes, Skip barked his orders.

Hicks and his team-members were standing on the platform about eight yards from Daggard and Anderson. If any shooting started, the tactical advantage was Daggard's. He would be shooting up at a slight angle, and not down like the CIA Agents would have to do. Plus, they would have to turn first.

"All right now agents of the mole patrol, pay attention because if any one moves out of sequence, I start shooting. I am going to give you my complete instructions first, then you'll perform the moves in cadence."

Kristine had finished her business, dressed, and had moved up to Skip's left side. He took six sidesteps to his right.

"We have you covered. Between the two of us, we have twenty rounds locked and loaded. Hicks, do I need to explain any farther?"

"No, goddamn you! Don't any fucking body move!"

"Good! Now, I want all weapons placed in the left hands. Then place them on the ground on the left side of your left foot. On my command, all of you will kick your weapons towards me using your left foot to do so, meanwhile keeping your hands high in the air. Everyone except you, Halbrooke. I want you to move to the right, front corner of the platform near the wall. Since your weapon is holstered, you can keep it.

"Now, you know the drill, move your weapons. Place them along your left feet. Kick them towards me!"

All thirty-five agents complied.

Some guns went off the platform into the water.

"Ok, Kristine, gather up the guns still on the platform and deposit them in the water after you remove the clips and rounds from the chambers."

Skip had them turn around to face him keeping their arms and hands extended into the air. "Hicks, I am going to ask you a question;

therefore, I suggest you answer it truthfully the first time because that's all you're going to get. What's this about my mother?"

The CIA Agents became frightened. Many of them started shifting their weight. All of them calculated bolting for the tunnel.

"None of us here had anything to do with your mother, Daggard," Hicks choked out his words.

Skip shifted his focus to Halbrooke. "Hal?"

"From what I understand, Skip, that was Rickard's idea. He was the one who sent three agents to get your mother, and bring her to him at the White House. General Hanalin had sent Furgeson, Tenny, and myself to her. We got there shortly before the CIA."

When Halbrooke did not proceed, Skip prompted him to continue.

"When the CIA kicked down her front door..."

Skip's eyes narrowed to slits. His face turned red, and his body began to tremble. Kristine was at his side immediately, holding him and soothing him with her words as his breathing became ragged.

Once Skip had regained his composure, he nodded to Halbrooke to continue.

"My men and I faced off with them at the threshold; however, your mother drew her own gun and had us drop ours. All of us! Then she fed us breakfast. Afterwards, she ordered us out of her house. She told us next time she wouldn't be so hospitable.

"Hanalin ordered us back to NSA with the CIA Agents."

Skip smiled. "That's my mom! Thanks Hal. I owe you one.

"Now, I am going to say this once and only once, so listen closely. Hal, you stay put. The rest of you have five seconds to be outta my sight."

It took two seconds for the agents to process Skip's words before they began scrambling over each other to run down the tunnel away from Skip's sight and gun-muzzle.

Skip contained his laughter until the CIA Agents were out of sight, but Kristine did not possess Skip's self-control, and she fell into the water laughing so hard she began to cry. When Skip finally let loose his uproarious laughter, it was directed more at Kristine's dilemma than at the hilarious scene of the agents fighting amongst themselves trying to escape.

Skip allowed himself twenty-seconds of jollity, before he turned it off like someone flipping a switch. He reached down helping Kristine to her feet, then looked up at Halbrooke.

"How goes the "war", Hal?"

Hal chuckled. "Chief, you're a real son of a bitch. I bet those guys pissed themselves before they got down around the bend. But to answer your question, General Hanalin and Toomey have about three hundred troops standing by at Tipton, ready to attack if you go down."

Daggard weighed Halbrooke's words for thirty seconds. "Kristine, get the envelope out of my pack, please."

She did so, then handed the brown envelope to Skip. "Hal, you need to beat-feet to NSA, and deliver this package to General Hanalin, immediately. Tell him I said, don't send in the troops because good soldiers and agents will die for a traitor who isn't worth it. I will take care of the situation. Me and my KGB partner, here." Skip said as he pointed to a wet Kristine Anderson.

Halbrooke crinkled his face in bewilderment.

"Oh, yeah!" Skip stated, "I just found out today, that my misses-to-be is a KGB mole."

Halbrooke jumped, *"You're joking?"*

Skip looked over at Kristine. "No joke!" She said to Halbrooke.

"Now, how's that for a boot-in-the-ass, Hal. I discovered a traitor in the White House and the only person I can trust to help me terminate the bastard is an enemy agent right out of "Little America," Georgia, Russia."

Halbrooke wiped his brow. "No Shit?"

Skip shook his head. "Now 'git,' Hal."

Skip and Kristine stood quiet in the ankle-deep water, listening. They could hear the water trickling down its watercourse, and its minute splashing sounds as the water splashed over their boots.

The ancient musty smell of the tunnel was like sniffing one thousand dirty wet dogs.

Skip allowed Kristine to climb the ladder first. He did this not just because it had been a courtesy learned from his mother, but a value he had leaned in war as well: The most capable hold the line, allowing the less capable to withdraw. He didn't really expect Hicks and Company to return, but why take chances.

As Kristine neared the top of the ladder and the closed manhole lid, Skip petted the inside of Kristine's left leg up to her crotch, caressing her.

Kristine kicked her foot at him but missed. "Skip Daggard, you're incorrigible! And if you think..."

Skip chuckled. "No, honey," he said looking up at her, "no lovemaking now. Things have changed. Now, I'm the hunter, and on a mission. I just saw an opportunity to stroke you, so I took it." He gave her a genuine smile, and she responded in kind.

"Now," he began to instruct her, "this is a sealed hatch similar to that on a ship. Turn the latch wheel counter-clockwise to open the hatch. Then push the lid open. Don't worry about holding it; it will stop at eleven o'clock."

Once Skip had ascended the ladder, he pulled himself through the manhole into another tunnel system. Then, he and Kristine lowered the lightweight lid over the manhole. Skip secured the lid by turning another wheel on top of the cover.

"Near as I can figure, Kristine this is a drainage system completed around the turn of the twentieth century. However, it is not listed on any maps that I had found. The noise you hear are vehicles passing overhead."

Skip leaned into her so his lips were tickling her right ear. "This tunnel will take us to our ultimate goal-the Washington Monument, providing we don't run into another team of agents."

White House
Washington, D.C.
Sunday - 1745 hours

While President and Mrs. Mantle were preparing to receive their dinner guests, Director Rickard was throwing a temper tantrum in the West Wing Conference Room.

Hicks and his team-members were standing by as Hicks received the brunt of Rickard's dissatisfaction.

"Tell me, you incompetent, worthless excuse for an agent, how the fuck does one goddamn piece of shit disarm a platoon-sized team? I want to know because it boggles my mind. All one of you had to do was drift back into the pack, turn and shoot the son of a bitch."

"As I was trying to tell you, Chief, before you cut me off, that we came upon Daggard and Anderson quite suddenly, and he had the drop on us."

"Yeah! Because he was ready and you fucking fuck-ups weren't. Now I have to go to the President before he sits down to dinner, and inform him I can't deliver the packages because my people are fucking duds."

You know something, Sir? I don't need your bullshit abuse. If you think you're so fucking good, then you go down in those filthy tunnels and take them out yourself. I can retire and start a Private Investigations business. That's what went through Hicks' mind, but he didn't verbally express himself to Rickard because he wasn't quite ready to retire yet.

"You take your team over to the Federal Building to get guns. Then you all hustle your asses back down into the tunnel and pick up Daggard's trail where you last encountered him. I'm going to inform the President that we will have his packages on ice within the hour. Now get out of my sight!"

While President Mantle and the First Lady were walking towards the reception room, Director Rickard was leaving the West Wing Conference Room heading towards the Banquet Hall. Hicks and his team were exiting the White House through the West exit on their way back to the Federal Building, while Halbrooke was just driving onto the exit ramp from Route 295 at the NSA-Fort Meade exit.

Under the streets of Washington, Altman and Boulder's teams were on a collision course with Chief Daggard and SFC Anderson.

Chapter Fourteen
Director Rickard makes a Decision

Drainage system
Pennsylvania Avenue
Washington, D.C.
Sunday - 1750 hours

Skip and Kristine had moved five feet to the right of the manhole cover with their backs against the damp, slime-covered stone wall. They were standing in about one inch of stagnant water. The only light in this system came through the run-off holes along the curbs, which were spaced about forty yards apart.

Daggard had his eyes closed. He was gently holding Kristine's right hand in his left. Skip was beginning his process of slowing down his vital systems, controlling his heartbeat, the rhythm of his pulse, and the flow of blood through his veins. Standing in the darkness, his subconscious allowed another image to maneuver into his conscious.

The rice-paddies were pitched in blackness. The five floodlights, which were strategically positioned around Bank Pla, cast an eerie, subdued glow creating deep shadows in every corner of the MI compound. He had stood in the dark shadows of the foyer between the outer and inner doors of the Command building, just as he was doing now, letting his eyes get accustomed to the darkness. His senses had warned him then as they were warning him now, that the next step he took was the step leading him to his death. And on that night in September 1968, when he stepped through the outer doors of the Command building, the happy-go-lucky, flower-sniffing Skip Daggard stepped into the waiting guns of three hundred Vietcong.

Kristine could feel Skip's tension as it pulsated from his hand through hers. She could make out his silhouette in the darkness, and sense a change coming over him.

Skip Daggard slowly raised his eyelids. His transformation was complete. He could see farther into the darkness now, and the hunted had become the hunter. He did not look at Kristine when he spoke. "I didn't want sex," he whispered, "when I caressed your thigh, Kristine. I just had a need to feel you.

"Things have changed. Now...I am on the offense. Not the hunted any more, but the hunter. All of my emotions and senses are geared towards my mission... there's nothing else."

Kristine squeezed his hand. She realized the meaning in his words. What stood before her now was the *man*, the *operative*, the *real* Skip Daggard who had caused such a wide range of emotions in people such as hate, love, admiration, and despicable anger.

"I have tried not to harm any Intel people. But now," he declared as he turned his head towards her, "now...it's war."

Skip released his hold of her hand. He turned her so Kristine's back was to him. He lifted the flap on her pack and took out the .45 plus two clips and refastened the flap.

"Turn and face me. Put these in your chest pockets." He handed her the two clips. Then he handed her the handgun.

"I have no doubt that we're not getting out of this system without a fight." He paused. Then he pulled Kristine to him.

His breath was hot against her forehead. "If there's an engagement, I will fight it out with you. But, if I determine we'll be taken, I will leave the fight to you, and beat feet to my objective."

Kristine lifted her head. They were standing close, their noses touching, and she looked into his eyes...vacant.

Skip gently squeezed her. "Save your last bullet for yourself, honey. You can't be taken prisoner."

"I won't let you down, Skip. This is for both our countries...and the world."

He placed a kiss on the wrinkles of her forehead and let out a heavy sigh as he continued to hold her in the darkness.

"I'm a soldier. But I can't tell you how many nights I've prayed to God not to let someone go insane, so I could awake to peace and not war. I hate war, Kristine, and I can't believe how naïve I was when I was young. I gave up a full scholarship and a teaching position to go to war. There is no glory in war...only death and destruction. But when a country is attacked like we were at Pearl Harbor and the World Trade Centers and the Pentagon, a country doesn't have an alternative...at least not America—we fight."

She laid her head on his shoulder and hugged him. "God," she thought, "how she loves this man."

"People of other nations don't understand us, Kristine. Hell, half the time we don't understand ourselves. I think Charlie Daniel's said it best, 'We may fight amongst our selves, but you outsiders best leave us alone.'"

From the things Skip was and had begun to share with her during the past twenty-four hours, Kristine was learning that her man was not a monster. He had values and beliefs. And that his people were his precious commodity, that his blood and his heart and his life belonged to them. Yet, even though he had feelings, Skip could turn them on or off instantaneously. He could recall combat situations, burst out into tears, then stop crying, suck it up, and continue to march—just like now.

"It's time to go."

Just as Skip and Kristine began to move south down the long, dark passageway, Agent Altman and his team were entering the same system at Pennsylvania Avenue near the White House, heading north.

NSA Conference Room
Fort Meade, Maryland
Sunday—1800 hours

Agent Halbrooke entered the conference room and walked directly to General Hanalin. As he handed Hanalin the brown envelope, Halbrooke said, "Chief Daggard is going to kill the President."

General Toomey slowly rose to his feet, leaning his knuckles on the oak table and stretched forwards over the table, "*What?*"

Halbrooke continued to address General Hanalin. "There's another thing, Sir..."

Hal felt the eyes of the sixteen officers bore through him as he gulped air. He was wondering what their reaction was going to be to his second piece of news because it directly reflected the competence of the agency.

"Chief Daggard told me, and Sergeant Anderson confirmed it...she's KGB."

209

No one moved. The silence was indicative of his statement. It felt like his announcement had sucked the air from the room's atmosphere.

General Toomey fell back into his chair. His shoulders slumped as if he was Atlas, and his burden had become unbearable.

General Hanalin choked out a whisper as if he had been shot, "My God, we put a Russian spy in the White House. We put a goddamn Russian spy in the President's home!"

Before the silence could envelop them again, Agent Halbrooke pointed to the envelope in Hanalin's hand. "Sir, Chief Daggard ordered me to get that package to you right away."

Mac Hanalin ripped off the Scotch tape with trembling hands. He found it difficult to work his fingers. He bent the silver clips together and lifted the flap of the envelope. He pulled out two sheets of paper, looked inside, and then dumped the remaining contents on the table.

"This is the original printout of the decoded message…"

"What's in the canister, Mac?"

"I don't know, Tim! But there's a letter here from, Skip. I'll read it aloud."

General Hanalin,

By now you know my mission.

The printout is the original that I had decoded yesterday morning at NSA.

By now you are aware that DAESY's operators are in hiding. Their taking to a hole was my idea for their protection.

Well, Mac, it certainly has been a long road from Nam to here. Go figure, that after all these years, I'd be pulling your ass out of the fire…Again!

Hanalin chuckled as the other officers smiled. Hanalin began to read again.

So here's the deal, Mac, do not send in the troops. The President's a traitor.

He wants to start World War Three so he can become a martyr. I can't allow that to happen, so I'm taking him out this evening.

The tape I had spliced from the White House commo recorder is in the canister.

Mac, that's the encrypted message between Kelly and Schmirnoff which started all of this shit. But here's the kicker, my lovely, SFC Anderson, is a KGB mole.

Yeah, Mac, she still lives.

This comment brought more chuckles from the officers as General Hanalin continued.

Now, this is how I'm going to pull your ass out of the fire and make NSA the good-guy. Thirty minutes after the President is dead, you hold a news conference explaining that we were working with the KGB to foil the President's plot to start WWIII. We tried to arrest the President, but unfortunately, he surrounded himself with FBI, CIA, and BATF agents.

There was no alternative but to shoot him.

But there is more to this conspiracy. The Soviets have a large communist army hidden somewhere. Neither the KGB, nor the Russian Secret Service has been able to locate it. The Russians believe that once the war was won, the Soviets planned to turn on the US.

I don't know what's going to happen, Mac, but if I fail, you go to the White House and blow the traitor's brains out.

Chief Warrant Officer

SD
Skip Daggard

Silence gripped the officers.

General Toomey stoked his pipe while General Stone lit up a cigar.

General Hanalin removed the lid from the canister and took out the ribbon of tape. "I suppose there is no reason we should check this?"

General Toomey shook his head as he lit his pipe.

General Stone spoke softly, "Now we know—which makes us part of the conspiracy."

Silence filled the room again as smoke-circles rose into the atmosphere from Toomey's pipe and Stone's cigar.

It had to be said, so MSG Milan said it, "Well, that clears up why the President has been so hell-bent on getting rid of Chief Daggard."

General Hanalin considered recalling Colonel Hempden and her troops, but he decided to wait.

Federal Building
Washington, D.C.
Sunday—1815 hours

The early evening sun was waning yet it was pleasantly warm. Rolling dark clouds were beginning to form in the east indicating a possible approaching storm.

Rickard decided to postpone his meeting with the President and go to the Federal Building instead. He knew Higgins had gone to speak with Kitchen, and he desperately wanted to share the news with Higgins that Agent Halbrooke had shared with him.

As Director Rickard left the White House through the west gate, he was formulating an alternative plan, contradictory to the President's program. He was beginning to suspect that President Mantle was either aware of the plot, or that he was personally involved in his own assassination scheme. By either scenario, it made the President a traitor.

Director Higgins paced the isle in the large room between the two rows of desks with his hands clasped behind his back.

Agent Kitchen sat at his desk watching his leader.

"Sir," Kitchen broke the silence, "I think we should pull our people out."

Higgins stopped near Kitchen's desk looking at him. "What *I* don't understand, Ken, is why you and your team are here and not *out* there."

"Sir, I'm going to make this short; none of you know who you are dealing with. Director Rickard should have shot himself the moment he decided to mess with Chief Daggard's mother. You think Daggard is trapped? Well, he's not. This is his game, and he's been at it for thirty-five years. Vietnam was his training center, and he learned."

Director Higgins studied Ken Kitchen's face while Ken spoke, but he couldn't detect any fear in Kitchen's eyes.

"Skip will show up here. And when he does, I am hoping that our time together in Hell will give me the edge to explain why my team and I are here, and not out hunting for him. And...he won't kill us."

As Kitchen finished, everyone jumped drawing their weapons, and looked towards the door to see who had just come in.

"Higgins, I need to speak with you," Director Rickard said as he marched down the aisle towards Higgins ignoring the guns aimed at him.

Higgins led Rickard into his office and closed the door.

Rickard collapsed into a chair positioned three feet in front of Higgins' desk.

Higgins sat down at his desk studying his old friend. *How worn-out he looks.*

"Hig, I'm tired! And I cannot fathom just what in the hell is going on." Rickard mumbled. "I think I am going to pull my people out," he said defeated.

Director Higgins sat straight up, shocked.

"I know that bastard is down there somewhere, but I have been giving some thought to what Kitchen had said earlier; 'none of our people have been hurt.'

"I just learned from NSA's Agent Halbrooke that NSA has about three hundred soldiers ready to attack if a shoot-out starts between our people and Daggard. He also let me read something."

Rickard used the armrests to help him rise from his chair. He stepped close to the desk and leaned forward. "That goddamn, no-account, Kelly has conspired to assassinate the President," he whispered, and then looked around the room.

"*What!*"

"I'm pulling my people out. I suggest you do the same. Let NSA deal with it."

"What about BATF?"

"BATF's one hundred agents have been assigned to me. I'm pulling them out as well.

"Like I said, I'm going to let NSA handle this fucked up situation. Obviously, Daggard knows something else no one else knows. Let him do what he's going to do, and be the fall guy.

"Then you and I can step in, get him and that bitch, Anderson, and be heroes."

Rickard sat back in his seat.

Director Higgins' smile started small, and then it spread out over his entire face. "I like it. Besides, Kitchen had just advised me to do exactly *that* before you had walked in…to pull our people out.

"We have to be at the White House in twenty minutes. Who's going to tell the President we're pulling our people out?"

The two directors came to an agreement and shook hands just as Altman's team and Skip and Kristine were closing in on each other.

Drainage System
Under Pennsylvania Avenue
Washington, D.C.
Sunday—1830 hours

Skip believed that in the scheme of all things, destiny was preordained. A person's life had already been written in the Big Book at birth, and the Fates guided each human being down that prearranged trail. Problems arose only when humans tried to alter their course when they arrived at crossroads in their lives. It was at these crossroads where things went wrong. If hate or greed overruled a person's values, then usually bad or wrong decisions were the result, which caused a ripple in the normal scheme of events.

Skip Daggard knew, at the age of seven, that he was going to be a soldier. Everything he did from that point on was in preparation for his goal. He played war, studied tactical maneuvers while playing with soldier figurines, and began his marksmanship training by testing the limits of the two WWII rifles he had been given as gifts, and a Marlin .22.

He discovered the Italian 6.5 made in Japan was a piece of shit, but the US M1 Carbine was a precision killing tool. He also learned that the .22 round was the most powerful cartridge ever made. It was about an inch tall with a quarter inch lead bullet, but was capable of killing at a distance of up to two miles away if the bullet was placed right.

In April 1967, when he stood at his first set of crossroads that would dictate his future, Skip was in a hallway on the second floor of Morristown High School. He had been offered a free scholarship and a teaching position. There had been no hesitation on his part—he refused the offer. One year and two months later, he was in Vietnam. He had achieved his dream and life-long goal—he had become a soldier.

Now, thirty-seven years later he was silently, stealth like, maneuvering through a drainage course seven yards under Pennsylvania Avenue on his way to kill a traitor, the President of the United States of America. He didn't hate President Mantle. In truth, Skip felt sorry for the bastard because when the President stood at *his* crossroads, he had allowed his selfish pride and greed to win-out. The President's ego trip left Skip with no choice—the traitor had to die.

Skip and Kristine had traveled three hundred yards when Skip stopped. He had been agonizing over whether his solution regarding Mantle was the correct one or whether there was another alternative. At the end of his final analysis, he realized to his dismay, there wasn't.

Chief Warrant Officer Skip Daggard stood in the damp, darkness of the system with Kristine breathing down his neck. He understood and finally accepted the responsibility the Fates had placed before him. It wasn't that he considered himself a hero; it was simply his values and beliefs that he had learned from his parents and life which had placed him here. He now stood at another crossroads in his life. He could leave Washington and retire, putting all of this behind him, or he could continue on his course terminating the President and stopping another war.

Skip let out a heavy sigh.

Kristine wrapped her arms around him, hugging him close to her.

Suddenly, Kristine felt Skip's body tense. Then she heard the noises Skip must have heard.

Listening to the noises of people moving ahead of them, Skip knew that the Fates were mobile. He accepted his destiny, drew his weapon, and quietly ordered Kristine to do the same. They lay down on their bellies side-by-side in the shallow, cold water with their arms extended, waiting. They were seventy-five yards short of the Washington Monument.

NSA Conference Room
Fort Meade, Maryland
Sunday - 1835 hours

The officers were sitting down to eat. Food had been ordered, and brought in from the Four Winds dining facility, which served the MI troops stationed on Fort Meade. Normally, food would have been delivered from the dining facility in NSA, but General Toomey preferred the Four Winds menu of roast beef with mashed potatoes and vegetables and assorted desserts over the fish and meatloaf NSA was serving.

It was a somber atmosphere in the conference room. No one seemed inclined to talk for fear of ruining the fine meal. Fifteen minutes after dining in silence, General Toomey spoke, directing his comment to General Hanalin. "When do you think Skip will terminate the President?"

"Sometime this evening, providing he can get out from under Rickard's tight grip. Maybe we can draw Rickard's people off. Give Skip an opportunity to move."

General Toomey worked the idea over in is mind as he finished his meal. "I don't think that is a good idea. First, we have no idea where Skip is. Second, if he has already exited the tunnel systems, and is taking up a position, we could end up drawing Rickard's people to Daggard. Besides, Skip told us not to send in the troops. We'll let it lie for now, Mac. I don't want to spoil this fine meal."

Everyone agreed, and went back to eating just as Master Sergeant Milan entered the conference room. "I have located Skip, Sir," he said to General Hanalin, "both he and Anderson are in the Washington Monument.

"I had I-Spy rotated at a slow speed, and a voice synchronization module connected to our fluxes with their voice recognition synchronization codes encrypted into the program. It's a filtering device which picks up only the voice modulation of the synthesized input deleting all other voices."

"That's it then. He's in position," said General Toomey.

General Hanalin clasped his hands together, resting his chin between his first and second fingers. "My fellow officers," General Hanalin said as he stood up, "we are about to become co-conspirators in the assassination of our President."

General Hanalin addressed Agent Halbrooke, "Hal, what exactly did Daggard say to you?"

"Sir, he told me he was going to terminate the President."

"History is about to be written and or changed," General Hanalin said, "I have made up my mind on where I stand. The rest of you have three options: You can remain here with me and let the events unfold in Washington; you can resign your commissions and take your leave; or you can try to stop what is about to happen.

"I must inform you that if you elect the latter, I will have you shot. Therefore, you really only have two choices. Decide now!"

"Oh Mac, so dramatic! You should have been an actor," said General Toomey, "you know damn well none of us are leaving this room. Milan, lock the doors."

As the doors to the conference room were secured, General Hanalin called Colonel Hempden. "Heather, stand-down and return to the Garrison area with your troops and stand by."

Drainage System
Under Pennsylvania Avenue
Washington, D.C.
Sunday—1837 hours

Agent Altman halted his team at the left bend in the system that they had just approached. He turned on them furiously because of the amount of noise they had been emanating during the last thirty yards of their advancement through the system. His nostrils flared while he chastised them in a low voice.

Altman was a seasoned hunter. He did not allow his team to use flashlights or their infrared lights on their weapons, and he knew he should not have allowed the noise to continue for as long as he had.

Agent Altman led them on with a stern warning, "Keep your damn mouths shut, and pick up your fucking dragging feet."

As they rounded the bend, Altman froze. He and three members of his team had just rounded the bend when he heard the clear distinct slide-action of a weapon. Before Skip Daggard could say anything, Altman moved back around the bend, and grabbed for his cell phone because it had just begun to vibrate.

Everything was black. There was no light. Nothing. No one could see…only hear. Skip and Kristine waited.

Skip knew only to well that the first one to move would be the first to die. He had played this game too long. However, it was during his thirty years of hunting White-tailed deer that he had learned to fine-tune his senses for the hunt as an operative. He learned too, how quick the hunter can become the hunted.

This important lesson had happened during the second weekend of the firearms season in 1977 while he was stationed at Fort Lewis, Washington. He and his hunting partner, Ron Mack, had walked up a logging road on the lower west slope of Mt. Rainier. They saw deer tracks on the edge of the road heading down a slightly over-groan old logging road, so they decided to follow the trail in hopes of coming up on some meat.

About one hundred and thirty yards down the trail, they came upon very fresh bear sign, and saw where the bear had just darted through the underbrush. They had looked at each other and decided to hunt somewhere else. Just as they made it back to the main logging road, a huge brown bear stepped out of the trees to their left about forty yards up from them. Skip had been closest to the bear so he returned the bear's growl and mimicked the bear by waving his right hand back at him. Bear and humans went in opposite directions in quick order, but Skip had learned from that experience.

Skip had also learned to listen to the forest sounds and to feel the change in an atmosphere. When Death is stalking, the air stops moving causing goose bumps to rise on your arms and the hairs to stand up on the back of your neck. The forest goes completely silent...every living thing holds its breath. It is during this type of silence when the hunter and hunted realize Death is close. Usually, man or beast will try to blend into their surrounding. Man is impatient and an animal can be spooked, so the first to move is the first to die.

Skip Daggard had learned how to be patient. He had sat in blizzards, rains, sand storms, and blistering heat, and never flinched when rattlesnakes, cobras, and other poisonous creepy-crawlers moved over his body. So far, he had always been the one to walk out.

Now, he waited, but he wanted to reach over and ring Kristine's neck. The sound of the slide-rail being pulled to the rear and sliding forward slamming shut was thunderous in the quiet tunnel. He had told her it was loaded. She had watched him chamber the goddamn round. The round that she had just ejected had pinked off of the wall and splashed into the water in front of them.

Altman held his cell phone in his left hand and his 9mm in his right, pointing his weapon down the tunnel. The damn phone wouldn't stop vibrating. Sweat beaded up on his brow and began to trickle down his face and back.

Should he just start shooting while he answered the goddamn thing, or get the hell out of there? He moved his team farther back around the bend, then answered his cell, "Who the *fuck* is this?" he whispered into the mouthpiece breathing heavy.

"Altman, this is Director Rickard. Pull out and return to headquarters. Go to your respective sections in the Federal Building, and wait there for further orders. *Understood?*"

"Yeah!" He hung up his cell phone and put it away. "Fucking idiot. You almost got us killed," Altman mumbled into the darkness.

Now, he wondered how this was going to go over with Chief Daggard. Altman knew damn well that Daggard and Anderson weren't far from his position.

Just as Altman was about to call out to Daggard, Boulder and his team came up behind him.

"Altman," Boulder whispered, "did you get the word to withdraw?"

"Yeah. Daggard and Anderson are just around the bend. We have enough; you want to take them out?"

Boulder thought about it for a few seconds. "No. But I can understand your reasoning for wanting to finish it here."

Altman flinched. "You think he'll hold it against me? After all, I was only following orders."

"Ask him."

"Fuck you! You ask him."

"Hey, guy. I wasn't the one who went and kicked down his mother's front door."

Altman wanted to shoot Boulder right then and there.

Boulder turned on a flashlight. He saw the fear in Altman's eyes. "All right, I'll save your nasty ass.

"Chief Daggard, this is Agent Boulder. We have been ordered out and back to HQ. We're leaving."

Daggard did not respond.

"We know you're there so don't shoot. We're withdrawing."

Again, Skip did not respond. He followed their retreat with his ears. Yet, he still waited thirty minutes before he sat up crossing his legs. He looked over at Kristine. Without warning, he slapped her, and snatched the gun from her trembling hands.

She was frozen immobile. He had never struck her before. She wasn't going to cry. She wouldn't give him the satisfaction. She didn't rub the left side of her face even though it stung and burned.

Skip sat in the water staring at her, a barely visible silhouette. "You watched me load the goddamn thing," he finally hissed at her.

It took Skip a few minutes to calm down before he reached for her.

Kristine pulled back away from him. "You... *hit* me!"

Skip didn't know how to respond because he had never hit a woman before. He had tortured them...killed them...but he had never struck one; it was against his principles. He had witnessed the physical combat between his parents. At the age of fourteen, Skip had made a conscious decision, *he would never, ever strike a female.*

"I'm sorry. It was the only thing I could do. It was either slap you or shoot you.

"You've never killed anyone before have you, Kristine?"

"No!" She began to rub her face.

"FNG'S. Fucking new guys or simply newbies. That's what we called replacements in Nam. They were the same way, honey...frightened. Hell, we were all frightened. But newbies would make too much noise going down a trail, or they would end up shooting each other or vets when shit happened.

"It didn't take long to start putting the newbies in front of a patrol, so if they started shooting they might hit the enemy, but the instant they began to turn...we shot them."

"S—kk-ip, I w-a-s so fri—ght—en—ed I cou—ldn't move, and my breath...it was jammed up in my throat, and my mouth was so dry."

He pulled her to him. She allowed him to this time. He lifted her up onto his lap, and she wrapped her legs around his back. He gently kissed her lips; she allowed him to, then she pulled back and punched him straight in the nose. He was caught completely off-guard.

"You *ever* strike me again, Skip Daggard, and they'll have to surgically remove your balls from your throat."

His demon flared up, especially when Skip saw his blood on his hand after he wiped his nose, but he quickly regained control. "Yes, Ma'am."

They rose to their feet as Skip tested the atmosphere with his sore nose. He was still rubbing it. He let the dampness of the tunnel wash over him. He could feel sensations vibrating...pulsating along the tunnel and over his skin. He sensed the tunnel's stillness yet, he still waited, reaching down the dark passageway with his senses giving freedom to his warning devises.

Kristine stood beside him waiting.

"I'll be go-to-hell! They *did* leave!"

"Are...you...*sure?*"

"Absolutely!"

Skip Daggard didn't waste any time. He could not figure out any logical explanations for the withdrawal, but he was never the one to complain; however, he still proceeded with caution although he moved rapidly.

Skip and Kristine stood at the bottom of a ladder gulping air just as Director Rickard and Higgins approached President Mantle at the receiving line.

White House
Washington, D.C.
Sunday - 1845 hours

The President and First Lady stood just inside the banquet room greeting their arriving guests. President Mantle was dressed in a dark tuxedo, which resembled his mood because Rickard had failed to capture and kill Daggard and Anderson. The First Lady had refused to let events spoil her dinner party, so she had donned a sky blue evening gown, which showed the upper parts of her ample bosom.

The first guests to arrive were three of the Joint Chiefs of Staff with their wives. The men were dressed in their formal dinner whites, and their ladies wore evening gowns of floral prints celebrating the arrival of warm weather after a nasty winter.

Next came the Russian Ambassador with his wife. The ambassador wore a dark colored tuxedo with a red shoulder and body sash. His wife was wearing a blue sleeveless floor-length dress with matching jacket and gloves. Next in line was the ambassador's secretary, Schmirnoff and his escort.

The line of guests continued for ten minutes. During the next hour, the partygoers mingled over cocktails and hors d'oeuvres.

Even though the President had changed his dinner party from Tuesday to Sunday, he was unable to achieve a festive mood because Daggard and Anderson were still at large. Schmirnoff had approached him twice. Once to inform President Mantle all arrangements had been made, and the second time to see if Agent Daggard had been dealt with. "No, Mr. Schmirnoff, he has not. But I have been assured he will be very soon."

At 1910 hours, President Mantle was able to get Directors Higgins and Rickard aside. "I have assured Mr. Schmirnoff you two will have taken care of the problem shortly. I want to know exactly when your people will deliver my packages."

Director Rickard looked off towards Mrs. Mantle who was in conversation with the Russian Ambassador's wife.

So here it was, the final curtain thought Rickard, "should he tell the President he had pulled out his people or lie."

Rickard looked over at Higgins. Higgins seemed to be staring off into space.

"We will have him soon, Mr. President. Two of my teams have them trapped in a section of a drainage ditch under Pennsylvania Avenue."

President Mantle sighed. "So, it will all be over soon." It was a statement rather than a question.

But Director Rickard answered anyway. "Yes, Sir. *It will all be over soon.*"

Chapter Fifteen
Villains or Heroes

George Washing Monument
Washington, D.C.
Sunday—1905 hours

"All right, Kristine, up the ladder."

She looked at him for a few seconds then said, "No. You go first this time."

Skip smiled. "Okay, honey, I'll go first."

As Skip stepped down on the second rung, Kristine reached up and goosed him.

Skip jumped and almost slipped off of the wet iron rungs. He looked down at her, startled.

"How did *you* like it, sweetheart," she said sarcastically.

"I liked it. Can you do it again?"

"*Figures!*"

They continued to climb for ten yards before they reached a trap door. Skip took out a key from his right vest pocket and unlocked the heavy duty silver lock.

"How come this door lid is different, Skip?"

"Because it's at the base of the monument, honey. We've reached our destination."

Kristine reached up and gently placed her left hand on Skip's thigh. He looked down at her. "Do you think they will be waiting up there for us."

Skip smiled, "No, Kristine, they won't be waiting."

Skip unlocked the padlock, slipped the chain from the hinges of the door and ceiling, and raised the cover. "See! I told you they wouldn't be waiting," he said as they climbed into the tight, small chamber.

"I don't know why the contractor included this section to the monument. Perhaps for stability, or maybe because of the War of 1812, and the government wanted a strategic location for a sharpshooter in case the Brits decided to opt for a repeat performance."

Skip lowered the three-inch thick oak wood lid. Using the lock and chain, he secured the door from inside the monument.

The interior of the structure was the same as that of the side visitors viewed, except this passageway was only shoulder-width wide, and instead of a stone-spiraled staircase, an iron ladder was bolted to the wall.

Kristine had to go up the ladder in order for Skip to close and secure the lid. The iron ladder was on the opposite side of the monument, which put Skip and Kristine's backs towards the White House.

"I'm not going to kid you, Kristine, it's a long way up. If memory serves me right, I believe there are 255 steps to the top on the other side of this wall," he pointed to the brick wall to his left, "there are two rungs to each step. Do the math in your head. What I'm saying is...take it slow and easy. And I promise to keep my hands to myself."

"You *promise*?"

He shook his head. "Now climb, honey."

Sunday—1925 Hours

The sun was warm and bright as the agents who had been involved with hunting Daggard and Anderson were reporting back to their respective sections at the Federal Building as ordered; Hicks and his team had never left the building. The BATF agents went into the CIA sector.

Many of them were so tired that they had sought chairs, slumped down and fallen asleep. Others began to converse in low murmurs about the operation, and discussing plausible reasons to why Rickard had called an end to the mission.

And there were some that didn't care, like Kitchen, because they believed this whole search and destroy mission was bogus from the beginning.

Skip and Kristine finally attained the plank platform at the top of the monument. Kristine had to open another wooden door before she could climb through the opening onto the platform. Skip heaved himself through the opening, and then he closed and secured the latch by sliding a metal bar into a steel bracket screwed to the floor. It was a tight-squeeze; the tiny room was four feet wide and five feet long.

Kristine helped Skip remove his pack and rifle. Then Skip helped Kristine with her pack.

Once their ordnance had been set aside, Skip took two small steps to the outer south wall, knelt down on his knees and gripped an oblong stone. He wiggled it back and forth until the five inch thick, eleven inches high, and seven inches wide slab came out of the wall into his hands. He placed the slab stone on the floor to his left.

"Look!" Skip said to Kristine.

She knelt down beside him. "My God! You can see up to the Capital Building, the White House and the lawn area up to the Reflection Pool, and the monuments."

"That's why I believe this section was added to accommodate a sharpshooter."

Skip scooted back along the floor. He retrieved his rifle, set the tripod, and positioned his weapon. "When I lie down, I have to bend my knees; my toes will be resting against the wall."

Kristine stared at him with a quizzical look on her face.

Skip broke a smile. "Once, I laid up here in a prone position for twenty-four hours, Kristine, observing."

"Hmmm! I should have known."

When Skip was satisfied with his position and the height of his rifle, He took out a ground cloth from his backpack. "Kneel, so I can lay this down."

Once the cloth was in place, Skip took up a prone position and practiced several scope sightings at the Oval Office window behind the President's desk. When he was satisfied, he let Kristine lie next to him on her right side. He was almost ready—just two more items. But Skip's attention was distracted when he looked down, and saw a man and woman playing Frisbee with their dog. He became somber.

Kristine looked to see what he was staring at. "That's adorable! Why don't we have a dog, Skip?"

Skip looked over at her, staring for a few seconds. *"Do you really want to know?"*

Kristine wasn't sure now if she really wanted to know because of the way that he had asked his question. "Yes!"

Skip looked back towards the portal, and then he lifted up so he could look down at the couple and their dog. He sighed. "They're in my food-chain."

When Kristine failed to respond, Skip looked over at her. She had heard him all right; her face was red.

It had taken her a few seconds to digest his words, and for comprehension to set in. "*What?*"

Skip was looking out the opening again. He sighed because he wasn't sure he wanted to discuss this subject.

"What the hell do you mean, they are in your food-chain? Hadn't you ever owned a dog?"

He could see he wasn't going to be able to sidestep the issue. Skip wished he had kept his mouth shut.

"Yeah, I had a few dogs while I was growing up. That was before Nam."

Skip looked over at her. "That's what I think I've been trying to tell you, Kristine. I was one person before Nam, and another person after Nam.

"Sometimes I would be in the 'bush' for thirty days. The mess hall didn't deliver like Domino's, so I ate what was available. That usually meant bugs, snakes, dog, or whatever else was around.

"I had eaten snake and dog on a stick…you know the way pork is done-up in a Chinese Restaurant? I've had 'em fried, raw, boiled with vegetables, and made into hamburgers. And on cold nights when the temperature dropped from 130 degrees in the shade to eighty or so, I'd cut open a snake and drink its warm blood. Sometimes animal's fluid was the only drink available."

Skip looked into her eyes. He saw disbelief, awe, and shock.

Kristine didn't know whether to believe him or not.

"There had been so much shit that had happened to us over there, Kristine. That's why I never talked about it. Lay people can't understand because they haven't experienced the loss of innocence…in combat. Vets don't need to share with each other…we can feel each other's pain. You know…empathy, empathizing."

Skip shifted in his position. He stared out the portal into space, thinking. He was thinking about how he was overloading his mouth, and why couldn't he stop?

Kristine lay on her right side with her head resting in her hand. Her arm was bent at the elbow, and she was staring at Skip, amazed because he had shared more with her in the past fifteen hours than he had in the entire two years they had been together. She knew that mentally he was gone. His breathing was slow and deliberate, and she could see that his face was void of any expression.

Skip lay in a prone position with his right hand resting on the top of the scope of his rifle. His chin was resting on the top of his hand, while he stared out at the "Wall" across the plaza.

It was quiet in the confines of the tiny room. Light filtered in through the small opening creating shadows of their bodies in the dark areas.

"I returned from Augsburg in May 1982, to NSA," he said, "I had been on special assignment," Skip raised his head to look at Kristine, "but that's another story.

"Sometime during the summer, a controversy began to boil over the construction of a Vietnam Memorial. For me, and several vets I know it was the "Wall." I became angry," he looked at her, "enraged."

Skip laid his chin back on his hand remaining quiet and still for several seconds.

"But when the purpose of the "Wall" was finally explained by its creator, I could accept it." Skip stopped talking again.

"When I look at it, Kristine, that polished granite, I see my tombstone."

Skip raised his head and looked at her again. This time there were tears in his eyes. Some had streaked the dirt on his face. "My generation is buried there, Kristine," he pointed towards the "Wall."

"I don't understand, Skip!"

"We died, honey. All of us who served in that forsaken land…we all died."

She watched tears swell up in his eyes as Skip stared through her.

"We faced death, embraced God, surrendered our souls, and…we died. We believed that we had been abandoned by the people we went to help, our government, and *our* people."

Kristine shifted slightly in her position.

"You can't win a war if war hadn't been declared. And you can't win in any conflict if you don't take real estate."

228

Kristine watched Skip rest his chin back on his hand. She was wondering if she should ask, but her words came out before she had finished formulating her question. "Is that why America lost in Vietnam?"

"That and other issues I don't care to discuss."

"Cold and hard," that was her Skippy she thought.

There were a few moments of silence, then Skip Daggard began again.

"I went to the "Wall" once. It was the spring of 1985. I was a First Sergeant for a MI company at Meade. It was the Company Commander's idea. I tried to fight the visit, but she pulled rank. We took about one hundred and twenty troops. I stood before the granite stone looking at the items that had been placed there: Jump boots, Jungle boots, dog tags, flowers, letters, a few helmets, and framed pictures. Some pictures were of soldiers with their families-others, just the soldiers themselves.

"I couldn't look at the names, Kristine. I kept staring at the ground where the base of the stone met the earth. I didn't want to know...who had died. I didn't want to see the names, embedded forever, of the guys I had known and served with that hadn't made it out.

"But I forced myself. I finally did it; I looked up tilting my head. Yet I couldn't focus...all those names! Instead, I heard voices, 'I'll be go to Hell if I'm surrendering my rifle.' 'Skip, you have to promise me you'll never tell.'

"There were the sounds of laughter, crying, and screams. Of explosions and gunfire and that horrible sound of all...ripping flesh."

Kristine saw pain chiseled into the skin of Skip's face. She pulled him close to her as his tears fell freely to the wooden floor. In the two years they had been together, he had never shared with her. She was learning things that only veterans knew. She was being inducted into the horrors of war.

"I didn't want to see...I wanted to remember. Remember those guys dancing, smoking and joking, and cramming a lifetime into a few hours of liberty. I wanted to imagine that they all got out, but I knew they hadn't.

"There was this hillbilly from Tennessee. The army was the first time in his life he had three hots and a cot and shoes. He sent his entire pay home every month to his mom. Then he fucked-up…he reenlisted." Skip squeezed out more tears. "The VC shot him down over Saigon."

Kristine witnessed Skip's body violently tremble and wretch.

"Then there was Roberts. He gets a Dear John in one-envelope and divorce papers in another. He was derelict in his duties that afternoon because he sat in the club, drinking. None of the NCO's thought it proper to call him on it, so they let him be. Along about twenty-three hundred hours, old Roberts ups with a steak knife from the club and charges the jungle…only thing…he must have forgotten about the four strands of concertina wire…we watched him thrash about for an hour before he finally died.

"One night on liberty, I met a homey, Bud Crandel. We had been neighbors for awhile. Went to the same high school together. He was on R&R with three other Marines. They were getting tea-totally smashed. Then they begin to cry. I became mighty uncomfortable. Bud put his arm around me…"

Again, Kristine watched as Skip broke-down in a fit of wrenching and an outburst of tears. This fit lasted approximately forty seconds. She wiped his face and eyes.

Five minutes passed. "They had been in the Battle for Hue."

Kristine saw a burning hatred and anger in Skip's eyes as he faced her. She felt a shiver ripple up and down her spine.

Skip's voice came in a whisper at first, then loud and venomous.

"Our circuits had been burning with traffic, but Bang Pla was only a relay station to Saigon and the Pentagon and NSA. The messages were in code and of the highest priority. The "Tape Apes" had three seconds to log and send the messages back out, so they didn't have time to decode…just receive and transmit.

"We knew something big was going down, but had no idea that the Battle for Hue was taking place."

Kristine watched as his tears began to fall again.

"It was Christmas, 1968, Kristine. A night that haunts me 'til this day," he paused, "and I wasn't even in the battle.

"It was in a barroom in Saigon. I was bellied-up to a trough in a coed restroom recycling my beer, and having a slurred conversation with a bar girl, who was squatted over a hole in the floor, when in comes this GI. He steps up to the trough to my left between the girl and me.

"Just as he begins to pee, he realizes I'm talking to someone. He looks over and sees the girl. He tries to put himself back in his pants while he's still peeing. It was the funniest thing...the poor guy didn't know what to do.

"The girl finally stopped laughing and said, "Hang it out and finish, GI.' I thought I was going to bust my gut.

"Then I looked at him closely. And I couldn't believe it; it was Bud Crandel, a homey from Morristown, New Jersey. A kid I hadn't seen in over three years.

"There we were in some restroom in Saigon recycling our beer and hugging each other. The girl called us queer in Vietnamese and left the room, laughing.

Bud explained he was there with three other Marines, and he invited me to his table."

Skip went silent. Then, without warning, his body shuddered violently, and he burst into tears. "He told me the story."

Kristine reached out to hold Skip but he pulled away. She recoiled, watching his eyes narrow.

Skip allowed himself thirty seconds for his breakdown before he sucked it down and turned it off as if it had never happened.

Kristine reached over and wiped his tears from his face. She was trembling now, and cried as well.

"I can't remember if Bud said it was his brigade or division that had been ordered down to support the South Vietnamese, but when the Marines arrived, the South Vietnamese had all but been driven out of the city.

"The Marines were ordered into Hue. The battle was furious and vicious. Inch by inch, seesaw, and hand-to-hand. Our boys were outnumbered and outgunned, but they fought. They were being driven back with heavy casualties. Then," Skip paused again as tears swelled into his eyes, "... the unforgiving happened...the enemy began chopping the wounded Marines to pieces beginning at their feet. Their screams were louder than the sounds of the battle.

"A rage gripped the Marines and they rallied, charging the VC and NVA without any thought but to kill. Once again they were driven back leaving more wounded."

Kristine watched Skip fade away. He got that far off look in his eyes and he was gone. Now, she knew where he went when he withdrew into himself...Vietnam.

His chin was resting on his right hand again. His breathing was shallow. "The new wounded, those guys, those who had witnessed the atrocities, they began screaming and shouting to their comrades, 'Kill us! Shoot us for God's sake. Please don't let them butcher us.' The Marines rallied again, but the charge was short-lived. Screaming and shouting obscenities and crying, the Marines began shooting into their wounded. However, as they were driven from the city, they began carrying as many of their wounded as they could, and fighting their way out.

"When the Marines married up with the ARVN, at first they were stunned speechless. But, as recognition took hold, the officers and noncoms walked away. The troops opened fire on the ARVN...instead of going in to help the Marines, the South Vietnamese forces sought shelter beyond the city, and were gambling amongst themselves on who was going to take Hue, the enemy or our Marines."

Kristine sat up. She had to wipe tears from her eyes.

"I try not to go there, Kristine. But every once in awhile...but looking out at the "Wall"...I can still see myself standing there that warm spring day...looking but not seeing...I never looked for Bud's name...I didn't want to know...I wanted to live with a hope and belief that he made it out. I never looked him up when I got back. I want to believe that he's alive..."

"But he might be alive, Skip!"

"I don't want to know, Kristine because...I want to remember him that night and the funny on how we met; me and that girl laughing so hard we were crying as Bud pissed all over himself trying to stuff himself back in his pants. That's what I *try* to remember."

Kristine lay back down near Skip. She looked at him, seeing him in a new light.

The only noise was their breathing for what seemed an hour.

Kristine couldn't bear the silence any more. She had her head resting back in her hand and was lying up against him. "Skip, what secret were you never to tell?"

Skip's body language told her she had overstepped her boundaries, again.

He glared at her. "Questions again, huh?" He stared back out of the portal. Then, slowly he turned his head back so he could look at her. "It's a secret I've kept for thirty-five years, Kristine. It's a secret..." Skip paused, "One night I learned, Kristine, the *real* reason an MP company had been assigned to our site; that MI types are not allowed/authorized to be taken prisoners. And that is another story I will share with you some day."

Washington Monument
Washington, D.C.
Sunday - 2001 hours

The sky was three shades of golden hues on the western horizon. Skip lay with Kristine next to his side angry with himself for allowing such an outpouring of his buried demons. *Why did he do that*, he asked himself silently? Perhaps, he felt it was time for Kristine to know the son of a bitch she was going to marry—the real Skip Daggard. Or, to be more precise, the animal that came out of Vietnam.

All of them, those that returned to the 'World' were forever changed. Zombies going through the motions of living yet waiting. Waiting to go home...waiting to die.

She watched his face turn somber again as he looked out at the "Wall."

"It was the end for us, Kristine."

"What was?"

"Hue. By mid January 1969 the horror had been illegally transmitted by every commo section to all the American forces in the Theater of Operation. A hate, a rage, and an anger strangled us— choked us...we wanted to kill all Vietnamese. We wanted to pack up and leave."

To her surprise, Skip started chuckling. "What's so amusing?"

"I had an attitude back then..."

"*Then?*"

"Hmmm! Make the call."

"Before I do, aren't you forgetting something?"

Skip looked around. "Oh, yeah!" Then he removed two cartridges from his right vest pocket and placed them down on the ground cloth on the right side of his rifle.

Kristine glared at him. "Not those! I mean the windows in the White House, Skip. Aren't they bullet proof?"

"Yeah, so what?"

Skip smiled that cat that ate the canary shit eating grin only he can muster. "I guess I negated to provide you with a small piece of information which you really don't need to know. You know what I mean? *Only on a need to know basis.*"

Kristine reached over to slap him, but pulled her hand away remembering the last time she tried in the past twenty-four hours.

"So, we're back to *that* again, are we?"

Skip smiled at her. "I'm not going to go into great detail, honey, but there is a chemical research area between routes 198 and 197 near the Patuxent Wildlife refuge that is overgrown and looks unoccupied. Besides working on chemical agents, they do work for Military Intelligence."

Skip lifted one of the cartridges, "This is called a Molecular Modulation Cartridge, or simply put, an MMC. I call it a GMFC. The MMC puts bullet proof glass on the endangered species list."

"A *what?*"

"A, gotcha motherfucker, cartridge. The MMC explodes on impact disrupting the molecules of an object. In other words, the bullet creates a three-inch whole in solid objects 1/16th of an inch to three feet in depth no matter what structure the material is. The chemical turns solids into a Jell-O-type substance"

"You're going to set off an explosion at one of the windows in the White House? Are you crazy?"

"It's instantaneous, Kristine. Right after firing the MMC, I squeeze off the killing round," he picked up the second cartridge, "this is also a special round. I had studied the killing power of a .22 bullet for years. In 1982, I asked the guys at Patuxent if they could make me a cartridge with a lead bullet the same grain-size as that of a .300 Winchester Mag. They shortened the bullet by 3/8's of an inch. I can shoot a gnat off a bull's ass two miles away.

"Besides, by the time anyone hears the explosion, my target will be terminated. Now, take out your cell phone and make the call."

Kristine did as she had been ordered. She dialed the President's "red" line, which some people, like Skip, called the BAT line.

As it rang, Kristine looked at Skip, "How long do you think it will take before President Mantle notices the blinking light," Kristine asked.

"*Now how the fuck do I know*! Let it ring until the traitor picks it up."

At 2105 hours, all the guests were seated and enjoying their dinners. President Mantle noticed the flashing red light in the upper right corner of the banquet hall. He pleasantly excused himself taking Director Rickard, Secretary of State Kelly, and Director Higgins with him to the Oval Office.

"My secure line is ringing," President Mantle said glaring at Rickard, "perhaps it's that damn thorn in my side that you have failed to pluck out!"

Higgins and Rickard stared at each other as they followed the President along the West Wing towards the Oval Office. No one was speaking, but Director Rickard was thinking, that when Daggard terminated Kelly, *he* was going to assassinate Mantle and blame it on Daggard.

Rickard was sure he knew the significance of the blinking red light. Once they were in the Oval Office, Kelly would be terminated.

Once again Skip lay in a prone position with the stock of the rifle seated in the pocked of his shoulder. Like magic, President Mantle appeared behind his desk picking up the red receiver, "*Where are you?*" he shouted into the mouthpiece.

Skip sighted, placing the cross hairs of his scope on his target. He inhaled and exhaled slowly, then held his breath.

"Mr. President, this is Sergeant Anderson…"

Skip aligned the cross hairs of the scope on the center of the back of the President's head.

"Agent Daggard is on his way to see you.

"Yes, Mr. President. Right now…"

Kristine watched the rifle buck twice against Skip's shoulder. Then she turned off her cell phone.

Skip raised up onto his knees smiling. He leaned forward and gently slid the slab of stone into the opening. "God loves me," Skip said as he looked over at Kristine, "that other traitor, Kelly, walked in front of the President as I squeezed off both rounds...both traitors heads exploded simultaneously."

Skip and Kristine rose to their feet. Skip hugged her, then placing his hands on both of her shoulders, he pushed her to arms length. "In thirty minutes, General Hanalin will be holding a news conference from the lobby of NSA. In one hour the world will know the truth," Skip said, pulling Kristine in close and hugging her tight. He gently kissed her right ear softly breathing out his words, "We'll let history decide, Kristine...whether we're villains or heroes!"

ABOUT THE AUTHOR

T. S. Pessini
www.qcol.net/tppublications

Tom enlisted in the United States Army in August 1967 in electronics communications, and served nineteen months in Vietnam. His next assignment was Ent Air Force Base, Colorado Springs, Colorado. After completing eight months at Ent, he separated from active duty in August 1970.

Once he returned home to Morristown, New Jersey, he worked as a lineman for AT&T for two years.

In February 1973 Tom reenlisted in the army, and served with the 3rd Armored Division in Frankfurt, Germany, the 9th Infantry Division at Fort Lewis, Washington, Military Intelligence and Military Police in Augsburg, Germany, and NSA and the 519th MP Battalion at Fort Meade, Maryland. He served a short tour in Korea as a Site Commander with the 293rd Signal Battalion, and retired from active service in March 1990.

Some of his awards and decorations include: The Good Conduct Medal with six oak leaf clusters, the Vietnam Service Medal, the Vietnamese Cross of Gallantry, the Army Achievement Medal, an Army Commendation Medal, the Meritorious Service Medal, and four Service School Ribbons.

"Writing has been a passion of mine since I began telling stories at the age of seven."

He didn't begin writing in earnest until 1987, when Tom joined Writer's Digest School for Writers. "I had trouble with criticism back then so I dropped out about three months into the course. However, I stayed with Writer's Digest Book Club and magazine."

Tom Pessini now resides in Friendsville, MD with his wife, Erroll Jean and their seven dogs, where he writes and substitute teaches.

CPSIA information can be obtained at www.ICGtesting.com
Printed in the USA
LVOW10*2131020615

440923LV00001B/27/P